Praise for
Someone You Love Is Gone

"A beautiful, haunting story of one family, spanning generations
and continents, as they face life's inevitable losses, struggle
with grief and reach for redemption."

— SHILPI SOMAYA GOWDA,
New York Times bestselling author of
Secret Daughter and *The Golden Son*

"In this brave and beautifully written novel,
Gurjinder Basran shines a light into the darkest corners
of one family's emotional inheritance."

— ALISSA YORK,
author of *Fauna* and *The Naturalist*

"The ability alone to weave this moral complexity into her
stories makes Gurjinder Basran a novelist worth reading."

— *The Globe and Mail*

"Although epic in scope, *Someone You Love Is Gone* is
economically and poetically written."

— *Toronto Star*

"A realistic and emotional portrayal of grief."

— *Kirkus*

Praise for
Everything Was Good-bye

"A tender novel about identity and the search for belonging that is both humorous and heartbreaking. In Meena, Basran has created a feisty, complicated and irrepressible heroine."

— THRITY UMRIGAR,
author of the bestselling *Honor* and *The Space Between Us*

"A brave book, and also a pleasure to read: emotionally engaging, sensuous, vibrant and beautifully observed."

— KATHY PAGE,
author of *Dear Evelyn* and *The Two of Us*

"Exceptional."

— *Vancouver Sun*

"Basran's writing is by turns elegant and poetic."

— *Quill & Quire*

"Thought provoking and compelling . . . a timely and engaging read."

— *Winnipeg Free Press*

Help!
I'm Alive

A novel

Gurjinder Basran

This book is also available as a Global Certified Accessible™ (GCA) ebook. ECW Press's ebooks are screen reader friendly and are built to meet the needs of those who are unable to read standard print due to blindness, low vision, dyslexia, or a physical disability.

Purchase the print edition and receive the eBook free. For details, go to ecwpress.com/eBook.

Published by ECW Press
665 Gerrard Street East
Toronto, Ontario, Canada M4M 1Y2
416-694-3348 / info@ecwpress.com

Editor for the Press: Jennifer Knoch
Cover design: Michel Vrana
Author photo: Karolina Turek

Library and Archives Canada Cataloguing in Publication

Title: Help! I'm alive : a novel / Gurjinder Basran.

Other titles: Help! I am alive

Names: Basran, Gurjinder, author.

Identifiers: Canadiana (print) 20210344393 | Canadiana (ebook) 20210344407

ISBN 978-1-77041-630-7 (softcover)
ISBN 978-1-77305-928-0 (ePub)
ISBN 978-1-77305-929-7 (PDF)
ISBN 978-1-77305-930-3 (Kindle)

Classification: LCC PS8603.A789 H45 2022 | DDC C813/.6—dc23

We acknowledge the support of the Canada Council for the Arts. *Nous remercions le Conseil des arts du Canada de son soutien.* This book is funded in part by the Government of Canada. *Ce livre est financé en partie par le gouvernement du Canada.* We acknowledge the support of the Ontario Arts Council (OAC), an agency of the Government of Ontario, which last year funded 1,965 individual artists and 1,152 organizations in 197 communities across Ontario for a total of $51.9 million. We also acknowledge the support of the Government of Ontario through the Ontario Book Publishing Tax Credit, and through Ontario Creates.

 ONTARIO CREATES

 ONTARIO ARTS COUNCIL
CONSEIL DES ARTS DE L'ONTARIO
an Ontario government agency
un organisme du gouvernement de l'Ontario

 Canada Council for the Arts Conseil des arts du Canada

 Canada

PRINTED AND BOUND IN CANADA

PRINTING: MARQUIS   5 4 3 2 1

MIX
Paper from responsible sources
FSC
www.fsc.org   FSC® C103567

For Arun & Amit

It is a waste to be asking the question when you are the answer.

— JOSEPH CAMPBELL

Day 1

It's morning.

Ash knows this before he opens his eyes. The spring light has a way of turning his lids orange and they open all fluttery and confused like butterflies. Outside the birds are doing their thing and he listens for a minute before reaching for his phone, scrolling and scanning through the messages, all variations of:

holy shit, did u hear

He's gotten a dozen Snaps about it in the last ten minutes, at least twenty texts, and it won't be long before the Facebook posts with the crying emojis start. Britt messaged him at least thirty times, make that thirty-one.

?

He's left her on read and she's pissed. Like he needs that today. His phone's blowing up: the ladder of notifications is too much to take; he tosses it in the nightstand drawer and pulls the covers tight under his chin. He could just stay there, avoid it all, but if he does, he'll have to deal with his parents. Last night he heard them whispering about it, that loud and soft rhythm of parents not wanting their kids to hear. He grabbed the pillow, pulled it tight over his face and screamed into it, bending his whole body until that *what the fuck* feeling collapsed.

He sat in the blue dark, gaming, racking up kills.

This morning, the TV was turned off, the controller was on the bedside; he knows his mom must have checked on him at some point. She usually comes in, readjusts the covers and brushes the side of his face with her fingertips, imprinting just like she did when he was a baby. Even if he's awake he pretends to be asleep so she can have that moment where everything is okay, where he's a boy, still peaceful and content in this small room and she is the last one up, the one to turn off the lights, to lock the doors, to shut out the world. Ash wishes it was like that still, but trying to shut out the world is like trying to dam an ocean. It finds a way in.

He grabs his phone, checks if the video is still up and is relieved that it's not. The shared links are dead and for a moment he lets himself believe that Jay's alive and that they could be best friends again, just like they were in grade five.

Ash had been the new kid at school and Jay showed him around because that's just what you did. On that first day, they went to the skate park at lunch. It was October, the sky was a crazy blue, as if someone had put a filter on it, and when Jay talked, Ash could see his breath, words coming out in little puffs. "You can't overthink it," he said, demonstrating a quick pivot of his board.

Back then it was Ash, Jay, Sullie and Joe — friends for life, secret six-move handshakes, touch football at lunch, sleepovers and all. But after a while it was just the two of them and the others were the hangers-on who found new people to hang on to. Then in grade eight, so did they. Ash became that guy — the kind who teachers love and hate, the kind who makes jokes and delivers a solid C+ effort, the kind who girls twirl their hair around. Jay didn't change much. He still loved to skate, mostly hung out at the pit perfecting his ollie, made friends with the stoners and then eventually Winona. Thinking back on it now, Ash can see that's where things went wrong and they stopped hanging. Sure, they nodded or chin-upped when they saw each other in the hall and occasionally they dropped a fist bump, but they never really talked again. That's the thing about getting older, everything that was just drifts away and a best friend becomes someone you used to know.

Ash gets out of bed as his mom comes in to tell him it's time to go and she can drop him off on her way to work and all of that other stuff she says on rinse and repeat, only today he tells her, "I'm good, I'll walk."

Pavan sits on the edge of the bed real gently as if she's trying not to spook him, and he can tell she's worried. Parents always think things like this are contagious and that they need to talk about it, make it a teachable moment. Ash glances at her to show her that he's fine. Her eyes are puffy from crying, but still she tries to make that longer *oh honey* eye contact. Ash turns away not wanting to deal with her concern, not wanting to encourage the extra "I love you" that'll get tacked on to the end of every sentence. He makes a show of opening and closing dresser drawers, rooting through his clothes, before she finally gets the hint; only now she's hovering, the way she does when she's looking for the right words.

"I'm fine," he says.

"I know." Her eyes narrow. She knows he's not fine but lets him have the lie. "I'm here, if you want to talk."

"Maybe later," he says, even though he has no intention of ever talking about it, about Jay. All he wants to do is forget but he knows she'll keep trying; it's what she does.

"Sure," she says.

Ash holds eye contact with her so she can get a good look and see that he's okay, that he's solid, that she doesn't need to worry in that big clouded way she usually does. It's too much to carry, her guilt, the fear, the worry of messing up. Sometimes he wishes she'd care less.

"Ash." She pauses, adding an "I love you," just like he knew she would.

He asks her to shut the door on the way out.

At school, the halls are crammed with backpacked bodies like always, but there's this extra feeling, like the heaviness you get in your chest when you're keeping a secret or telling a lie, only it's not contained, it's alive with a virus-like spread. The popular girls are crying in huddled masses, mascara runs down their cheeks as they work at mastering sentiment, sullen expressions, and the not-too-ugly cry — they don't know how to do anything but pose and pretend. And the boys, they just nod and look away, never quite making eye contact. Head down, hands tucked in pockets, he avoids them all, weaving and maneuvering his way through the day as if he were a rat in a maze.

An announcement is made after first bell. "We are shocked and saddened by the sudden passing of Jacob McAlister. Our hearts and prayers are with his family and friends." No mention of the details, only that there will be counselors on hand for the next few weeks. People who didn't know him act sad. People who did know him are legit stunned. Teachers whisper out one side of their two faces, gossiping about Jay's mom and how she must be feeling. Ash wants to tell them to stop talking about Jay like he's an event, like some epic winter storm that they'll recall when they're old. And Jay's mom? How she's feeling is fucked, not in her usual too-many-night-shifts, cash-strapped, chain-smoking way, but in the *life is never going to be good again* way. Ash feels bad for her; Lisa tries hard, like most moms do. He can still hear her calling down the street as Jay skated away. "You come back here, Jacob McAlister," his name caught in the whirring of the wheels, syllables eaten by asphalt.

No one saw this coming. He was a happy kid; he had a girl-friend. Sure, Winona was a bit weird but still he had someone. Jay wasn't like the cutters who carve at their arms in the bathroom stalls or like the bullied kid who hanged himself in the art room. That's what everyone's saying at least. Now that he's gone, every-one wants to know him, to know why, to insert themselves into the story and make it mean something.

But there's no making sense of it.

Jay jumped off the Lions Gate Bridge.

And even though Ash saw it, he doesn't want to believe it. The sky was too blue that day.

A bunch of Ash's friends skip third block to go to the skate park, even Britt stops him at his locker, hassling him about why he's not going. She's wearing dark jeans and a hoodie, plain-faced, her blond hair in a high pony, nothing extra about her, which is what he likes. She's pretty without trying.

"Are you alright? You didn't answer my texts last night."

Ash pulls his binder down and shuts the locker door. "Sorry, just needed some space, I guess."

"Space? Really?" She squints her eyes and nods as if she's getting ready to tell him how he should be a better boyfriend. He braces himself. "Don't talk to me about space. If I don't message you back right away you freak, but you, you just leave me on read and that's supposed to be okay." She's talking with her hands, her face close to his. When she's like this, he can't focus on the things he likes about her, the freckles on her nose or her hazel eyes; all he sees is her mouth moving.

"Look, what do you want from me? My best friend just died."

"Oh, so now he's your *best* friend?" Her eyes are buggy, disbelieving.

"He was . . . Would you just stop?" Ash says this louder than he meant to and she goes silent. He reaches for her arm, wanting to apologize, but she backs up and yells for her friends to wait up. He turns around, resists the urge to hit the locker door and stands there, head pressed against the cold metal for a full minute before he goes to next block.

In class, he sits in the last seat of the first row, two rows down and three seats back from where Jay would have sat. He usually skipped anyways, but today when some new kid tries to take his seat, Ash tells him, "That's Jay's."

"I didn't know," he says, quickly moving along.

Everyone else whispers and side-stares. Ash is relieved when a sub walks in. He'll be spared Mr. Larson who, like all the other teachers, would have tried to connect in that way teachers do when they fake-care. The sub scrawls her name across the board as if this is the start of some made-for-TV movie where she, Mrs. Kaye, is going to make a difference. She's old-lady artsy, with short cropped hair, a *look at me I'm worldly* tunic and an oversized turquoise necklace. By the looks of her droopy tits, Ash figures she's probably a staunch feminist who burned her bra back in the day. Mrs. Kaye announces that they're watching a video on World War One and for this, Ash is grateful. He'll be able to sit there in the dark and disappear. With some difficulty, she loads the archaic film reels onto a projector and the black-and-white images of soldiers marching, bombs dropping, shrapnel flying fall over the edge of the screen. She wheels her AV cart back and the image resizes and falls into the frame. The guy doing the voice-over has that old-school TV dad voice but it's hard to hear above the whirl and clicks of the projector. Ash leans forward, elbows on desk, cupping his ears, watching the grainy footage of dead men. There are some jumpy close-ups of the soldiers' faces, all young and perfect, square-jawed and steel-eyed. He can't look and closes his eyes until the bell rings.

After class, he grabs his backpack from his locker and ducks out before anyone sees him; so far he's managed to avoid all of his friends, to ignore their question mark texts and their *u ok* attempts at connection. Ash walks through the ravine, where he and Jay used to ride their bikes. The trees are starting to bud, light passing through the dark boughs of evergreen. The ground is soft and springy, a mulch of fallen pine needles. If he squints, he can see Jay riding ahead, standing tall and pedaling hard. Ash picks up his pace, but still he loses him.

By the time Ash arrives at the skate park, there are only a handful of guys skimming the sides of the bowl. Near the gated entrance is the beginning of a makeshift memorial for Jay — grocery-store flowers next to his yearbook photo, an unlit tea light set against the chain-link fence. Winona walks up from behind him. She's wearing all black today, channeling her namesake from the movie *Beetlejuice*, all pale and thin. Ash wonders if she stopped eating and is counting her ribs the way the girls said she did. Without a word or a sideways glance, she kneels down and lights the candle. Ash stands there not knowing what to say, watching the flame, listening to the skates grinding and popping on concrete.

She takes out a cigarette, lights it up and offers him a drag. He takes it from her and for a few minutes they do this back-and-forth until finally she catches his eye.

"Do you know why he did it?"

"Nah," he says, shaking his head, looking over at the graffiti wall, bubble letters and random tags from stoner wannabes. "Do you?"

"Why does anyone do anything?" She taps ash into the flowers.

He stays with her there by the chain-link fence saying nothing, his mind empty, sunshine on his face. It's the first good feeling he's had all day.

Across the street a black Mercedes pulls over and honks. "My ride," she says and drops her cigarette.

Clean and Tidy's Mini Cooper is parked in the driveway and Ash wonders if his mom came home early on account of everything that's going on. He tries to sneak by her but the floorboards squeak and she waves at him, pointing to her headset. He can tell by her smiley voice and quick laugh that she's talking to a new customer; her everyday tone doesn't have as much singsong in it, and in general she's not easily amused. She's a serious person, not in a boring bad way, just in a practical way; having a cleaning business, as lame as it is, suits her. He listens for a few minutes, thinking she'll finish her convo and they can get the "How was your day?" over with but she's still full-on talking about natural cleaning products, listing off ingredients like vinegar, baking soda, and tea tree oil with such hype that he can't help but deliver a solid eye roll. She gives him the *five minutes* palm up and he heads to his room, drops his bag and collapses onto the bed. Ash can hear Anik listening to music downstairs, some sad retro shit on vinyl that he ordered from Amazon. He closes his eyes and imagines their rooms stacked one on top of the other like a dollhouse, each of them lying in their twin bed staring at the ceiling. Anik doesn't come out of his room much. His dad says it's a phase, some collegiate quarter-life crisis. His mom says that he needs some time to get it together and take control of his life. Ash doesn't know what to think. Anik's smart, talented and good-looking in his own way, but he hides in the basement eating microwave meals and playing weird-ass minor chords on his keyboard. Ash can't remember the last time he had a full conversation with him. They used to talk a lot. He takes his phone out of his pocket and starts to text him.

need to talk. J is dead. don't know what to do

He looks at the message, rereads it and then deletes one letter at a time until the only word left is *need*. He stares at that four-letter word, the blinking cursor and closes the app.

Day 2

Pavan scans the floral stand.

Potted yellow daisies and white lilies wrapped in cellophane are lined up in two neat tiers. The nearby pails of spring flowers are picked over, with only the wilted ones left standing in shallow water like exotic birds. She wonders which ones Ash would want to take to the skate park memorial and glances at the refrigerated floral arrangements and roses sold by the dozen. He told her not to be cheap about it. She didn't like the way he said it but she let it go; it wasn't worth the argument.

"Excuse me," she says to the woman at the counter.

The clerk, who is tying curling ribbon on an elaborate bouquet of orange and pink gerbera daisies, doesn't look up. "I'll just be a minute," she says and motions to the man a few feet away. "Here you go, and congratulations!" The clerk has a perfectly amused expression that annoys Pavan, an overt cheeriness that reads as simpleminded — she's the kind of woman who watches *Jeopardy* and crushes on Alex Trebek, the kind of woman who sits by the lotto kiosk with her scratch cards and coffee or the kind of woman who makes those useless doilies sold at local craft fairs. Pavan tries to get the clerk's attention again by wandering around the displays of daffodils and Easter balloons. She's awkward in moments like this when she needs to be noticed, when she needs someone's help. Her years as a single mom instilled in her a DIY resourcefulness that's made her overly competent; waiting to be served by others seems entirely unnecessary to her now. After a few moments, she clears her throat. "Is this all you have?"

The woman comes out from behind the counter. She adjusts the ties on her green apron, puts on the glasses that hang around her neck and surveys the flower stand. "I'm afraid so. What's the occasion?"

"No occasion."

"Oh, how nice, to have flowers for no reason at all. If you ask me, more people should do that." She laughs a little and clasps her hands as if she's pleased with herself and this annoys Pavan even more. She imagines the woman as a *Price Is Right* contestant, the type who wears Christmas sweaters and undercuts everyone by bidding one dollar.

"There is a reason — it's just not a happy one." Pavan's flustered, having to explain. Her speech falls into a staccato rhythm. "It's for my son to take to a memorial." She runs her palm across the back of her neck, a physical reminder to get a grip, to calm her nerves. The whole thing has rattled her.

"Oh, I'm sorry. Is it for that boy at Laurier High School?"

Pavan nods, delivers a weak smile.

The woman lowers her head and Pavan can't help but notice her graying roots, the age spots at her temples, her ashy potato skin. "It's so sad. A lot of kids came in with their parents today to buy flowers. Most bought the single stem yellow roses." She points to the few that remain.

"I was thinking of something more elaborate," Pavan says, remembering what Ash told her. "Maybe you could put a few roses together with some of the lilies?" She takes charge and gathers a few bunches of flowers. "Something like this?"

"Of course," the woman says, taking them from her. "Would you like me to wrap them?"

"Yes, that would be nice." Pavan follows her back to the counter where the clerk wraps the bouquet and measures multicolored ribbon, curling it with the edge of her scissors. Pavan doesn't know where to look and focuses her attention on the twirling coil.

"Did you know the boy?"

"No, not really." Pavan's not sure why she lied. She did know Jay and she has spent the day thinking of him as the boy she knew. Freckled and pale, his hand-me-down clothes, his second-helping appetite. He used to stay for dinner at least a few times a week and even went camping with them one May long weekend. That was his first time camping, and he and Ash spent all day exploring the woods and all night by the campfire telling scary stories with a flashlight under their chins. The next day they woke up with hives, and Pavan slathered calamine lotion on them, covering their torsos and faces with the chalky film. Even the itch from whatever rash they had didn't stop them from having fun, and for the remainder of the day they pretended to be ghosts haunting the forest. When Jay stopped coming around Pavan was sad about it and asked Ash if they'd had a fight, which of course they hadn't. Boys don't really have fights — friendships don't break up in high-stakes arguments, they just fall away. She saw Jay a few times after that, usually in the mall, and she'd stop to talk, taking in the way he changed — the curl in his hair softening, freckles fading in adolescence. He was always so polite, never rushed her, happy to answer her boring adult inquiries: "How is school? How's your mother?"

The flower lady's still talking, rambling really. Pavan opens her wallet, signaling her readiness to pay, to leave. The woman doesn't notice and continues at her slow menopausal pace. "I feel terrible for his family. His mother, that is. How hard it is for a single mother, and now this?"

"Do you know his mother?" Pavan asks, thinking of Lisa now. How awkward she was when Pavan would call to see if Jay could stay over. It always seemed as if she was trying to find a reason to hang up quickly, to go watch TV or take a burning cake out of the oven. She rarely picked him up, and when she did, she never came in to meet them. They only met the one time, when Pavan insisted on driving Jay home because it was after dark. Lisa was friendly enough that day. She even invited her in, but Pavan could tell that she didn't really want to, that she was only trying to be polite for Jay's sake, so she thanked her, suggesting maybe another time. But that time never came, and now this.

The woman shakes her head. "Know her — no. But it's still sad, just the same."

"Is it? Sad — just the same?" Pavan plunks down her credit card.

It starts to rain on her way home, a springtime shower that makes everything smell like dirt and memory. Petrichor. That's what she told Anik the scent was called when they planted the magnolia tree in the front yard. Planting that tree was a way of putting down roots after so many years of moving around and trying to make ends meet. Anik was in charge of picking out the tree and the two of them made a day of it, visiting the local nursery where Anik, with his wide eyes and thick glasses, peppered the garden specialists with questions. He was a curious boy and so he came to know everything about that tree, from its proper species name, *Magnolia denudata*, to its history as a symbol of purity in the Tang dynasty. Pavan remembers him as a very specific child, maybe never a child at all on account of those first few years, always trying to control and catalog everything he came into contact with. He even named the tree, calling her Petra, so he would always recall the name of how that morning smelled. She remembers his little hands in root and soil, happy to let the worms wriggle through his fingers as he patted the dirt in place. He was five and full of a wonder, a wisdom beyond his years. He marveled at Petra's first blooms and collected the scattered petals and pressed them into the pages of his beloved atlas — the world cut up, quartered and flattened inside the thick volume, almost too heavy for him to carry. She should have known then how it would be for his bird-like heart, beating and humming in the noise of the world. She should have prepared him; she should have protected him. She should have told him that the world was not at his fingertips, it was not his for the taking, it was not his for the saving. But how do you let your children hope and dream when all you want is to keep them safe?

When the boys were younger, motherhood was a physical *go here, do this* checklist and schedule, and now it's a mental exertion of shoulds and worries, a depletion of self with so much guilt and shame at having done it all wrong. She believes all of their hardships and missteps lead back to her not having done something that would have made it better or easier for them. She's always to blame just as her mother was. And now this. Part of her wants to call Lisa and talk to her and tell her it's not her fault, but surely it must be, for without blame and guilt what else does she have but a dead son?

Pavan sits in her parked car and stares at Petra for a few minutes before stepping out, bouquet in hand.

The ground is littered with fallen petals, fleshy and pink.

Day 5

Anik hasn't left the house in months.

He hasn't left the basement for three weeks and today when he does venture out, no one's home and he's relieved. Ever since Jay died, their house feels heavy, and at times it's like the entire main floor is going to buckle with all of the things they aren't saying and they, along with the floorboards and beams, will cave in and come crashing in on him. He knows he should do something but doesn't know what or how so he stays tucked away in his world of one.

He takes in the aboveground silence. He likes the house when it's empty like this, when there's no deep bass coming from Ash's bedroom, when the TV isn't on, clipping from channel to channel on top of his parents' idle chatter. He likes it when he can hear the hum of the refrigerator, the sound of the furnace clicking on and off, even the sounds of the construction crew that has systematically dismantled the neighbor's house and is now building a second-story addition. There's almost a musicality to the tempo. The hit and slice of hammer and saw remind him of how things come together. From Ash's bedroom he watches the crew hoist the two-by-fours and frame them into walls — making rooms out of felled trees, turning one thing into another. This is what he thought of when his mom and Peter took him to see the totems at Stanley Park. It was the first time he'd met Peter, and though Anik was more interested in learning how the trunks were carved, his mother was overly concerned that they got along, always hovering and cajoling him into conversation.

"Do you like him?" she asked while Peter stood in line to buy ice cream from a concession stand. Anik said yes to make her happy. He didn't like Peter, but he did like the totems. They towered over him and he, in awe, seemed to understand that they were trying to announce their history and place in the world. As they ate their ice cream, Peter told Anik that the totem poles were made by Indians.

"I'm Indian," Anik said. "Can I make totems?"

Peter laughed and mussed his hair. "Well, that's not what I meant, buddy . . . but, yes, of course you can."

"What's that one with the big wings and green face?"

"It's a thunderbird. Do you like it?"

"Yes, but thunderbirds aren't real," he said, licking the ice cream drips off the side of the cone. "I've never seen one."

"It's a mythical creature." Peter knelt down to Anik's level. "You see, sometimes totems tell stories of a family and sometimes they just tell stories."

"What, like a fairy tale?"

"Sort of."

"I don't like make-believe stories — except for dragons. I like them even though they aren't real."

Peter smiled and stood up. "If you were going to make a totem pole, what animal would you put on the top?"

"Maybe a killer whale or a wolf," he said and snapped his jaws up at Peter's face.

Just then Pavan walked over and stood between them, taking their hands in hers.

"I'd be a raven," she said. "They're magical creatures. In some Indigenous cultures they're known as Tricksters. When I see one, it reminds me that things can change, or better yet that things aren't always as they seem."

Anik nodded. "I like magic, but it's not real."

When he turned sixteen, his mother gave him a ring with a raven carved in silver. On the inside, an inscription — *the world has its own magic.* Sometimes he thinks about that when he's twirling the ring on his finger. Is the world real? Is it a Gabriel García Márquez novel, a trick, a slip of the hand, something to disappear into, to carve yourself up inside of? Sometimes he can't make sense of it all.

Most days he can't even remember where he was going or what he wanted. He hadn't meant to stay locked away but his room felt safe the way nothing else did. He couldn't explain away the fear, the anxiety, the way it crawled on him like a thousand thin-legged spiders. There was no reason for it, and since there was no reason for it, there was no solution for why his life, without warning, had stalled. At first, he blamed it on the long winter, gray days and tin skies, but even with spring brushing into the frame, he's still choked up, like an engine turning over, coughing and sputtering, a failure to ignite. Pavan was the first to realize something was wrong. He wasn't excited about studying music, even though it used to be all he'd ever wanted. His grades slipped and he flunked a semester and then didn't bother showing up for the next one. He stopped playing the piano in any meaningful way, he abandoned the classical standards and tuned his ear to the beautiful melancholy of minor chords. He'd strain his ear to the ivory, to hear how a note seemed to puncture the air and disappear, the same way a spark of light dies in the dark. Sometimes he'd open the top of the piano so he could feel the vibration coil through his ear. Pavan, recognizing the signs of depression, took him to a doctor, who prescribed antidepressants and therapy. Neither worked for him, not really. He remained numb, sick of himself, his anger turning inward, the beginning of his self-imposed exile.

At first, he likened it to meditation.

Like the Buddha who sat under the Bodhi tree for forty-nine days in search of enlightenment, he too was on a spiritual quest.

While sequestered, he read his mother's copy of *The Art of Happiness* by His Holiness the Dalai Lama and every other text about spirituality or religion on their bookcase. She had dozens of books on philosophy, monotheistic movements and New Age basics like Eckhart Tolle's *The Power of Now*. He devoured all of her self-help books, from the classics like *Man's Search for Meaning* to the dumbed-down *Chicken Soup for the Soul* series. It was hard for him to believe that his mother had ever read them; she's a hard-shelled pragmatist, prone to mini meltdowns when things don't go her way. He couldn't reconcile her with someone who'd tried yoga, meditation and mindfulness; who read theology, dogma and New Age bestsellers. But there it was: bookshelves of proof of her longing for wisdom and purpose, which clearly he'd inherited. Hope — that's what they were both after. In so many of the books, gratitude and happiness, or happiness through gratitude, seemed to be the pursuit, the goal and the measure. Anik found that hard to believe. Happiness is birthday cakes and Santa Claus, a word for children who don't know any better or for people who are content with the con. But in his reading, he learned that happiness was not to be confused with pleasure and that subtle distinction was what pulled Anik in and put him on a spiritual quest in earnest.

Like all good quests, there must be a purpose, a profound cause, a question for the hero's journey. For him they were one and the same: *why?* With a thick black felt marker he wrote a question mark on his wall, a reminder that everything starts with *the* question, not a question.

A few weeks into his exile, he got himself organized, cleaned up his desk, set up a red-tabbed binder full of loose-leaf paper and spent at least two hours a day devoted to his spiritual studies. Each morning, after eating his instant oatmeal, he tied his shoulder-length hair back, undressed and wrapped his bedsheet around himself, fashioning it like a Kasaya. Of course, he looked nothing like the ordained Buddhist monks in saffron robes. In fact, when he looked at himself in the full-length mirror, the white bedsheet wrapped around his thin frame made him look like he was in a Mahatma Gandhi Halloween costume that needed a bald cap. Regardless, something about nudity and the thinness of the sheet allowed him to shed himself and do what he named his "soul's work." He even started to listen to Oprah's *Super Soul* podcast. He took notes, highlighted bite-sized wisdom, forged his own spiritual text and distilled his learnings to three spiritual tenets:

Life is suffering and suffering comes from desire and attachment.

Our inability to accept suffering creates more suffering.

The only moment is the present; stay in the now.

Point three was profoundly simple yet complex in adaptation. No matter how much he meditated on it, he didn't know how to remain in the now. How could he act with a higher purpose and remain unattached to outcomes? How could he keep his mind from the backward slide of regret? How could he keep himself from casting hope for futures that don't exist? Over time, this idea of nowness, of purpose without attachment equaling faith and happiness, seemed naive, the work of a charlatan. The question that launched his crusade was the very one that ended it. Why bother? For if there could be no attachment, no conclusions, no assurances, then what was it all but a pile of wishes and hopes strung together like fairy lights — all ambience and no illumination.

After thirty days he abandoned his red binder, washed his sheet and put it back on the bed where it belonged. He trenched in, took refuge in the safe harbor of his bed, the comfort of a down quilt and the distraction of Netflix, Facebook and Instagram.

The phone rings. He doesn't try to answer it and just waits until it clicks over to the answering machine, listening to the message in real time. It's the school calling to tell his parents that Ash missed class again. He heard them arguing about it yesterday. It was the kind of argument that never resolves, the kind where each person makes their case in a loud emphatic way but nothing actually changes. A year ago, Anik would have intervened. He was always the peacekeeper, the good-natured one in the family, but ever since he pulled away, they seemed to have fallen apart or shifted their orbit. That's how he sees all of them — forever floating in space, never getting anywhere.

In the living room Anik replays the tone-deaf message of "concern." He can't believe they're concerned about attendance at a time like this. Jay's face flashes in front of his eyes and he's filled with regret for not telling Ash he'd come by a few days before he jumped. Anik tells himself it wouldn't have made a difference, or maybe it would have, but it doesn't matter, not now. He shakes his head but what he really wants is to shake his fist, to rattle the cage, to find a way out. It's then that Anik realizes that he and Jay aren't so different. He googles information on his death and finds none. Suicides aren't reported on. Jay never made the news; he'll be forgotten as soon as everyone can muster the strength to move on, because moving on equals progress and progress is where it's at, the currency of a good life.

Anik listens to the message once more before deleting it. He sits down, feeling good about having erased it, having covered for Ash, but he knows it's the least he can do. He's been a terrible brother.

Most days, he watches life unfold on his phone, letting envy eat him up. He still comments, he still likes, he still shares, he still acts like he's part of it all. He's even on Tinder, swiping left and right, going through the motions and then ghosting them all.

Day 7

She's lying on her bed like Jesus on the cross.

Her eyes are closed tight against the spring light and beneath her lids she watches her own kaleidoscope unfold. Patterns of gold, green and red rush, expand and collapse — a whole universe inside. Winona stays there, counting breaths. Her therapist says meditation is a good way to calm her anxious thoughts, to slow down moments to manageable chunks. It's never worked for her before; her thoughts circle and find new places to nest. Even the meds don't help. They just numb her out, make her soft and sad, make her insides dark and deep like an ocean. Sometimes she can swim inside herself and other times she floats around killing time, but eventually the panic swirls and pulls her under. It's moments like those that make her want to cut, to feel something — anything. She exhales again and tries to empty her thoughts. She's listening to ambient music, but the tones and bells don't drown out the sound of the twins playing in the other room so she grabs her headphones and clamps them over her ears, turns on the noise canceling until even her own breath goes seashell quiet. She imagines herself sitting in the pink inner tube, floating circles in their pool the way they did that last summer when everything was still good. The sky was so blue, the kind of blue there isn't a name for, the kind that makes you want to skywrite declarations of love. She did love him and now she thinks that he'll never know. As the song fades into the next, she hears her stepmother's muffled voice and opens her eyes.

"What the hell, Winona?" Trish is leaning over her, arms crossed. She'd look pissed if it wasn't for the Botox that gives her an always-surprised face.

Winona takes off her headphones and sits up. "What?"

"The school called," she says, pausing. "About you missing classes again?"

"So? Everyone skips. It's not a big deal."

"Well, I guess it *is* a big deal because they asked us to come in."

"Us?"

"I called your father and he's on his way."

"Thanks a lot," Winona says.

"Look, I'm sorry, I did try but I can't keep covering for you."

"Whatever." Winona puts her headphones back on.

Trish yanks them off. "Come on, get yourself together. He wants you to go with him." Trish pats Winona on the leg twice as if she's a horse needing a giddy-up.

"Why." She says it like a statement and then reluctantly gets up to shut the door behind Trish. She checks her look in the mirror and smooths out her bedhead. She's more pale and gaunt than usual, her eyes red from staying up late — '90s heroin chic. She turns away from the mirror and pulls off her T-shirt. She doesn't mind seeing her face but avoids the rest of herself. She knows her deficiencies by heart. The visual assault of small breasts; her no thigh gap; her disproportionate hip, waist, bust ratio; her silhouette — a beaker rather than an hourglass. She slips on a fresh white tee and turns back around, pulls her hair into a high pony and wears her glasses for a studious effect.

Downstairs, the twins rally, five-year-old voices chirping, "Daddy, Daddy."

From the stairs, Winona watches him hoist them up the same way he used to gather her in his arms when she was little.

"Jon!" Trish rushes over to greet him as if she's a '50s housewife. To Winona, Trish is a try-hard in every way. She tracks her steps, her sleep, her calories; her entire life is flattened into fifteen-minute intervals and scheduled onto a sticker-laden family calendar. She's a part-time yoga instructor, she's a book club member, she's a classroom mom and she cleans the house before the Clean and Tidy maids come by every Tuesday — only she'd never call them maids, she'd never call things what they are. As far as Winona's concerned, she's alright in every basic boring way except that her very presence is a reminder that her own mother is dead.

Winona leans over the banister. "This is such bullshit. Everyone ditches."

Jon hands the twins off to Trish. "Well, you're not everyone. You have a history. Grab your coat."

Winona follows her father out to his car. She connects her phone and streams David Bowie extra loud to deter whatever car lecture he has planned.

Jon taps the beat on the steering wheel. "Did I ever tell you that this was the song your mom and I danced to at our high school grad?"

"Like, only a hundred times," she says and turns it up even louder to drown him out. He can't carry a tune the way her mother could and he doesn't tell the story the way she did. She danced with him because she felt sorry for him. He was standing by the exit sign the entire night. "That's what we do as women," she once told Winona after having had one too many glasses of wine. "We rescue men from themselves and let them believe that they are the heroes in the story."

Jon pulls up to the school, parks in a reserved spot and reminds Winona to let him do the talking. She follows him into the office where the principal and guidance counselor are waiting.

"I'm Jonathan Winter, Winona's father. Call me Jon."

"Yes, of course, we've met before," Principal Carter says, shaking his hand, pumping one too many times. "This is Sheryl Kind, our school counselor."

"Ms. Kind or is it Mrs.? What a perfect name to have in your role," Jon says, disarming her with his smile.

"Sheryl, please." She's flustered the way women get around him. Winona snickers.

"Well, you all know my daughter already," he says looking over at Winona.

She flashes a pretend smile. There's an awkward moment where everyone is just staring at each other, waiting.

"So." Jon sits down without being asked, and the rest follow suit. "What's all this about?"

"Yes, right to it." Principal Carter smooths his tie as he collects his thoughts. "We're concerned because we haven't seen Winona at school much since the unfortunate incident."

"The incident?"

"Yes, with Jacob McAlister," Sheryl says.

"Oh, I see," Jon says. "And you're concerned because?"

"Well, they were friends, and given some of Winona's challenges in the past, we were obviously worried." He looks to Winona, clearing an opening for her.

"I'm fine. I just didn't feel like being at school. It's depressing." She watches her father's blank expression, the way he nods; she knows his half-day parenting seminar on mental well-being did not prepare him for variables, did not give him the compassion to go off-script, and she takes his discomfort as a personal victory.

"You know we have counselors available," Mrs. Kind says.

"Winona has all the support she needs," Jon says.

"Yes, it's just that leading up to the — incident, the art teacher had expressed some concern about Winona's final project."

"I'm sorry. I don't follow," Jon says.

"Mr. Winter, have you seen the art installation?"

"No, I can't say that I have."

She nods as if something has been made clear. "It might make more sense if you see it for yourself. Shall we?"

Winona follows them down the corridor. She watches as her father peeks into open doors as he passes; he's never been to parent-teacher nights. That was her mother's job, and after Lara died he ignored the school notices and teachers' requests to meet until they called him to tell him that Winona was in the hospital.

By the time he got there, her stomach had been pumped and she was sitting up in her bed, staring out the window. Sobbing, he rushed to her bedside where both of them muttered tear-soaked apologies and made promises that things would get better, promises neither could keep. She stayed at the hospital for a few weeks before she was released to outpatient care. He went to family therapy with her and, after each session, resolved to be a better father. Things got better for a few weeks. She stopped cutting. She started eating. Then it all went back to the way it had been, playing out over and over in its sameness like a video clip cycling back a few frames at a time.

"Here it is." Mrs. Kind points toward the back of the room.

Winona watches Jon stare at the installation, taking in the scope of its floor-to-ceiling dimensions. He steps closer and examines the layers of feathers, tissue paper and twigs that are fashioned together. Coins, newsprint, bottle caps, all chaotic and purposeless up close. He adjusts his perspective, moving around the installation — the image comes through best from a distance.

"It's a 3D portrait of Jacob McAlister's face," says Mrs. Kind, "but as you can see, the image itself is made up of thousands of small objects. It's really something. Your daughter is very talented."

"She gets it from her mother. She was an artist . . . a painter." He takes a closer look at the canvas and then backs up again to see it in its entirety. "Up close, it looks like nothing but random junk, but from further back — the face. Remarkable." He pauses for a second and without looking at Winona asks, "What inspired you to do this?"

Winona shrugs. "I don't know." If she tells him about the chaos of her mind, the things it holds onto, junk and meaning, beauty and hate, how all of it makes her who she is and how her perspective is both lost and found in the accumulation, he would only worry for her. Jay was the only one who truly understood.

"If you look closely, there's a repeated use of small plastic blue whales and broken doll parts to build up the eyes," Mrs. Kind points out.

"Yes, I see that," he says, reaching out to touch the plastic whales. "But I'm afraid I don't understand why you brought me here. Why the concern?"

"Well, obviously we are worried about her well-being, given her close friendship with Jacob, his recent passing and this," she says, pointing to the installation. "In some ways, it's unsettling."

"My late wife, if she were here, would tell you that art is meant to unsettle."

"Of course," Principal Carter says.

Jon, seeming to have forgotten the principal was even there, turns toward him. "So your point being?"

"We just want to make sure that Winona is alright and that you were fully aware of their friendship."

"Thank you for your concern. But Winona is fine. Aren't you, Winona?"

She nods.

"Good then. I think we're about done."

"There is one other thing," Mrs. Kind says. "The use of the blue whale motif."

"What of it?"

"Well, 'blue whale' is associated with an online game that's been linked to numerous deaths."

"What kind of game?"

"Perhaps we should speak alone? Maybe, Winona, you could wait outside."

Before Winona moves, Jon tells her to stay. "Please just say what you need to say."

"I really don't think —"

"What game?" he asks, his voice slightly raised.

"It's an alleged suicide game. Teens are lured into completing tasks over the course of several weeks, the final task being . . . a filmed suicide."

"Alleged," Jon says, in the same tone Winona's heard him use when he's preparing for a trial.

Principal Carter steps forward. "Yes, nothing official here, but dozens of teen suicides are linked to it overseas."

"And you think my daughter is somehow involved in this alleged game because she used tiny plastic whale figurines to make the blue of an eye . . ."

"Well, given her history and recent events. We thought it best to be cautious."

"The installation is distressing, I'll give you that. But your assertion is alarmist and unappreciated."

"Mr. Winters, we certainly didn't mean —" Principal Carter stops short.

"Didn't mean what?"

"To offend you."

"Well, you have. A boy is dead and to suggest that my daughter had something to do with it or has some knowledge of it just because she's had her own mental health challenges is preposterous." He opens the art room door and stands with his hands on hips as if he's in a standoff. "Winona, let's go. We're done here."

He doesn't say anything to her until they're in the car, doors locked. "What the hell is blue whale?"

She's chewing gum, snapping small bubbles. "It's a marine mammal and the largest animal to have ever existed on Earth."

"Don't be smart. I know what it is. You heard what they said in there, so what I'm asking *you* is is it anything *else*?"

"No. They're just being assholes. " She pulls her sweatshirt sleeves over her wrists so he doesn't finally notice her whale tattoo.

She glances at him. He's got that look in his eyes that he used at therapy, his attempt at patience.

"And this boy, Jacob? You've never mentioned him before."

"He was just a friend," she says.

"Be straight with me. Is there anything I need to know, Winona?"

She stares out the window, thinking of all the things he should know, all of the things he should have known, like how he should never have married Trish, how starting a new family was a betrayal to everything that ever mattered to her. But she doesn't say anything and presses her head against the window.

Trish rushes to the door when they get home. "Everything okay?" Her question upturns in a way that shows her age.

Jon kisses her as he steps inside. "It's fine. They're just being cautious since the thing with that boy Jacob. Maybe a bit too vigilant but . . ." He doesn't have a chance to finish his thought.

"You know, Jen at the studio said that she heard he jumped off the Lions Gate Bridge in the middle of the day. I bet he was high or something, I hear he was a real messed-up kid."

Winona gives her a murderous look before running up the stairs to her room, where she sits cross-legged on the bed, opening her laptop to Jay's Facebook page.

Rest in peace Jay

You were the best

I hope you find some peace RIP

She reads the posts, mouthing the words, but doesn't like or comment. She scrolls through his pictures and saves each one, keeping what she can before life takes him from her in pieces, the way it took her mother. She was only nine when her mother died, and now she barely remembers the sound of her voice. But what she can't forget is how her mother looked in the hospital, her bald head and gaunt face, a dainty but somewhat pained smile and big blue oval eyes just like her porcelain dolls'. Winona threw them all away after her mother died.

The most recent post is from a girl Winona doesn't recognize: *For any of you struggling, reach out, I will be there for you.*

Winona's thinking of all of the things she wants to say to all of the randoms posting: They didn't know Jay. They won't remember him. Tomorrow they'll be Snapchatting their filtered faces and #IWokeUpLikeThis vanity posts and they'll forget. But not her. She can't forget.

Day 11

Ash isn't religious.

He doesn't know anyone who actually goes to church on the regular, but his friends all agree that the minister must be cool on account of his messages on the church sign. Last week he posted, "Forgive your enemies, it messes with their heads." Today the signboard is blank and Ash stares at it as if it means something like death is a great void, a blank space, an unknown. He shakes his head, trying not to overthink. Out front, there's already a line to get into the chapel and he queues up. He can't help but hear the girls around him talking random shit, as if the funeral is some social event. They've been talking about it all week, in classes and online, asking who was going, what they're wearing and what they're going to do after the service. A bunch of Jay's friends brought their boards with them and are going to the skate park after. By the looks of it, some of them are already stoned. Can't really blame them.

Inside, the church smells like old people and damp coats. Sun streams through the narrow stained-glass windows, lighting up every other pew in a weird orange-soda glow. The chapel is standing room only; the wood-paneled walls are lined with randoms and faculty making a show of being there. Ash didn't want to come, he wanted to remember Jay in his own way, but his parents, who are waving at him now from their seats, insisted they make an appearance "out of respect." They're always talking to him about doing the right thing; it's exhausting and today he's got *give up* written all over his face. Whenever the school called home about him skipping classes, or sent an email about his lack of attention and missed assignments, Pavan sat him down and told him that life was full of doing things you don't want to do and that he needed to learn that it isn't all about him.

Ash asked her once, "If my life isn't about me, then who is it about?" Obviously that didn't go over well and Peter looked up from whatever he was doing to double down and give some fatherly advice. Classic good cop, bad cop. "Just put your head down and do the work, buddy."

And though Ash got what they were saying, he figures the reason teachers singled him out was partly their fault. They taught him to think, told him not to be a sheep, but then whenever things get real, they just want him to fall in line like the rest of the flock. He's learned to nod a lot, to say "I'm sorry," to tell them what they want to hear.

Ash sits down, avoiding eye contact with them and everyone else by focusing on his dress shoes — Anik's shoes actually, a half size too big for him, but his mom insisted he take off his Jordans and put them on, even if it meant wearing an extra pair of socks. Now he wishes Anik had come with them, but as always he wasn't up to it. His parents argued about that in their shortcut way, the way they do when it comes to their kids. They don't really fight; they simmer, never quite boiling over. Sometimes, Ash watches as if he's a spectator looking in on their house from above and sees the smallness of it. Table, chair, bed, walls, all props for their little charades. Everyone wants something. Everyone wants what's best and no one knows what that is, just that it's slightly out of reach, always. Try-hards. That's what Jay used to call people who were always striving, the straight-A kids with their hands pointed high in the air, an answer at the ready. It's not that he didn't like them; it's just that he liked people more when they didn't try so hard. But everyone's trying — trying to fit in, stand out, hide out, come out, blend in, so many ways to be and not be at the same time. Broken people always gravitated to Jay, because he didn't see them as broken, and to them, he didn't seem broken either — until now.

Ash looks up at the chapel ceiling — no vaulted arches, no Renaissance inspiration, no fancy stained-glass Jesus, not even a Last Judgment blue-sky fresco.

Jay's video loops through Ash's brain, and though he's tried to stuff it away, it plays at random — unsteady shots of sky, Jay's voice broken by that high-up wind, the inlet below, all of it boomeranging in his mind.

When he first watched the clip, he didn't think Jay was going to jump. When Jay went live, he, like everyone, thought it was just another stunt. Last year on a dare, Jay climbed a crane on a construction site and the year before he joined a charity group rappelling down the side of a high-rise to raise money for firefighters — not because he cared much about raising money, but because he wanted to know what it felt like to free fall. Jay was always thrill-seeking. Lisa's standard goodbye to him was "Jacob, be careful." Even when they were kids, he was always doing dumb stuff. He once convinced Ash to follow him up the tallest oak tree in the park, showing him which branches to grab as they climbed higher and higher into the canopy. Unlike Jay, Ash couldn't see the foot holds and fell, breaking his arm. He had to wear a cast for the rest of the summer, but not Jay — he had never broken a bone in his life.

It's a closed casket. Some kid, whose uncle's friend was a paramedic on the scene, told Ash that Jay's head was smashed from the force of the fall, that he was identified through dental records and other markers, like the stick-and-poke whale tattoo on his arm. It's the same tattoo that Winona has. People are talking about that too. That somehow this is her fault. Ash hasn't seen her since that day at the skate park. She hasn't been at school, but even if she had, he probably wouldn't have talked to her. Something about her makes him feel weird and okay at the same time. Ash keeps staring at his shoes until the minister breaks through the organ music.

"We are gathered here together to say farewell to Jacob McAlister and commit him to the hands of God."

Ash looks up at the minister. He expected a better intro from this hipster guy with the funny church sign but he's coming off as normal — just a short dude with trim blond hair, a Disney jawline and perfect teeth. He's smiling and talking with the full expanse of his arms about God's plans without any funny reference to Drake. He's such a disappointment and Ash isn't really listening — not to his sermon, not to the terrible hymns that follow, and no, just no, to the slideshow soundtracked to Green Day's classic "Time of Your Life." Ash's knee is bouncing up and down and he can't seem to concentrate on anything but the shiny black casket, thinking how soon that box will be lowered into the ground.

The song lyrics punch in and he glances at his mother. She's tearing up and taking in short breaths, wiping tears before they fall. Pavan pats his hand, in her *it's okay* way, only it's not and never is and it's exhausting. She's exhausting. He pulls his hand away and stares straight ahead. The only other funeral he's ever been to was for his mom's mom. It was weird to think of her as a grandmother because he'd never known her and seeing her dead in her casket, her face gray and waxy, was the worst way to meet her. The service was in Punjabi but he didn't need to know the language to understand they weren't welcome. Later that day Ash heard his dad telling his inconsolable mom that the funeral was the closure she needed to let go of her old life, and now as he sits here he wonders if that's why they insisted he come. Closure. As if.

After the slideshow is over, he follows his parents into the long line of people waiting to pay their respects. Some nod at the casket as they walk by and others touch it, leaving sweaty palm prints on the black lacquer finish. Ash tries not to look at the palm prints but he can't help it and discreetly wipes them as he walks by. He glances at the large easel-mounted portrait of Jay; he's wearing a suit and tie, his hair is slicked back and he's got a studious look about him. It's the kind of picture a grandparent would frame. It looks nothing like him. As Ash walks past the portrait he gets the feeling that imposter Jay's eyes are following him and it makes his insides melt.

"We are so sorry for your loss," Peter says. Lisa's sitting in the front pew, stoic, her thin frame all limbs and angles held tight. She has a hard-lived face, sunspots and bags under her eyes, loose skin, the kind of face you might see on the street, weathered and numb, the kind of face that hides all her goodness. Her boyfriend, Paul, is by her side, wearing blue jeans and a denim shirt with a red tie. His sleeves are rolled up, revealing his shitty skull-and-roses tattoo and his long thin hair is pulled back in a ponytail.

Ash steps ahead of his parents, heading for the exit while others stand around. Their small talk gathers and rises, amplifies in his ears and makes it hard for him to think of anything beyond "I need to get the fuck out of here." He's barreling toward the door when the minister steps in front of him and places a hand on his shoulder.

"Hold on there. Are you alright, son?"

He shrugs his hand off. "I'm not your son," he says and pushes the wooden doors open. The air slaps his face and instantly he feels better and even a little sorry for being a dick to the minister. He checks his phone; it's mostly funeral stories on Snapchat. He keeps his head in the screen as people file out into the parking lot, pretending not to see Britt as she walks over.

"Hey," she says.

"Hey."

"We're going for sushi," she says, pointing to their friends. "You want to come?"

He glances at them, huddled up and curled into their phones, thumb swipe after thumb swipe, taking in nothing. "Can't," he says, not bothering to make an excuse, not bothering to look at her for more than a second at a time.

"Oh. Are you mad at me or something?" She's twirl-yanking a piece of long hair in that way she does when she's feeling insecure, when she needs to be told she's not fat, that she's pretty, that she's good and perfect just as she is.

Ash doesn't give her what she needs and just says, "No."

"Okay, then. Call me later?" She walks away, looking back every few steps. He watches as she rejoins her friend circle and how after a moment they crane their head his way. She probably told them that he was being a jerk and of course that was true, he didn't know why he was, only that it felt good to care less.

His parents come out a few minutes later, suggesting they make their way to the cemetery for the burial.

"I don't want to go," he says.

His mom tilts her head, a sure sign that a speech is coming.

Peter rescues him. "It's okay. We don't have to go if you don't want to."

"But Peter."

"It's fine," he says, cutting her off. "We paid our respects and that's what we set out to do."

They pile into the car.

"Can I get a slushy?" Ash asks, remembering that as kids, he and Jay used to get them every Friday after school.

"What? No. It's hardly the time," Pavan says. "We've just been at a funeral."

"I didn't know that funerals and slushies were mutually exclusive."

"Don't be like that."

"Like what? Thirsty?" He snaps his seatbelt in place.

"Ash, please, not today."

"What's the big deal?"

Her jaw muscles clench momentarily, as if she's biting down, swallowing something bitter, but she doesn't say anything and he takes it as a win. Peter pulls into the gas station and tells him to go inside.

"I needed gas anyways," he says before Pavan can object.

Ash is the only customer in the Mini Mart and it's eerily quiet like that moment in a horror movie when something bad is about to happen. The cashier, a thin Indian guy with a turban, is watching the security camera monitors as if it's a TV. He looks nervous and sweaty and Ash wonders if he's sick or whether he just looks like every other freshie, kinda ripe and grimy. From the back of the store, Ash waves at him. He looks up from the monitor and gives a meek smile and part of Ash wants to go and chat with him for no reason, the way his dad does with people.

Every time Peter comes home from a business trip, he tells them about some cabbie he met who was an engineer or doctor in their home country but has been forced to drive a cab to make ends meet here. He says this as though he's impressed with them. He shares their story — how many children they have and how many hours they drive a day. The last cabbie he told them about was studying for his citizenship test and told him all the Canadian factoids he was learning. "Don't all Canadians know these things?" the cabbie asked, listing off prime ministers' names and accomplishments. Peter admitted that they should but don't. He said the cabbie nodded as if he understood. "It's hard to know what you are when it's all you have ever been. For me, I am Indian, but soon I will be Canadian, a proud one at that." At this part of the story Peter slapped his thigh and said, "Can you believe that? This guy has given up so much of his life, he's driving a cab so his kids can have more opportunities — and not a hint of bitterness." Pavan said something about the grateful immigrant syndrome, but Peter just went on talking, saying that he told the cabbie that he was married to an Indian and then tried to speak a little Punjabi, a few words like Sat Sri Akal, paaji, which of course made the cabbie laugh. He told them all of this like it mattered, like they should care.

Pavan says, "Dad makes friends with everyone," like it's a bad thing, but now as Ash glances at the cashier and thinks of how tedious it must be to work inside a plexiglass box, he realizes why his dad does it.

"Excuse me," he says, and grabs a big cup, "do you have a favorite flavor?"

The guy eyes Ash with suspicion. "No. They're all good."

Ash nods, disappointed that he doesn't even have an accent. "Alrighty then," he says and presses the button, pouring a layer each of Coke, cream soda and Orange Crush into the clear cup just like Jay would have. Ash snaps the lid on and goes to pay — he hands him the money and forgets the niceties. As he pockets the change, the door chimes open and Winona walks in wearing all black. To him, she almost looks normal, except for her bug-eyed sunglasses that are too big for her face. It's not even that sunny outside.

"Hey, classic rainbow. Good choice. Jay's fave."

Ash takes a sip, trying to avoid the small talk.

"How was the funeral?"

"Good, I guess. I don't know."

"Which was it? Good or you don't know? Can I have some?" She takes a long sip before he can answer. "I love that feeling." She scrunches her face up for a full five seconds. "You know brain freeze is literal, right? Like your brain is actually cold because it's right above the roof of your mouth."

"Interesting." Ash glances outside. "I gotta go."

She grabs his arm. "You know how you can get rid of brain freeze? You just put your tongue to the roof of your mouth for a few seconds to warm it up. Like this," she says, demonstrating, her words rolling up at the back of her mouth.

Ash heads out the door, turning back before it closes. "Hey, why didn't you go the funeral?"

She doesn't answer. She just stares at him, bug-eyed and swipes a stash of gummy bears into her pocket.

"Who were you talking to?" Pavan's on her phone, scrolling and talking, doing the very thing she tells him not to.

Ash buckles up. "No one. Just some girl."

"A friend of yours?" She has a way of continuing even the most mundane conversation as if she's on a covert operation, investigating and researching.

"No. She was a friend of Jay's."

"Odd, I didn't see her at the funeral." She clicks the phone off.

Ash knows she's waiting for him to respond. She always does this. She makes a statement and waits for a minute, thinking he'll fill up the silence with some tidbit without her having to ask. It's a benign parental thing she does but he doesn't feel like dealing today. He takes a sip of slushy. "Want some?"

She takes a long sip and hands it back quickly.

"Brain freeze?" He can see her pucker face in the side mirror.

She nods, still pinch-faced.

Ash doesn't tell her how to get rid of it.

Day 11

Ash doesn't talk on the way home.

He just keeps sucking back that slushy, and as much as Pavan wants to fill the quiet she doesn't bother.

"Talking makes things too real," Peter once told her. "Boys talk without saying the things —"

"Without saying the things that need saying?" she said, interrupting him. She'd noticed that whenever she did this, his shoulders dropped a little as if she'd stolen a punch line but hadn't gotten it quite right.

"Well, no, but — yes. It sounds crazy but it's just that way with boys. They'll figure things out. We all do."

"Really?"

"Yes, but in our own way. Not everyone is you."

She knew he said this as a reminder but she took it as an insult. Her way of doing things is so particular that there's little room for anyone else, yet what she wants most is for each of them to find their way, and to find it easier than she had, but of course they don't see that. All they see is control, her every effort a lever or restraint.

She stares out the window and watches the suburban sprawl, mostly fast-food restaurants, low-rise apartment blocks and strip malls with their dirty little parking lots and their overcrowded signposts: Nail Salon, Pho Vietnam, 24/7 Fitness, Dollar Mart. The strip malls are what she hates most about suburban life, the horrid soulless convenience of it all. The only thing she misses about England is the high street — proper shops and friendly locals. Everything she'd needed was within walking distance, but here at home it's all drive and buy. In the side-view mirror she catches herself — stern-faced and tired — and wonders if that's what she looks like and if that's what other people see. Resting bitch face — that's what Ash called it when he asked her why she looked so upset one day.

She looks at her reflection again and widens her eyes, grins a little and tilts her head just so. "That's better," she thinks and tells herself that she should make a point of smiling more. People have always told her that — such a pretty face, if only . . . if only you lost some weight, if only you tried a bit of makeup, if only you smiled more. Her ex-husband was always after her about the way she looked. "Make an effort," he'd say, not realizing that she had, she really had. She had gone to Boots and the woman behind the cosmetics counter had sold her all kinds of powders and concealers, that once at home, Pavan couldn't remember how to apply and in what order she was to apply them. Concealer, corrector and then powder or primer? Corrector and then powder? It was no use; she was simple and a highlight powder or a pallet of frosty nude eye shadows wouldn't change that. Her simplicity, at first, had been a virtue. Obedient, family-oriented, quiet — this was how her mother had described Pavan to her soon-to-be in-laws as if they were adopting a dog, not seeking a wife for their son.

She glances over at Peter. His green eyes, sun-kissed complexion and deep laugh lines disarm her even after all of these years. She was twenty-six when she hired him to handle her divorce. As her lawyer, Peter came to know everything about her — he knew the most intimate details of her life and had offered her tissues as she'd cried recounting the details of her abusive marriage. After having shared so much, she felt connected to him even though she knew very little about him. Later, she realized that he had that easy way about him that made people feel comfortable. Maybe it was the slight drawl in his voice or his sunset-quiet tone that made her feel as if she was sitting on a front porch talking to a friend, or maybe it was just that he was the first person to ever listen to her. Really listen.

In the end, her divorce came down to a few signatures and time. There was no property, no real assets, just an unborn child that Bal wanted no involvement with. And so after several months, she signed a paper and Peter told her, "That's it, you're free." She stared at her signature and held on to the pen as if it was a knife, something that cut her ex — along with her entire family who'd disowned her — out with a definitive stroke. She tucked the pen, Knight and Associates printed on it in gold, into her purse and there it stayed, a reminder of that day. Over time the *and Associates* brushed off but his name remained.

She didn't see Peter again for another few years, by which time he too was divorced and had left family law for a career in life coaching. They chatted in the produce section of the grocery store, though the energy between them had its own language. She can't remember who said what, just that they were standing by the tomatoes and root vegetables and that he remembered her name. That was enough.

She looks at him now as he's singing along to some Top 40 song on the radio.

"How do you know all the lyrics?"

"Ash was playing it on repeat the other day," he says, tapping the steering wheel and moving his head in some mock hip way that Ash would normally say was cringeworthy. Pavan turns around laughing, expecting Ash to groan or at least make some comment about his dad's terrible singing but he's got his earbuds in and is staring out the window. He hasn't noticed a thing.

When they get home, Ash heads straight to his room, ignoring Pavan's "Are you hungry?" followed by her suggestion that he should eat.

"It's awful," Pavan says when she hears his bedroom door slam shut.

"What is?" Peter drops the keys on the kitchen counter.

Pavan opens the fridge and stares inside for a minute before shutting the door. "Everything, I guess. I don't know what I'm supposed to do."

"You're not supposed to do anything. It'll be okay. It'll take some time but now that the funeral is done, he can start to move on."

"I still think we should have gone to the cemetery. They were friends for a long time."

"It's a lot to ask of a kid his age. We've got to let him take this at his own pace."

Pavan shrugs and leans against the counter, stretches her neck both ways. "Why do you think Jay did it? You know there wasn't even a note. His poor mother — always wondering why."

"Who knows? None of it makes sense."

Pavan watches as Peter takes off his jacket and places it on a chair back. She makes a point of picking it up and hanging it in the hall closet.

"I was going to do that," he says. "You just didn't give me a chance." He kisses her on the cheek and she pulls away, suddenly annoyed by his charm, his goodness.

"Do you think Lisa saw the video before it was taken down?"

"Who?"

"Lisa — Jay's mom."

"I don't know. I hope not," he says, loosening his tie. "I've got to change. Hockey practice." He kisses her again. "I'll grab dinner with the guys."

She sits down at the kitchen island, envying his ability to compartmentalize, to stay on the surface of things, and wonders if that's what it means to be the simple man he's always claimed to be. But for his coaching clients he's all in, sorting out their complex lives, building ten-step programs to personal success and life balance, as if there was such a thing. Sometimes she watches his now-famous TEDx Talk, "Love Is a Four-Letter Word," and tries to heed his advice but wonders if his shtick of self-love first and foremost is his way of justifying an unearned selfishness. After that talk's viral success, he ended up on the morning show circuit, and his story resonated: *Ex divorce lawyer turned life coach has advice for your relationship*, with his headshot — handsome man, scruff-shaved, bedroom-eyed poster boy. His brand appealed to both women and men over thirty-five; men wanted to be him, and women wanted to be with him. His TEDx Talk views sky-rocketed to eighteen million and opened the door to a book deal and a nationwide workshop tour. He crisscrossed the country, preaching self-love as a way toward intimacy while Pavan stayed at home with the boys. He'd call every night, completely jazzed by how many people he was helping while she dealt with bath time and bedtime stories. She realizes now that solving the everyday problems of family life would never be enough for him compared to fame and adoration. He can inspire strangers to change their lives but rarely remembers to pick up milk on the way home. He says domestic details are her thing, and he's right; she's always been completely obsessive about every little thing, and now she's obsessed with Jay's death.

Last night she googled the video and was disappointed that she couldn't find it. She was left to only imagine how it must have been — a boy falling, the landscape tumbling, the crash of water and then what? She wonders what darkness plagued him and how he went from the boy with the sweet big eyes and curly hair to the boy who's being buried today.

She glances at her watch and wonders if there's still time to go to the graveside service. She takes her purse from the counter and pulls out the funeral program. She unfolds it and with a flat palm irons out the center crease that cuts across Jay's face. As she rereads the details, she wonders what will happen to all of these leaflets. Will they be recycled, tossed in the trash or left in purses only to be found weeks or months later — perhaps some of the pocketed programs will be forgotten and end up in the laundry until they are pulped and dried into a wad of fiber and lint? His school photo stares back at her and she decides there's no point in going now; it's too late. How would her being there help anyways? She tucks the program into the side pocket of her purse, careful not to crease it even more and thinks if only someone had intervened for him the way someone had for her.

Like Jay, she hadn't left a note. She'd simply walked out. She wandered for hours until she realized she had nowhere to go and ended up on Tower Bridge staring into the water. She'd never learned to swim and was always terrified by the idea of drowning. Yet there she was contemplating it, not thinking of anything beyond letting go, beyond falling. Her marriage had never been a happy one; he'd never loved her. She was a concession he'd made to his parents, and now — a baby. She placed her hands on her abdomen, telling herself it was still a nothing, only a few cells, smaller than a seed. She gripped the rails and just as she was about to step onto the ledge, a man approached. She still remembers how he looked at her with a half smile, how his innocent "Can you take our picture?" in his Australian accent surprised her. He motioned to his two small children and wife and handed Pavan his camera. She took it from him as if he was offering up something more. She waited as they gathered into the frame, the city behind them, the midday sun glinting on the river. She pressed the button, clicked the frame forward and clicked again. She handed it back to him. "I took two in case one doesn't work out." After they walked away she followed them, keeping a distance behind. When they stopped for ice cream, so did she. Pralines and cream. She can still remember the thick caramel swirls coating her tongue and throat. Sweetness was all she could taste.

When she was thousands of miles away she called back, over the ocean and across the time zones, and told Bal she was filing for divorce. She often wonders about that family on the bridge, that roll of film, whether they developed it and placed the photo in an album and that album on a shelf. Whether somehow, by accident or on purpose, her thumb made it into the frame.

It's always been a reminder to her of how things work, the small interventions. When we're the luckiest we don't even know it's happening. We take it for granted that life finds a way despite our best attempts at ending it.

Day 13

Anik is trying to meditate again.

He can hear Ash's heavy footsteps above, the slam of his bedroom door and the blinds drawn shut. He imagines Ash sitting
on his bed, scrolling a screen while he sits below, lotus position
on a yoga mat, tea lights lit, pretending to be at peace. He tries to
concentrate on his breathing, pulls his shoulders back and down
away from his ears. He extends his spine, imagining a thin silver
thread running from his sacrum to the top of his head. He inhales
through his nose for four seconds, holds it for seven and exhales
for eight. The process always makes him a little light-headed, not
clearheaded the way it's meant to. He repeats the four, seven,
eight breathing pattern he learned on YouTube, but he can't find
enough personal Zen to block out the music that's now thumping
above him. Anik doesn't recognize the artist; he prefers post-punk
and is sure that Ash's affinity for rap culture is a rebellion against
his parents' Leonard Cohen loving ways. Anik, having written an
essay on the history of hip-hop for his contemporary music class,
told Pavan not to worry. "Rap is just the protest music of now; it's
misunderstood by the masses that are scared of the social and cul-
tural realities being overtly voiced."

"So, you think it's a reflection of our times?" Pavan said, still
unsure but interested.

"The world contains multitudes, Mother," he told her, reminding her of her own wisdom on perspective. People can be many
things, life is a study in contradictions — the world, a meditation

on slow justice. She said this thing about multitudes over dinner, after watching news coverage on yet another mass shooting in the U.S. perpetrated by a seemingly normal white guy. Anik can't remember which shooting it was, nothing seemed to stick in his mind after the horror of Sandy Hook, the images of small children walking out of the school single file, hand in hand, frightened and obedient. He was fourteen at the time. Though Pavan tried to show him that people were inherently good and often talked about changemakers and thought leaders, the brave and bold throughout history, he couldn't help but notice that good did not prevail. He knew his mother felt this way too, even though she tried so hard at hope. She started listening to Marvin Gaye's "What's Going On" and "Mercy Mercy Me" on repeat when Donald Trump became the U.S. president.

Sometimes Peter would make her a vodka seven and they'd sip and slow dance in the living room the way they used to. Anik liked to think of them that way, coffee table pushed to the side of the room, Peter twirling her under his arm, the to-and-fro, back-and-forth sway, head-thrown-back laughter of being in and out of sync. The boys would tease them as they passed by the room, yet there was nothing better than to see them together like that, a sort of hope at its simplest. When they were little, they'd peek through the doorway and they'd giggle, their hands in front of their mouths, and slowly sneak away to the family room where they played on the vintage Nintendo Pavan had picked up at a garage sale. While other kids had new consoles, they were left with the clunky cartridge decks and wired remotes of their parents' generation. Thinking of it now makes him nostalgic, and he searches his closet for the console. He pulls it down from the top shelf and blows off a layer of dust, using a nearby T-shirt to wipe away the rest. He carries it into the family room and hooks it up to the old TV that stands like a black monolith in the corner of the room, among all the other relics. The family room houses a vintage StairMaster, a treadmill and a mishmash of furniture no longer nice enough for upstairs but still perfectly functional. An overstuffed leather sectional, a glass and brass coffee table and all of Peter's promo material, including a life-sized cutout of him that he uses at workshops and speaking events. Two-dimensional Peter in his squared-up stance, arms crossed over his chest, confident expression, stares back at Anik, judging. Anik picks Peter up and turns him around, placing him in the corner. He's sick of seeing his know-it-all, well-meaning face; he's tired of his thoughtful lectures, his SMART life-goal planning, his emailed article links on how to develop a growth mindset. After a while, Anik became sure that Peter's concern is just ego worry that someone will find out that Mr. Life Coach can't help his own son. Correction — stepson. What a perfect public relations escape hatch, a nature over nurture loophole if anyone were to find out about him.

Anik texts Ash:

> want to play vid games

Sure, be online in ten?

> no, downstairs

??

> old school super mario

k

Anik sits down, his knee bouncing. He hasn't really spent time with Ash since Jay died. They've texted a bit about it but that's it. He knows he should have gone to the funeral; it would have been the right thing to do, the decent big brother thing to do. But the gap between knowing and doing has widened for him. From the kitchenette, he grabs a bag of chips and a bowl. It'll be just like it was when they were kids and would binge on junk food, drink Orange Crush and play games, trash-talking as they leveled their way through the game.

Ash knocks on the door before opening it.

"You don't need to knock." Anik unwraps a packet of buttery popcorn and tosses it in the microwave.

Ash flops onto the couch, glances at the small room crammed with junk. His parents always meant to rent the basement suite out, a mortgage helper they called it, but then Peter's video went ape and money suddenly wasn't a thing anymore. As kids, they spent hours down there, building forts and playing hide-and-seek, but Ash hasn't been downstairs since Anik took over the suite and fell into his depression. Pavan doesn't like him to use the word *depression*, she prefers *funk, rough patch,* and *phase,* any grouping of words that helps her believe that things will be okay with time. While Anik waits for the microwave to beep, Ash hops onto the StairMaster and starts stepping, ratcheting the tension up and pressing down hard. It looks like he's walking in slow motion, like some superhero in the action sequences they played at when they were young. Anik doesn't say anything and lays out the snacks on the coffee table as if he's hosting. He puts a handful of popcorn in his mouth and motions to Ash with the controller.

"Just a sec." Ash, winded, steps off.

Anik starts the game and is first up. He plays with his whole body, torso tightening and head bobbing up and down as he runs and jumps through the levels. "I'm sorry. I should have gone to the funeral."

"It's okay."

"How was it?" he asks, not averting his eyes from the screen. "Never mind, dumb question." He keeps on playing to the end, jumping Mario onto the flag and into the next level. He debates whether to tell Ash that Jay had come by the week that he jumped, that Anik didn't answer the door, but decides there's no point. "It sucks — what happened, all of it. He was a good guy."

"Yeah, he was."

Anik realizes how strange it is to use the past tense and thinks how odd that Jay will be forever remembered as he was. Unlike him, Jay won't get old, he won't have a house and a car and 2.5 kids and a dog. He won't adult, he won't have to get a job, pay bills and deal with everything that sucks. He'll be forever young, like that cheesy song Peter likes so much.

"How are Mom and Dad? Are they being weird about it?"

"Totally weird. Mom watches everything I do like I'm in some control group, you know?"

"Yeah, she's just worried. It's what she does." Anik drops the controller. "Fuck," he says, as his Mario falls off a cliff. "Your turn." He hands off the controller. "And Dad? Is he coaching you through it?"

Ash groans. "Thank God, no." He races through the level with ease. Neither of them says anything and the video game soundtrack fills the awkward silence. "Mom's worried you're depressed. I hear them talking." He pauses as he captures the coins onscreen. "Are you depressed?"

"Nah. I'm just trying to figure some things out." Anik glances at him. He doesn't want Ash to worry, not about him, especially now.

"Like what things?"

Anik doesn't know how to answer without sounding like a self-indulgent idiot and says, "I don't know," which beneath the sound of the cheerful *Mario* song sounds ominous.

Ash hands the controller to Anik. "You know Jay had this girl-friend named Winona."

"Like the actress in *Stranger Things*?"

"Yeah."

"Weird. Why would someone name their kid after her?"

"I don't know; it's beside the point. Anyways what I was trying to say is that she, Winona, is this totally weird chick, some days goth, some days prep, a hard to figure out artsy type. Jay told me she used to keep a list of bad news headlines in a scrapbook. She cut articles and pictures out and glued 'em all into a collage and then she used all of that in this crazy-ass art installation of the inside of Jay's head."

"What? Why'd she do that?"

"Guess it reminded her that we are all messed up. That life is pretty bad. Self-fulfilling prophecy type way to deal and not deal."

"That's depressing."

"Exactly. She kept herself miserable and I think she made Jay miserable too."

"Now you sound like Mom. Depression isn't contagious."

"I know, it's just that if you focus on the negative, there isn't much room for anything else." Ash pauses, watching Anik play for a moment before adding, "Maybe that's why you're upset."

"Huh?"

"You're upset because you spend your time thinking about being upset."

"I'm not upset."

"Well, depressed then or whatever. I just think you have to get out of your head and get over it. Maybe leave this room as a start."

"I told you, I'm just trying to figure things out." He's annoyed now and tosses the controller. "This game is fucking stupid." He tries to remember his breathing but can't seem to count it out and exhales in small spasms.

"Are you okay?"

Anik nods, feeling foolish. He tries to channel his inner Buddha, conjures up the sound of chanting monks, bells, rain, anything that will bring him down. "I'm fine." He picks up the controller and passes it to Ash who expertly maneuvers his way through the levels, commenting only on the play until the music picks up to signal that time is running out. He narrows his focus but jumps a second too soon and Luigi falls, the synthesizer calypso tune slows and descends. Game over.

Day 17

Winona's sitting on the couch, under a giant furry blanket watching CNN. She convinced Trish to let her take a sick day and now that the house is empty and her absence from school excused, Winona settles in with a bowl of popcorn and Anderson Cooper on the PVR. She loves his silver hair, his alabaster skin, how it practically sparkles as if he's an elf from Middle Earth somehow made real. He's talking Trump in his perfectly dreamy way and she's fixated on today's morality pitch. She watches CNN mostly for the moral outrage, and when she's up for something a bit more *Jerry Springer*–like, she tunes into Fox and folds into the drama. Her mother used to watch soap operas. She recorded them and watched them after work while she made dinner. Winona would sit in front of the TV and do her homework, and every so often Lara ducked her head through the kitchen pass-through to catch the best bits. Political news to Winona was a lot like a soap opera and was one of the things she and Jay watched together. Since Jay didn't have cable at home, she recorded it and they'd watch, fast-forwarding to the good parts. He loved the extreme weather reporting. Hurricane season was his favorite with their boy/girl-next-door names, the Mother Nature doesn't care, in-your-face, fuck-you of it all. "Losing everything makes people better," he said, after Hurricane Harvey. She told him that was easy for him to say since he was sitting on her comfy couch.

"Maybe, but wouldn't you rather have less? Wouldn't you like the reminder that life isn't supposed to be work, buy, sleep, repeat?"

"Sure, but I wouldn't want my whole life washed away." Winona glanced at the on-screen footage of an elderly woman being airlifted from her rooftop. "Look at that poor woman. She doesn't deserve that."

"Maybe she does," Jay said, stone-faced. "Maybe she was an awful mother who beat her kids or maybe she kept them locked in a cage or some shit like that." She waited for him to crack. He had a way of saying bullshit stuff just to get a reaction. She was such an easy mark.

"You're horrible," she said, throwing popcorn at him.

"Do it again." He opened his mouth to catch the incoming kernels.

Winona sits back and tosses the popcorn in the air, trying to catch it in her mouth but gives up after several failed attempts. She mutes the TV, watches the soundless bobbleheads and makes up new lines for them to say in their newsy voices. "Jacob McAlister is dead. Sources say that he fell from a bridge while filming a stunt, while others close to him say that he'd been depressed in recent weeks and fear he took his own life." She repeats the phrase "took his own life" and sits with the strangeness of it, the abstraction of what it means to take something that is you, to take something that is you to some unknown.

"Where do the dead go?" she says in her newsy voice, imagining the variations of hell and heaven, purgatory and nothingness that she and Jay had talked about in a baked haze. He once told her that when he was seven he passed out from a fever and left his body and had what he was sure was a near-death experience. He floated over himself for a minute before being sucked into a swirling vortex of souls that tried to grab him. Some force propelled him out of that tornado and through a tunnel toward a pinprick of light, which opened up into a magnificence of colors, a swirl of turquoise, gold and violet, with starry arms like a Van Gogh painting come to life. And as beautiful as it was, what he remembered most was the smoky figures, the souls that stretched out from the sides of the vortex attempting to pull him in. For a while, he was obsessed with it and filled an entire art pad with drawings of it. His mom grew worried when his teacher called to show her the drawings. His shadowy black crayon tunnel, intricately shaded in stark contrast to his classmates' stick figures and sunshine rays. Lisa took him to the doctor, who explained it away as a hallucination. He stopped drawing the pictures but he never forgot the visions and once, while in a drug-induced haze, had suggested to Winona that they recreate the experience by playing the choking game. He'd wanted to try it on his own but was scared that he'd accidentally die, so he'd never got further than watching instructional videos about it. People said that the asphyxiation was like a high, but he wasn't interested in that. He didn't want to feel the euphoria, the fuzzy feeling of brain cells dying, the supernova-like explosion; he wanted to know what happened when things go dark, when the conscious mind is quiet and control shifts to the unseen all-knowing.

"So what do you think? You want to try?" He had asked it so casually, as if he was suggesting they go to a new restaurant. He made everything sound like a no-brainer.

She straddled him on the couch, wrapping her hands around his throat.

Jay told her to squeeze harder. She tightened her grip but couldn't bear down with enough force. They tried a few times but the minute his face turned deep red, the minute she felt his ropey ligaments, she let go.

"It was a dumb idea," he said, gasping.

"Damn right it was." She pushed her hands into his chest and slid off his lap. "Besides, even if it worked, I doubt you'd see that same thing again. It was just a hallucination."

"Yeah, you're probably right . . . but what if it wasn't? What if it was a near-death experience and that's what happens on the other side?"

"Well then, be glad you're not dead," she said and lit a bong. Jay took it from her, inhaled and then collapsed back into the seat cushions, both of them surrendering to a fuzzy chill afternoon of listening to her mom's records, jumping on the couch and singing along to Talking Heads' "Once in a Lifetime."

She pulls out that record and listens with her eyes closed but it's not the same and she drags the needle back, scratching it so badly that it skips, stuttering about the days gone by, over and over.

Day 28

Ash drops his backpack and kneels down in the dirt by Jay's memorial.

It's been pouring for a week and the whole thing looks like trash. The flowers are dead and damp-crushed. The lonely helium balloon tied to the chain-link has deflated, and the little one-eyed teddy bear holding a heart is dirt-streaked. He picks up the framed yearbook photo and wipes the raindrops off the glass with the cuff of his jacket. Jay's hair is long and wavy, grazing his shoulders and he's half smiling, not a smirk, just his regular *I got you* smile. Ash saw him the day this picture was taken. He'd been skating to school and stopped to walk with him.

"Hey man, sup?" he said, trick-flipping his board into his hands.

"Not much, you know."

Neither of them said anything else for about a half block and that was okay. They were cool like that. Quiet didn't bug them the way it did with Ash's other friend groups; the need to talk over each other, high-five, or clown around didn't apply to them. It's like when you know people for a long time you don't need to add all the pretend.

"You got your schedule?" Jay asked.

"Yeah." Ash listed off teachers and blocks.

"Ah man, that sucks. You have Grant for English."

"Yeah, I heard she's strict."

"Moody bitch too. Looks like we have Socials together." Jay glanced at Ash and half-smiled, nodded for no reason. Winona called from the top of the street where she was waiting, arms crossed, smoking. "Later," he said and skated away.

Ash watched the way they walked together — not quite boyfriend-girlfriend but still close like a secret. Now he wonders what secrets they did have. People are talking, saying they had a suicide pact, but looking at his face in that photo he doesn't buy it. Jay wouldn't have done that; he wasn't selfish that way. The photo's edges are blurred now, watercolored from the rain, bleeding blue and green, dreamy like. Ash tucks the frame into his backpack, cleans up the dead flowers and throws them in the trash along with the one-eyed teddy bear. It's been a month since Jay jumped. The fakers and trauma wannabes are back to normal life, obsessing over the spring fling dance and who's hooking up with who, and Ash hopes today's assembly doesn't change that. In a way it's easier to float along with the pretenders than to dive in too deep.

The gym is half-full by the time he gets there. It's a mix of different grades, some people he recognizes and a lot that he doesn't but that's the point of it, to get people out of their bubble, to get people talking, to "build community," at least that's what the announcement said. Ash tried to get out of going, told Pavan he didn't want to but she thought it would be good for him, help him process everything with Jay, as if it was that simple. So here he is ready to "Break Down the Walls!" in a half-day assembly. The student group that's leading the charge are wearing matching T-shirts, lanyards and khakis, like they work at an Apple store.

Principal Carter takes the mic, taps it a few times. "Testing, testing, can you hear me?" The audio feedback that follows makes everyone cringe. "Please take your seats." Ash and all of the others file onto the bleachers and after a few minutes he resumes. "It gives me great pleasure to turn the day over to Bill Mitchell from BDB, Break Down Barriers."

A white-haired, thin man jogs onto the stage to "We Are the Champions." Ash's insides collapse with the cliché of it. As the man talks about the format of the day, Ash notices that he paces across the stage the same way Peter does when he presents but unlike Peter, who speaks slowly and pauses for effect like Barak Obama, this guy is budget, talking fast and loud like he's selling knives on the shopping channel or evangelizing to the faithless. "Save yourself," Ash mutters to himself beneath the pump-up music and introductions.

"Each of you received a name tag when you came in and that name tag has a picture of an animal on it. Your first assignment is to go to the group leader who is holding up a picture of your animal. That will be your work group for the morning," says Budget Peter.

As everyone gets up to find their group, Ash sees some of his friends and goes over. "What did you get?" he asks, looking at their name tags. None of them have the elephant. They all start laughing. "What?"

Riley, the ringleader, the blond QB that all the girls fall over, points to the back of the gym where Britt is holding an elephant sign. "Shit luck," he says, slapping Ash on the back.

"Fuck," Ash says. "Switch with me."

"No way, man." He shoves him playfully. "Good luck."

Ash wanders over to the edge of the group where Winona's standing. She looks normal today, no getup. Her long hair is pulled up in a messy top knot and she's wearing an oversized hoodie and jeans. "Hey."

"Hey," he says, offering up a weak smile, a head nod.

"This is such a waste of time."

"Totally," he says, looking around the gym. "My parents made me come."

"Mine too. It'll be okay, I'll get you through. I'm a master at this type of thing. Years of group, you get good at sharing but not sharing."

Britt lifts her chin and freeze-smiles when she sees Ash.

Ash does an awkward wave, as if to say *it's not my fault*. She smiles, no teeth showing, just a big fake *oh my God* grin. She looks down at her clipboard and then back up again. She's trying for maturity; she dumped him, after all. Sure, he didn't return any of her messages after Jay died, but she was the one who hooked up with some douchebag after the funeral. Ash should've been mad about it, he could have peacocked like any other guy would have, but he just let it go and then she was mad about that, shit-talking him for not caring enough. Looking at her now, the way she's chewing on the inside of her cheek, the way her neck's gone all strawberry-splotchy, he can tell that he was wrong for not caring because clearly she still did.

"Is this going to be weird?" he asks, pulling her aside.

She shrugs. "You're with her now?" she asks, glancing at Winona.

"No, she's just" — he pauses, unsure of what she is to him — "someone I know. Look, if this is going to be awkward, I can get reassigned." He watches her face, the way she can't quite make eye contact. "It's not a big deal."

"Whatever," she says, blowing him off. "Do what you want."

"Okay then." He rejoins Winona who asks if he's okay, in a way that makes him realize she's actually asking. "Yeah, totally. I'm good."

Budget Peter calls the group leaders together and Britt is swapped out to another group. Their new group leader, Hardip, an international student who's become instantly popular because he has a cool British accent, takes them through the first activity. "Okay, people! Two truths and a lie, yeah? It goes like this: you have to write out two true things and one lie and guess which is the lie, right?" he says, handing out worksheets and pairing students off.

Winona and Ash sit cross-legged across from each other.

"Okay, here goes," she says, speaking loudly above the din of voices around them. "Number one: Winona Ryder is my mom's cousin.

Ash watches her face for the usual tells — excessive blinking, lip biting, stumbling over words — but she's not signaling.

"Number two: I'm a vegan."

Still, she's completely calm, and he finds himself studying her face for too long. Her large blue eyes, fair skin and dark hair remind him of Snow White, and somehow that puts him at ease.

"Number three: I love steak."

On this one she laughs a little and so does Ash.

"Okay, well, it's gotta be number two or three. You can't be a vegan and love steak. So, I'll go with door number three."

"Wrong," she says. "It's number one. My mom was a superfan, not a relative."

"Wait a second, explain how you can love steak and be a vegan?"

"I said I love steak; I didn't say I eat it. I'm a carnivore who abstains." She makes a weird growly face. "Okay, now you go."

Ash nods and holds up his paper. "Number one: I love Harry Potter. Number two: I'm an elite *Super Smash* player, and number three: I have a genius-level IQ."

Winona makes a show of thinking. "No offence, but I have to go with door number three."

"Wrong." He crumples his paper. "I do have a genius-level IQ. I'm just not willing to peak in high school, so I keep it on the down-low," he says, lowering his voice.

"Right," she says. "So which one is the fake?"

"I don't love Harry Potter."

"What? How can you not? He's awesome."

"Nah! He's just a dumbass with a scar. Everyone knows Hermione is the real deal, a kick-ass muggle-born."

Winona makes a surprised face. "So you're a feminist."

"What? No, that's not what I said. I'm just not that into wizards and shit."

"So number two, *Smash*? We should play some time."

"Yeah, sure."

Hardip calls the group to attention. "So what's the takeaway from this?"

One of the geeky kids pipes up. "We're more than meets the eye."

"Robots in disguise," Ash sings the *Transformers* cartoon jingle under his breath and nudges Winona, but she's actually listening to the kid and to Hardip, so he goes quiet for the rest of the talk, watching how serious everyone is, watching how hopeful they are that somehow things really will get better like all of the PSA videos promise. After a trust-building activity where they each have to let themselves fall back into the group's waiting arms, Budget Peter comes back on stage, motioning for them to sit down.

"Growing up isn't easy, in fact it's never been harder. Let's talk about what might be going on with each of you." He signals to someone at the back to dim the lights and a movie plays on the screen behind him. Close-ups of teen faces, sad piano music like the stuff Anik composes. "I didn't know what to do . . . I felt like ending it . . . I worried what my parents would think . . . I hated myself . . . I couldn't find a way out . . . I just wanted it to end . . . I just wanted it to end . . ." Ten minutes of artsy shots of empty rooms, empty chairs, heads down, eyes closed, hands out, reaching. "If only it could be different."

The lights come back up. Some kids are tearing up, red-faced, and seeing them makes Ash choke. He has a lump in his throat and swallows hard, grinds his teeth, clamps down. Winona is sitting cross-legged next to him, completely still, as if she's transcended.

"What you may not realize is that everyone feels this way at some point. You're not alone. Statistics tell us that twenty to thirty percent of you are probably depressed. Suicide is the second leading cause of death in young people." He pauses and, with his clicker, projects the sobering statistics on the screen. "I tell you this not to frighten you, but to arm you with the knowledge that you are not alone. I'd like you all to stand up and form one straight line."

"This is so dumb," Ash says to Winona. She doesn't answer and simply follows along. "Now step forward if you feel sad at least once a day." Ash watches as three-quarters of the line moves up. "Now step forward if you feel anxious." Ash doesn't step forward even though he does feel anxious most days. "Step forward if you hate something about yourself." Dozens of kids step forward. Ash doesn't; he picks and chooses what he wants to be honest about. Budget Peter goes on and on, listing ways in which people are the same and different, showing their challenges to each other one step at a time. "Step forward if you've ever thought of or known someone who harmed themselves." Ash thinks of Jay and steps forward. By the end of it he and Winona are far apart — she's stepped forward while he held back. Budget Peter tells them to look around and see each other. "You are not alone." Some people are crying and hugging, consoling each other while others, like Ash, are standing with their arms crossed, their faces in awkward twists. He starts to crack up the way he does when he's nervous. He quickly covers his mouth and orchestrates an elaborate coughing fit and is excused to the hall. He stays there for a few minutes, trying to catch his breath and talk himself down.

At the end of the session they're all given pamphlets with mental health information, hotlines and support groups, before being sent on their way. As cheesy as it sounds there is a general sense of community in the room and though Ash doesn't think it will last, it feels good and he goes along with the instructed high-fiving as the students file out of the gym. He's at his locker when Winona taps him on the shoulder asking if he wants to hang out.

"Today?"

"Yeah. You live around here right?"

He nods, grabbing a binder from the shelf.

"See you after school, out front."

Ash watches her walk down the hall as if she's floating along, as if there's a thread from the top of her head to the sky keeping her moving just so, immune from the masses.

She talks the entire walk home. She has a lot to say and normally Ash would be annoyed by her nonstop-ness but he finds himself actually paying attention to what she's saying. On the short walk home she's covered climate change, Black Lives Matter and feminism, and Ash knows she has way more to say and will probably cycle through again. As she talks, he glances at her every so often, taking her in bit by bit. She's nice to look at in a plain white T-shirt, washes-her-face-with-Ivory-soap kind of way, but she's not his type and he's glad; he doesn't need the distraction.

"This is me." He stops in front of his plain two-story house that, compared to the new gated houses nearby, must look small and regular. But if she thinks this she doesn't say anything and it makes him like her even more.

Ash drops his bag in the living room and sets up the console.

"Anyone else home?" she asks.

"Probably my brother. But he doesn't leave the basement much."

"Interesting," she says and sits on the couch, scanning the family photos on the nearby table. "This him?"

"Yeah, from a few years back, just after he graduated."

"So he's what, like, a hikikomori?"

"A hiko-what the fuck are you talking about?"

"It's Japanese for people who don't leave their rooms. They withdraw from socializing, isolate themselves, like modern-day hermits."

"I didn't know there was a name for it."

"Yeah, it's a real thing. Half a million of 'em in Japan, a lot of them your brother's age."

"How do you know this shit?"

"I don't know. I just know stuff. Usually the isolation is a result of some life trauma. Does your brother have trauma?"

"Fuck, I don't know. Who doesn't have trauma?" He hands her a controller. "So you want to play or what?"

"Heck yeah." She takes it and picks Princess Peach.

"Typical," Ash says.

"Just wait. I'm gonna kick your ass," she says and does this weird wink. She's way better than Ash expected and as she's playing he notices the small blue whale tattoo on the inside of her wrist.

"Did you do that yourself?" he finally asks, motioning to it.

"This?" She flips her wrist over. "Yeah. Jay and I did it."

"Cool," he says, unsure of what to say next.

"It's not what you think. It's not what people are saying."

"What do you mean?"

"Come on. I know everyone thinks we were playing some stupid game."

"And you weren't?"

"No, all of that shit is fake news."

"What is it then?"

"It's like . . ." She finishes her round and puts the controller down. "I saw this image online of a beached whale with garbage coming out of its mouth and it stuck with me. It was an art installation by Greenpeace — a protest piece on plastic in the ocean."

"So your tattoo is a protest?"

She shakes her head. "It's metaphoric."

"Okay," Ash says, still unsure.

"See . . . it's like whales are starving to death, because they can't distinguish plastic from food and are filling up on our garbage." She pauses, tracing the tattoo with her finger. "I guess the whale reminds me that we're killing ourselves too. It's symbolic. We're full of garbage and we're starving."

"That's intense."

"Jay thought so too. The tattoo was his idea. A way to remind ourselves to stay real."

They both go quiet.

"Want to hear what blue whales sound like?" she asks.

"Sure." Ash waits as she pulls out her phone and scrolls through the music app.

"I looped these together from sound files I found online. Jay and I used to listen to them." She passes Ash an earbud and they put their heads together, listening to the whale's mournful call.

Later that night, when Ash can't fall asleep, he plays the audio file she sent him. He closes his eyes and zones into the vibration. He imagines that he's floating in water, in space, and is overcome with a profound isolation, the experience of both a beginning and an ending.

Day 39

Pavan's sitting in her parked car eating a chocolate bar when she sees Lisa.

Like a scavenger, she's pulling out cardboard boxes from the recycling bin and Pavan watches this from the comfort of her car, windshield wipers clearing the view every three seconds before she finally drives over and rolls down her window.

"Lisa," she says, "I don't know if you remember me, I'm Ashton's mom, Pavan." Lisa doesn't say anything. Pavan realizes now that she should have minded her own business and just gone home to start dinner, but because she's been thinking about Jay, she took this as a sign. "Are you okay?" She hears herself ask the ridiculous question and wishes she could take it back. "I mean, can I help? Do you need a ride?"

Lisa looks around and then down at the pile of cardboard. "Paul was supposed to meet me with the truck." She checks her watch. "We're moving."

"Oh. That explains the boxes." Pavan pauses, unsure of what to say next. "Well, if you want, I'm going that way. I can drop you off."

Lisa checks her watch again before agreeing. Pavan gets out of the SUV and opens the hatch and helps Lisa load the boxes in.

"Thanks," she says and slides into the passenger seat. Her T-shirt is soaked through and she's shivering, shoulders curled in like a small injured animal. Pavan turns on the heater and adjusts the vent toward her.

"You're still in the same apartment?"

"Yeah, same one. It's hard now. Being there."

Pavan wishes she knew what to say but instead lets the silence linger. She imagines that Lisa's life is full of this silence now, this quiet of not having the right words, or enough words to occupy the time. She turns on the radio, switching from pop to classic rock to oldies, but it all seems wrong and she switches it off.

"So, you're moving?"

"Yeah, up north actually. My mom lives in Terrace and Paul's got a job lined up, so . . ."

Pavan waits, thinking Lisa will say more about it but she doesn't.

"How's Ash?" Lisa asks.

"Oh, he's alright," Pavan says. "You know how kids that age are." She wants to take the words back as soon as she hears them come out of her mouth. She didn't mean to sound so cavalier, so stupid. "I'm sorry." She pulls into the apartment complex.

"Don't be. It's fine."

"Jay — he was a really great kid."

"Thanks." Lisa stares straight ahead. The rain has stopped and clouds rush across the sky, unspooling silver threads. "Well, I should go. Thanks for the ride."

"Let me help — with the boxes," Pavan says and gets out of the truck.

"If you're sure you don't mind."

"Not at all." She grabs an armload of boxes and follows Lisa inside.

The lobby of the building is sterile, a few chairs and plastic plants clustered together in a sitting area. It reminds Pavan of the utilitarian medical offices she used to clean when she started Clean and Tidy. Those offices made her feel hopeless, as if the sick of all the patients was lingering, clinging to her as she mopped the floors.

"The elevator's broken. We got to use the stairs. Nothing around here works right."

Pavan follows her up the five flights, the flat-packed boxes tucked under each arm, shifting and slipping along the way. She's winded after two flights and can feel her blouse clinging to the small of her back but Lisa seems unfazed and climbs with ease.

"This is me," Lisa says, dropping the boxes to push open the door. "Paul!" Lisa calls out but no one comes. "I thought he might be home." She checks the time. "He probably took overtime." Lisa catches Pavan looking around. "Sorry, it's a bit of a mess. Packing and all."

"Oh, it's fine. Mess is what I do for a living."

"Oh right, I've seen your mini cars around town."

"If you need some help, I could arrange —"

"Oh, no, I couldn't afford that. Things are pretty tight, especially with the funeral and everything. It's . . . I'm sorry. I don't know why I'm saying that. Let me get you some water. You must be tired after the walk up." Pavan follows Lisa into the small galley kitchen. The walls are mint green, the oak veneer cupboards are chipped and the sink is full of dishes. "Sorry about the mess. I said that already, didn't I? Jay always said I repeated myself too much. 'Mom, I heard you the first time.'" She sighs and seems to drift away for a moment. "I started packing here but then I got sidetracked. I always get sidetracked. So much stuff to go through." She sees Pavan looking at the photo of Jay held up by a magnet that says "World's Best Mom." "He's nine months old in that one, had just started walking. Can you believe it? Advanced for his age." She fills up a glass of tap water and hands it to Pavan.

"It must be hard — moving that is." Pavan takes a sip of water.

"It is. Jay grew up here. We lived here since he was a baby. First steps, first words. All of it, right here." She walks by Pavan and into the hallway. "Right here, we'd mark his height every September on the first day of school." She runs her fingers over the dates, toward the most recent. "Leaving is hard but staying is hard too, you know."

Pavan doesn't know what to say and just stares at the height marker, the smudged pencil lettering.

"I'm sorry. I don't know why I'm talking like this." She wipes her eyes as if she's been crying, only she hasn't.

"It's okay. It's good to talk."

"So they say. Doctor has me going to a support group at the church. Says it's good to talk to people going through the same thing. But I don't know, hearing them talk about how much they miss their kid, how mad they are, how sad they are — I don't know that it helps all that much. Besides, I'm not much of a talker. Jay was the talker. Always talking. I'm sure you remember that about him. Your boy Ash and him. They were good friends."

"The best," Pavan says, choking down the moment.

"Jay always said real nice things about your family. You should know that. I want you to know that. Until I met Paul, it was just me and Jay, and well, him being able to spend time with your family was good. I wish I could have given him more." She drops her gaze for a moment.

Pavan wants to tell her it's okay and that loving her son was enough and all that he needed, but she doesn't say this because they both know it's not true. Love was not enough, it never is.

"I'm sorry. I don't know what's wrong with me. Here you are helping me and I'm just blathering."

"It's fine." Pavan fishes her keys out of her pocket. "I should get going and leave you to your packing."

Lisa smiles, her mouth a weak straight line. "Actually, before you go, I have a box of some of Jay's things that I thought maybe Ash might want. Do you want to take a look?"

Pavan follows her down the narrow hall to Jay's room. The gray walls are covered in posters, and the entire space feels cold and dark even with the lights turned on. The air is heavy and she resists the urge to slide the windows open the way she would if she was cleaning. She looks around, cataloging the preservation of time. The single bed is unmade as if he'd just woken up. There are clothes on the floor and textbooks on the bedside next to soda cans and Pop Tart wrappers. The record on the turntable is covered in a fine layer of dust.

Lisa opens the closet and pulls down a box. "I haven't opened it. He always said it was private."

"Are you sure?" Pavan asks, taking it from her. The cigar box is covered with overlapping images, a collage of cut-out letters that spell his name.

"It doesn't seem right to open it now." Lisa sits on the bed. "This room is the hardest. I don't know where to begin. I haven't touched a thing and now we have to be out next month."

"I'd be happy to help. If you like I can send a team in to pack everything up and label it for you."

"I really can't afford —"

"It would be no charge. Please let me do this for you. Jay was Ash's friend. I want to help." Pavan can tell by the way Lisa looks down that she's not used to accepting help and so she insists, not out of charity or pity but as a means to find her own way forward. "That's settled then." She tells Lisa that she'll call to arrange a time and sees herself out.

When she gets home, she hides the box in her bottom desk drawer and doesn't tell anyone where she's been. When Peter asks how her day was, she only answers with the routine "fine" and sets the table for three.

She takes a tray down to Anik and leaves it outside his door as she does every night. She stopped asking him to eat with the family months ago because he'd just sit and look at his plate, making comments on how distracting their chewing noises were.

Ash is quiet now too. Ever since Jay died, he spends more time alone. Pavan hears him late at night, awake and online, keystrokes and whispers, imagines him sitting inside the cone of a backlit screen in the dark of his room. She tries to ask him how he is, drops small questions about his day, but no matter how benign her inquiry is, he answers her with silence or hostility. She's not sure what she did to aggravate him but he's made her tentative and, perhaps like an animal that smells fear, he knows it. Sometimes she worries that she's lost both of her children, that they have moved deep inside their shells, like some prehistoric creatures hiding from unseen dangers.

As she and Peter engage in idle supper talk, Ash moves his vegetables around his plate for twenty minutes before asking to be excused. Peter says that it's fine and Ash leaves his food virtually uneaten. "I don't know what to do." Pavan picks up his plate and scrapes the remains into the trash. "God, I hate that I said that, that I always say that," she says, piling the dishes in the sink. "I'm worried. He's not seeing his friends anymore, he's just in his room doing I don't know what."

"Just give it time," he says, clearing the table. "He'll be fine."

"And Anik, will he be fine too?" she says this with an edge, more cutting than she meant, but she's tiring of his *wait out the storm* mentality in all things. His calm, which she once loved, now seems apathetic and unsettles her.

"Yeah, he will," he says, ignoring her tone. "It's his journey. We have to let him experience his own life."

She nods, eyebrows up, gnawing on his Tony Robbins–esque morsel. His fans may be satisfied by his charming quips but all she wants right now is to spit his words back at him. What use is *wait and see* when everything is falling apart now? When she reconnected with him all those years ago, she'd recently embarked on her own self-help journey and she thought it was admirable that he'd left law to pursue life coaching. He'd gotten tired of seeing people at their worst and wanted to help people be better, wanted to empower them, but now, to her, this desire to help, to simplify, to demystify, reeks of superiority.

She leans against the counter and exhales. A confession. "I saw Lisa today."

He's doesn't answer. He's busy, head down in his phone.

"Peter?"

"Hmm, what?" He still doesn't look up. "Sorry. Just reading an email about the workshop in Toronto. Apparently it sold out in an hour."

"So great." Her tone flatlines.

"My agent's talking about adding a second date."

"Fantastic." She flashes a fake smile. "Hey, can you finish this? I have some work to do."

"Yeah, I got it. You go," he says without ever looking up.

She shuts her office door behind her and from the drawer pulls out Jay's keepsake box. She runs her fingers along the collage, wondering what kind of mother would give her dead son's things away and for a moment considers driving the box back over to Lisa and telling her that she should keep it. But then she remembers the look in Lisa's eyes when she said that it was private. There's so much fear about not knowing your child, but perhaps even more fear about finding out who they were when there is nothing to do but accept it. She opens the box. Inside are a sports day ribbon with faded gold lettering, a small gift box tagged for Winona, a few baby pictures, class photos and even one of him and Ash standing on a cliff overlooking the ocean. Pavan had taken that photo and given him a copy the week after the camping trip. She didn't know that it was the last trip he'd take with them. Underneath the stack of photos is a journal and two joints. Pavan gets up and checks the lock on the door, cracks the bay window and lights one of the joints. Sitting on the window seat, she takes a drag and exhales into the cool air. She flips through the photos, examining each one as if it were evidence before finally opening his journal.

January 1

It snowed last night and the world, the way I knew it, disappeared. It was soft-edged and quiet, the sun was a dime — silver and so sharp that when I walked I had to look down and even then, the snow glare forced my eyes shut. How stupid I must have looked, trudging through the snow, my eyes half-open. I glanced at the houses, the Christmas card feel of the snow-covered rooftops, the lawn ornaments and inflatables, the crooked string lights that on any other day would've looked sad, looked peaceful. I stopped and took some pictures, but nothing I captured matched what I saw and that lack, that distinction of nothing is as it is, stayed with me for the rest of the walk. Maybe it was the day — New Year's resolutions and that promise of a do-over — that put me on edge. The edge is a dangerous thing because hope is always on the other side. I don't know where I heard that, or if I made it up, but it's true. Before I headed home, I unplugged one of the Santas and watched him deflate. The withered St. Nick made me laugh and I texted Winona a picture of the lump of vinyl in the snow, but she didn't reply. Busy in Hawaii with her family probably. At least that's what I told myself but still her not replying made me feel bad and then I felt bad about unplugging the Santa. Even now, hours later, writing this, I feel nothing but bad and can't do anything about it.

January 5

Mom's working nights, overtime, all the shifts that nobody wants. Paul left for Prince George to see his family. His grandma died. I'm glad that he left — not that his grandma died — but that he's gone and now I can have the apartment to myself and I don't have to hear him whistling or hassling me about doing stuff. He's always telling me to grow up and act like a man, like that's supposed to mean something. If he's the example of *be a man* — no thanks. Without him here, I don't have to feel bad about having been parked on the couch for three days playing video games and eating Pop Tarts. I'm wearing the Christmas sweater mom made me. It's ugly but warm — over-the-top festive red and green, but at least it's soft. Betty at the old folks' home taught her how to knit and since Betty never has any visitors, she helped her finish it. I put the sweater on right away so Mom could take a picture of me wearing it. She stared at the picture and then at me, saying I looked great and that she was so proud of me, but really I knew she was just pleased with herself for having knit the sweater, and that's okay because she deserves to feel good. She works real hard. Last week, I went to her work to pick her up. I sat and waited in the common room while she finished up with the residents. Residents, right — they should really call them prisoners. It was the most depressing place in the world. Clinical and washed out, weak light coming from small window slits. The room had an old TV with big fat recliners semicircled around it, a few shelves with crap books and outdated magazines and a couple chairs and tables. The old people just blended right into the furniture. They were all withered up, oatmeal skin, bobble heads on their hunched-up backs, just ragged skin on bone. I remember thinking, "If that's what I have to look forward to, just kill me now."

January 21

I went to the cemetery with Winona. We skipped school and took the bus into the city so she could visit her mom. Seems strange that there's a giant cemetery in the middle of Vancouver, acres of dead people in the heart of the living. Winona walked me through, showed me the oldest grave, 1887, a ten-month-old baby named Caradoc Evans. Caradoc! What a name. No one has good names like that anymore. I was kind of disappointed by the tombstone. I expected it to be big and old, covered in moss, but it was new and improved by well-intentioned people pretending at conservation. I tried to imagine what it all might have looked like 132 years ago, and as I pictured it, everything I saw turned to black-and-white except the trees. There would have been more trees. No — it would have been all trees, and now it's all stone and stump except for the few that remain. While Winona visited her mom, I climbed a tree to take in the view. Behind me, city sprawl and the North Shore mountains, and before me row upon row of dead people. From my perch, I could see Winona in the distance. A dark figure at the grave marker, head bowed down, like a bird searching for worms.

January 24

I'm not feeling it today. Well, not any day really, but today I can't quite fake it so I stayed home. Winona thinks I have seasonal affective disorder, but I'm not sure. I hate the label, why can't sad just be sad and not be an acronym for some mental illness? I didn't tell her that. I didn't want to hurt her feelings and who knows anyways. She's probably right. There's probably a million names for all the things that aren't right with me. I've googled it all and it scares the shit out of me. I took a bunch of those online mental health surveys:

Do you have suicidal thoughts? Yes. Are you having trouble sleeping? Yes. Have you lost pleasure in doing things you used to like doing? Yes. Do you have mood cycles? Yes. Have you been acting in ways that others would say was dangerous? Yes. Do you have trouble concentrating? Yes. Do you have racing thoughts? Yes. Do you have trouble getting out of bed? Yes. Have others said you don't seem like yourself? Yes. Do you think others would be better off without you? Sometimes. Are you engaging in reckless behaviors? Yes.

I didn't bother pressing submit.

What's the point?

January 31

Winona and I had a fight about the whale. I spent the day hunting and came up with nothing but wannabes and trolls with task lists. I know she's right that it's probably a hoax but a big part of me wants it to be real, wants there to be someone to help me get to the edge, someone to blame. It would be so much easier if there really was some perverse puppet master pulling strings and texting out daily instructions — death by numbers. But it's probably just another meme, just another Slender Man, an urban legend that keeps you up at night, scared and hopeful. Winona's tattoo has almost healed but mine's scabbed up, a bloody mess. I'll probably need to get antibiotics or something.

February 4

Winona sent me a playlist. All whale sounds except for one Cocteau Twins song called "Whales Tails." It's a dreamy track — mermaids and fairies, underwater whispers. Her way of saying sorry. I told her it's okay, it was a dumb idea anyways, let's forget it. Peace.

February 8

In Careers today we did one of those personality tests that tells you what to do with your life. Winona's said that she should be an artist. Obviously. She's been deep into her installation and has been talking about going to school in Montreal, New York, maybe even Tokyo. Tokyo, for real! She wants to get away. Don't we all? The only difference is that she actually can. She's actually got real talent and could make it out. She could make it big — loft living, eccentric-ass party people, bottle service, gallery showings. She's going to do it. She'll go, but I'll still be here. My results said that I should pursue a trade. I know there's nothing wrong with that, a lot of money in it too, steady work — but then what? Dirt under my fingernails kinda life? Work, pay the bills, six pack weeknights with the TV, a girlfriend if I'm lucky. It's all depressing AF. My whole life laid out like a flatline. Winona thinks I could be a writer, she says that I have a way of seeing things, which is why she bought me this journal and why I promised to write in it. But seeing and thinking are way different than actually doing. Besides, what could I possibly write about? My life pretty much sucks.

February 12

Saw Ash today and I should text him. He was with his girlfriend so I didn't stop to talk. It's kind of weird seeing him because it's like I know him but don't know him. We know these better, simpler versions of each other. I don't know how things got so complicated and how I ended up like this — always in my head. Sometimes I think I was just born like this but seeing him reminds me that I wasn't always this way. I was actually a happy kid, always grinning with big gut laughs, and every old picture of me is bug-eyed goofy-faced proof of that. He and I used to have so much fun and we didn't even have to try. It was so easy but then something happened. A switch flipped. I'm sure of it. It was like I was seeing with one eye. Life was up close, everything was in my face, loud and angry with something always missing. I told my Mom I felt different but she just chalked it up to growing pains. I tried to talk to the school counselor but it's hard to explain what you don't understand. Occasionally I feel better, but it doesn't last. It never does. Having Winona helps. Even though we aren't dating, I'm pretty sure we are because sometimes we mess around but it's not always so I'm not sure. She's fucked up in her own ways and we talk about stuff and talking helps but it doesn't change anything, not really.

February 14

Valentine's Day. Winona pretended not to care about the candy-gram I sent her in first block. I didn't bother with the ten-dollar single rose and helium heart-balloon combo and sent her a bag of cinnamon hearts instead. She said they were too hot, set her mouth on fire, and later when I kissed her, it was all I could taste. At the end of the day I snagged her a helium balloon and we took turns sucking out the air, talking in munchkin, laughing nonstop.

February 19

The other night I dreamt that I was folded like origami and tucked inside a black box. When I reached up the box collapsed and I was suddenly standing inside a white room with no walls, no edges. A water figure walked toward me and with each step the white room rippled. I reached out and put my hand through the featureless figure. Water dripped from my fingertips in perfect orbs and in each orb was a universe. I asked it where I was. It didn't speak and yet I understood its meaning as it shapeshifted, changing form in front of my eyes. I was in the everywhere place, where all that was, and will be, is. When I pinched myself to wake up, the water figure turned into a row boat and I heard the sounds of children singing. "Merrily, merrily, merrily, life is but a dream." When I said I didn't understand, the figure turned into a question mark, a clock, a calendar with days marked off to one hundred and then it turned into me waking up from a long sleep. One hundred days until what? The figure shapeshifted from human to animal to air to water to space to everything, cycling through faster and faster until it became a ball of light inside an orb. Then I woke up, the sunlight crashing in. I remember the dream so perfectly it feels less like a dream and more like a vision. Everywhere I went that day, I saw the number one hundred. I flipped open my math textbook to page one hundred, did the one hundred meter dash in PE, top one hundred songs appeared as a playlist, the history assignment was one hundred years ago today. I told Winona about it and she laughed it off as a tripped-out hallucination. Even though she didn't believe me, that expansive knowing, that tingly feeling of keeping a secret stayed with me all day.

February 27

I thought the dream was a sign. But nothing since. Maybe Winona's right about it being a hallucination. Nothing's felt right since that day. Today I did a solo jump from the roof of one building to the next and part of me actually hoped I didn't make it across, just so I could see if the everywhere place was real. I know it's fucked up, thinking of death that way, because it could just be a big nothing.

March 8

I haven't been doing much of anything. Winona even said I'm not myself lately, whatever that means, if it even means anything at all. My self . . . number one — so singular, so small, just a line on a page. Me me me me me — a needle in my brain. Winona's installation is almost done. I don't know how she did it but she got it right. It's amazing. Somehow she made me out of junk, she took all this stuff and actually showed me who I am, who we all are and how we're all disconnected. Big brain, for sure. People aren't gonna know what to make of it. She's got a life ahead of her, and that's a whole bunch better than days on a wall.

March 19

I've been thinking about dying a lot lately, way more than usual and at first it kind of scared me but in this upside-down headspace I'm in, it's perfectly good. We're not in Kansas anymore, Dorothy.

Man, I love that movie; it reminds me of being a kid. Watched it again with Winona a few weeks ago and we both laughed about having been scared of the flying monkeys. Favorite scene — when they try to run through the poppies to Oz and fall asleep before the snow breaks the wicked spell. There's a creepy song at the end of that scene that sticks in my head — something about being out of the woods and into the light, holding on to hope, and on and on it goes.

Day 47

Anik hasn't opened his eyes yet.

He's in that post-dream haze, where everything is soft-edged, pixelated and fuzzy. He tries to stay there, to remember his dream and find a way back, but the light filters in and there's no returning. Anik rolls over, untangling himself from a high-thread-count cocoon. His mother thought the Egyptian cotton would be better for his eczema and in truth the silkiness feels good against his skin; the dry rashes behind his knees have all but disappeared.

He is what some would call frail — a slight breeze could make him ill and as a child he was allergic to almost everything. Pavan used to send a list to his teachers of all the foods he couldn't eat and was making gluten-free cookies before it was the thing to do. She's always done small things like this to ease his suffering, acts of service are her love language, or so Peter says. As much as her hovering and helping annoys him at times, he knows she does it so he can feel normal and focus on himself. For the most part, he considers himself lucky to have such supportive parents. They encouraged his love of music from an early age; he'd been playing piano since he was five. It was all he ever wanted and it was clear to anyone who heard him play that it was all he was meant to do. Music teachers said he was a prodigy. He could play any instrument intuitively, any piece by ear, and unlike his peers who were hounded to practice he wanted nothing but to practice. For him playing music was akin to breathing. He doesn't remember ever deciding this. Desire and purpose for him were one and the same until suddenly the want had fallen away, and all that was left was the thorny obligation of having to do something with his life. That real-world heaviness pinned him down and he submitted to the years ahead as if they'd already happened and had led to an inevitable meaninglessness.

As he sits in bed he wonders if his spiritual life and creative ambition stalled because he hasn't suffered. His life is too comfortable, too predictable, even his contemplation is fueled by his privilege. How can he create something truly original without knowing struggle? How can he live when the living is too easy, too empty? It's not the first time he's thought this. One late night when he was bringing his dishes to the kitchen he heard his parents talking about why Jay did it, and he wanted to interject and say that he probably killed himself because he was lonely and hopeless and that's way worse than being sad. Despair is a neverland of thoughts and feelings — it's numbness, a black hole, a wasteland of apathy.

He throws his pillow and duvet onto the floor and lies down on it, his bones pressing on hardwood. He imagines what it might be like to sleep outside on the cold earth with nothing but a sleeping bag. Even when they went camping, his mother always inflated a queen-sized air mattress for him and Ash. They woke to the smell of bacon and eggs cooked on a camp stove, and when they explored the nearby woods they never veered too far from their parents' watchful eyes. He knows they are well loved and cared for. Nothing wrong with that, but there comes a time. He stands up, presses his shoulders back and looks at his thin frame in the full-length mirror and repeats out loud as if to convince himself. "There comes a time." He says it again, and the words float over his head and into a melody. He grabs his notebook and sits on the edge of his bed, scoring the words onto sheet music. An hour passes easily. It's the first original thing he's tried to compose in weeks; time falls away and he loses himself in the creative flow. He opens his laptop and plays the piano piece, looping and dragging it into a new track. He can't find the right drumbeat and searches for percussion loops online, ignoring all but one of the persistent pop-up ads: "Walk in the footsteps of saints."

He clicks on the image of a backpacker walking along a dirt road, rolling grass fields all around him: "The Camino de Santiago pilgrimage: claim your place in the ages, guided tours with accommodation and regional cuisine — book early and save five percent." He scans the photos of hipster hikers with their Patagonia sun hats and walking sticks and closes the browser, shaking his head at the saint's commodification. Though the spiritual pilgrimage is clearly nothing more than an adventure tour for bucket-listers and thrill-seekers, the idea of the trail piques his interest and he puts his music aside, spending the rest of the morning down a rabbit hole, reading blogs and articles on the Spanish walk.

That afternoon he falls asleep and dreams of walking through dusty heat with only the clothes on his back and a sweat-drenched rag wrapped around his head. He walks until his feet are raw and blistered, until he stumbles and falls asleep under a dome of animated constellations. When he wakes his mouth is parched, his feet are throbbing and his body aches. He sits ups slowly, once more distinguishing reality from his dream and glances at the clock on the wall. He stares at the white face, the black hands, the quick thin movement of each second ticking. He only slept for forty-five minutes but he feels completely alive as if he's journeyed beyond himself and returned with a higher purpose, a mission. He jumps out of bed, full of possibility and again looks at himself in the mirror, wondering why he never thought of it before. It seems so obvious to him now.

"Of course. I'll walk. I'll suffer. I'll create." He says this to his mirrored self before any doubt can creep in. "I'll go on a pilgrimage. I'll be one with nature. I'll write songs — no — I'll compose a modern symphony. A magnum opus!" He knows he's young to proclaim such a thing, but what does age have to do with art and wisdom? His Holiness was discovered at age two, Bob Dylan was in his early twenties when he rose to fame and Mozart was a child prodigy. Time is just something that people with power use to make other people wait. There is no waiting for your turn; there are no dues to be paid. He's going to get out, journey beyond what he thinks is possible.

He sits back down, reaches for his laptop and begins his research on pilgrimages around the world. He makes a list of his top contenders. Although he's looking for God, he's not religious, and the more he looks at the Camino de Santiago, the more he thinks that the entire tour seems like an overhyped, overpriced, millennial photo op. He crosses it off his list and moves on to the next. The Inca Trail to Machu Picchu, breathtaking and mysterious, is out of his budget. He crosses it off the list. The John Muir Trail in California's Sierra Nevada Mountains is too rugged for him so he crosses it off too. By far his favorite is the Kumano Kodo trek in Japan. Even though he doesn't have enough money for the plane ticket and he's crossed it off his list, he's mesmerized by the images and returns to it. The Kii Mountains with their lush forests and moss-covered roots are reminiscent of the Pacific Northwest. The old-growth fir trees, the weak light, the stillness of the wild and the ancient pull of ocean remind him of his boyhood summers in Tofino on Vancouver Island.

Every year until he was nineteen they rented the same beach-front house; the cedar planks with their silvered patina of wind and sand reminded him of home more than home ever did. On the beach he was free to wander with Ash and they would spend hours running in and out of the cold surf, building sandcastles and flying their dragon kites while their parents watched from the deck. Time didn't really have a place outside the sky; the sun's up-and-down dictated their movements. Even when the weather turned, they would bundle up in rain slickers and rubber boots and watch the waves crash against the black rocks. They'd walk along the shore, pushing forward into the wind, heads down, smiling.

They hadn't been back there for a few years. Ash had spent that last summer obsessed with *Pokémon Go*. He complained about the network connection that made the game impossible to play and the edge-of-the-world Wi-Fi needed a router reset every thirty minutes. Ash was full of sleep and teenage anger, a quiet violence beneath the surface of every word. Despite his parents' urging he wouldn't sit by the fire and roast s'mores or play Scrabble before bed as they had always done. His mood imprinted, left trails and residue like the tides that dragged in more than they pulled out.

"He ruined it." That's what Anik overheard Pavan say. They hadn't taken a family vacation since.

Anik opens another tab and googles "hike Vancouver Island."

The seventy-five-kilometer West Coast Trail takes the hiker through rugged terrain along the west coast of Vancouver Island . . . the journey through cedar, spruce and hemlock forests, along beaches and cliffs . . . across bridges and ladders will take an experienced hiker five to seven days . . . part of the Pacific Rim National Park Reserve, the trek is one of the most difficult in North America.

Though he knows he doesn't have the stamina for the West Coast Trail, he scrolls through photos of the temperate rainforest and wild beaches, clicking on tourist links, pausing on the aerial view of Tofino and Clayoquot Sound — dense forest mounds rising out of the ocean, small islands and rugged coastlines, desolate beaches. He opens his photo app and scrolls until he finds a photo of himself on that very beach. He's at the corner of the frame, his surfboard tucked under his arm, looking out at the ocean. In his mind the photo animates: the storm-sound waves, the catch of white wash on his heels, the weight of his wetsuit, the taste and grit of salt.

He opens another tab and maps the distance between here and there. He reviews the ferry schedules and coastal highways. He changes the navigation setting from *drive* to *walk*. The route doesn't change much. There's only one way out and one way back.

Day 52

Winona picks at her cuticles.

She's pulling at the snagged skin with pinched fingers as if she's ripping a seam, or clipping loose threads. She stays focused on her hands, avoiding the awkward eye contact of group therapy while others share in the "healing circle." Tonya, the bulimic, is talking about her body dysmorphic disorder while the other eating-disorder girls stare at her. Winona knows they're sizing her up, wondering if they are thinner than her, wondering if she's tried laxatives instead of the old-fashioned heave-ho of binge and purge, puke and retch. Normally she would be thinking these things, she'd be taking measured looks at Tonya, she'd be circling her thumb and index finger around her own wrist, cuffing herself, but today she's not that into it. She's not even sure why she's here. There's nothing to solve that hasn't been solved. The psychologists attributed all of her problems past and present to her mother's death; her mother was the root and stem of it all. It's easy to blame dead people and now she can add Jay to the list of the guilty. Jon sent her back to group after the visit to the school, a preemptive self-harm intervention to keep her from starving and carving. Her body records everything, flesh remembers even when the wounds close up and scars fade into silver braided threads. Besides her doctor, the only person who had seen it all was Jay. He wasn't horrified by it. He didn't ask why. He didn't tell her to stop. When he ran his fingers along the fresh cut that ran under her bra strap, he only had one question: "Does it hurt?"

According to her shrink, starving was her way to hollow out, to empty and numb, to feel the physical dread and grief of mother-loss. Not eating allowed her to become a shell, to disappear into herself, affording her a wakeful death. But cutting was different — it was a way to feel alive. Neither remedied her grief and for the most part she's given in to the mania in her mind that has her cycling obsessions; she's either drowning in her own thoughts, or stranded in the hopelessness of waiting for something to happen, something good and different. She isn't bipolar, at least that's what the doctors say; she has a general anxiety disorder and ADHD. As far as she's concerned she has all the symptoms of bipolar listed on WebMD and so did Jay, and so does every other kid she knows. By her estimation, everyone is sick. Everyone is fucked up and there aren't enough healing circles to do anything but spread this shit around and around on a fucking merry-go-round. She listens as Tonya circles the drain, the therapist guiding the way with his "tell me more" prompts. He sinks her deeper into herself, exploring and excavating. He's leaning in, and nodding, as if he's getting off on it. His name is "You can call me Rob" Robert; he wears loafers and a uniform of khakis and polo shirts. Winona imagines his life tastes as dull as the back of a penny. Copper and dirt, and dying electrical currents. He probably lives in a shabby bachelor suite that he tries to make cool with secondhand vintage shit and a collection of jazz on vinyl.

Last year, one afternoon when she was bored she made a Tinder account using her stepmother's photo and name. Rob's Tinder profile said he likes to hike, enjoys live music, Sunday morning sleep-ins and pancakes. His profile pic was pretty good — a selfie with a vivid warm filter that made him look extra approachable. She swiped right and so did he. They had an online love affair for a few months before she ghosted him. Winona and Jay took turns messaging him and both of them actually kind of fell for Rob. He was smart and good, a bit awkward but kind. The kind of man you feel sorry for, the kind of guy who jerks off in the shower instead of in bed because he doesn't want to stain his sheets. They messaged at least twenty different guys pretending to be Trish, using her old modeling shots and bikini pics as clickbait. Rob was the only one who didn't send a dick pic. He was the only one who didn't ask to hook up. That made him special and weird. After he messaged that he'd fallen in love with Trish, they deactivated Trish's account.

She wonders now as she looks at him if he misses Trish, if he thinks about her every day. She examines his pasty face and tries to reconcile him with the outdoorsy online Rob who likes craft beer and '80s movies. She wonders which is real or if he can be both. Her heart aches a little as she thinks of online Rob. Now that Jay's gone, she toys with the idea of reactivating Trish so they could be in love again and she could have someone to talk to. She wonders how he'd feel if he found out that he'd been catfished by two teenagers. Online Rob had fallen in love with two kids, which means that therapist Robert is really a giant flaming pedophile. No wonder he specializes in behavioral therapy for young people. He breaks them down, builds them back up, gets to be the savior and if everything goes to plan, he is loved for it. That's what he's doing now, breaking Tonya down and getting her to swim in self-loathing while they all watch, take note, internalize the lesson.

"So, why do you hate yourself?" Winona asks, interrupting the groupthink.

Robert motions that Tonya needn't answer. "That's really not appropriate, Winona."

"Why isn't it? Isn't that what all of this is about? We're messed up, we fuck up in crazy-ass ways and you, you're here to help us find forgiveness, self-acceptance and peace and all the other shit that people post and pin, gratitude attitude, be the change blah blah blah." She stands up, glances around at the circle of nodding heads. They all look the same: waif-like, pin-straight hair, pained faces with scooped-out eyes. She doesn't belong here anymore.

"Winona, I have to ask you to take your seat. This is highly disruptive."

"Oh, come on, lighten up, Rob," she says and looks at Tonya straight on. "Answer me. Why do you hate yourself?"

"I don't hate myself." Tonya shifts in her chair, twirls a blond lock of hair tight around her finger.

"Sure you do. Otherwise you wouldn't be starving yourself. You think you're not good enough and the truth is you're not. None of us are, and not eating isn't going to change that. Trust me, I've been there. You'll never be good enough so you might as well eat." She takes a chocolate bar from her bag and holds it out like an olive branch.

Rob stands up, getting between them. "That's enough."

Hands up, she takes a few steps back and turns around, addressing the other girls. "It's the truth. We aren't good enough, and if we can accept this we can stop this charade of trying to be better just so our parents don't feel so shitty about us." She drags her folding chair into the center of the circle and jumps up on it like a circus ringmaster. "Everyone repeat after me: I am not good enough." No one speaks. The girls just sit tight in their seats as if they've been strapped in, drugged up and let down. "Come on now. One more time with feeling!" She holds her fist out to them like a microphone but there's not a sound, nothing but the squeaking of her own chair as it wobbles. "Okay, then." Winona steps off and drags the chair back to her spot, its steel legs screeching painfully against the linoleum floor.

Straddling the seat and hunched over the backrest, she bites into the chocolate bar. With a death stare and slow chew, she glazes over as Tonya resumes talking about her childhood. Nothing bad happened to her; as far as Winona can tell Tonya had a perfect pink life. Maybe she's just buckling under the perfection, like a cake out of the oven too soon, a cupcake with so much icing that it tips over. Yeah, she's a cupcake for sure. All sugar and show, piped-up frosting with silver pearls, confetti sprinkles that look nice and taste like shit. The more Tonya talks about herself, chapter and verse — the ballet recital gone bad, her recent breakup — the more Winona barrel-eyed locks in on her. If her mother was alive, Winona might have been her. If she never met Jay, she might have been her — an insipid mouth-breathing moron. Ready. Aim. Fire. "Would you shut up already," Winona says.

"Winona," Rob cautions.

"Rob," she parrots. "No one cares. She's full of shit." Winona looks around the circle hoping for an ally, but most of the girls are just sitting with their arms racked against their chests, discreetly checking their phones. One of them is filming. Winona marches up to that girl and tells her to stop filming and when she plays dumb about it, Winona grabs the phone and tosses it against the far wall. Rob is yelling in the background, trying to regain some control, as the girl shrieks and runs over, picking the phone up as if it's an injured bird.

She holds up the cracked screen. "What the fuck." She lunges at Winona and grabs her by the hair and for a moment, they're both caught up in each other, legs and arms thrashing, fingernails clawing at each other. Rob, trying to pull them apart, gets an elbow to the face and ends up on the ground. He slides back, rights himself and calls for reinforcement, all the while telling everyone to calm down. Two security guards come in and tear the girls apart. Rob's nose is bleeding and before he can even ask what's gotten into them, they both point fingers and blame the other.

"Winona, out," he says, motioning to the door.

She folds her arms across her chest. "Why me?"

"Outside, now." The way he says it, so emphatically, with blood gushing out of his nose, impresses her and she nods, giving just a little, just enough. She follows the security guards through the double doors and into the office where she's told to wait while they call her father.

"He's away on business. You'll have to call my stepmother."

After thirty minutes Rob joins Winona in the office. He's cleaned up some but still has blood on his shirt and a wad of tissue up his nostril. He doesn't counsel or chide her like she expected and his silence makes her feel bad, as if she went too far, and she feels even worse when Trish, dressed in her studio leggings, walks into the office and his eyes soften.

"I can't believe you. I was teaching a class when they called. This acting out of yours . . ." She turns to Rob who's staring at her.

"Trish." He stands up. "What are you doing here?"

"What do you mean? Your people called me about Winona?" Annoyed, she shakes her head. "I'm sorry, have we met?"

"Well, no, not really but . . . I'm confused. You're here for Winona?"

"Yes, I'm her stepmother."

"When were you going to tell me that? Is that why you stopped returning my messages?"

"Messages? Look, buddy, I don't know what you're talking about. I'm just here to get Winona." She turns toward her. "Let's go, grab your stuff. You can explain it to your father when he gets back."

"Trish." He reaches for her hand.

"Don't touch me," she snaps, glaring at him.

Winona can see the moment he realizes it was never Trish.

"Winona?" Sitting down, he says her name like a question, a half-whispered realization.

"I'm sorry." She breaks into a nervous laugh. "I'm not good enough and neither were you." She feels a twinge of regret as she says it and balls up her fist so that her nails cut her palm.

Day 56

Ash is mindlessly scrolling.

He updates his story with a picture of his bedroom ceiling. Britt's posted a Snap of her trying on a dress at H&M for the spring fling. It's tight and short, attention-seeking just like her. He reminds himself that their breakup is not a big deal. He wasn't that into her anyways. Besides she was moody as fuck, always talking shit about other people and now she's talking shit about him. Normally he'd care, obsess about the details, but he's bored by the whole thing. He thought having a girlfriend would mean something, but she was just another person to worry about, another person to disappoint. He can hear Anik playing the keyboard downstairs and realizes he's onto something by keeping to himself, pouring himself into something rather than someone. People are trash. His screen lights up. It's Winona.

hey

He watches the dot-dot-dot cycle as she types.

what r u doing

not much

want to hang out

He thinks about it for a second. Sure, people suck but at least she's interesting. Real about her weirdness.

sure

pick u up in 20

k

He gets up and checks his look in the mirror, not that it matters. He knows he's got a look about him — perfect teeth, nice smile, broad shoulders and a strong jaw. He's glad he has the face he has; he'd hate to look like those dough-faced, weak-chinned guys who can't take a punch. He pops his earbuds in and runs his fingers through his hair before heading out.

"Hey, where you off to?" Peter asks.

He pulls one earbud out. "Just gonna hang with a friend."

"Your mom know?"

"Nah. Tell her for me?" Ash knows that if it was his mom, she'd be asking for the "411," whatever that means, and make him text her a few times so she'd know he's okay. She made Anik do the same thing even after he turned nineteen and was out past midnight. He'd send her texts in the middle of the night that said, "I'm alive," and that somehow made her feel better. She says she can't relax if she doesn't know where they are and that they're safe. But Ash knows that they're not okay, never safe — the world is a terrible place. Climate change kills, corporate interests rule, politicians are puppets and the average person is so self-absorbed that they don't even realize it. The text they should really send is "Help! I'm alive," but that would seriously mess her up and she's already a mess.

Winona pulls up in a black Mercedes, techno music blasting. Ash slides into the passenger seat. "Nice ride."

"Thanks," she yells over the manic beat. "It was a birthday gift."

"That's some present," he says, glancing at the leather interior and wood inlay.

"Huh?" She turns the music down a bit. "What did you say?" She doesn't signal as she pulls away from the curb and almost hits another car.

"Never mind," he says, realizing that people with money don't like it when you make a big deal about it. They always want to be seen as normal. "It's not important."

She lights a smoke and cracks the window.

"Cool tunes. I didn't figure you for a techno type."

"What, you thought that I'd be listening to emo, indie, singer-songwriter, death metal, depressed cliché sort of thing?"

Ash nods. "Maybe."

"Nah, I like a lot of music. Jay, he got me into the classics — the Doors, Queen. My fave is 'Radio Ga Ga.' Have you heard it?" She doesn't wait for Ash to answer and asks Siri to play it. A few seconds later, tinny synth drums fill the car and something about the sound and the speed that she's driving makes Ash feel like he's flying. Freddie's voice is God. "You've had your time," she's singing, tapping the steering wheel, cigarette ashes falling with the beat. Ash watches the suburbs fly by as they merge onto the highway.

"Where are we going?"

"Wait, wait," she says and turns it even louder. "This is the best part." Cigarette lipped, she urges him to clap along with the beat.

"Hands on the wheel," he says, interrupting her jam.

"I love that song." She turns it down and snuffs out her cigarette. "Jay liked 'Pressure' more, you know the duet with Bowie — the lyrics are totally relatable." She sings until he says that he knows it. "What about you? What music do you like?"

"The usual, I guess."

"Drake? That sort of thing," she says, mocking.

"No, nothing that basic."

She makes a face.

"What, you don't like hip-hop?"

"I do, I just thought you'd be different."

"I'm different. I have layers."

"Yeah, like what?"

"Like, Frank Sinatra."

"No shit, the Rat Pack?"

"What pack?"

"That's what they called the guys who rolled together in Vegas in the '6os. Dean Martin, Sammy Davis Jr."

"How do you know all of this weird shit?"

"My mom, she was an artist, always telling me about history, culture and art and stuff."

"She sounds way cooler than my mom."

"She's dead. Cancer. Not so cool."

"Sorry, I didn't know."

"That's okay. I was just a kid when it happened."

"That's rough."

"Yeah, it fucked me up good. At least that's what my therapist tells me." She goes quiet and hands him her phone. "Play something."

Ash makes his selection and watches her face as the opening bars of Sinatra's "I'm Gonna Live Till I Die" plays.

She cracks up. "Layered for sure."

"I told you."

"What's next, jazz hands?"

"Saving it for later." He picks another song, this one all ambient chill.

"I like the vibe." She relaxes into her seat, her eyes squinting against the setting sun. The glare cuts through the need to talk and they drive in silence toward the airport. She parks in the grassy lot where people usually come to hook up. He's weirded out but doesn't say anything. She grabs a blanket out of the trunk and tells him to follow her as she climbs up the hood and sits down on the roof of the car.

"Jay and I used to come here to watch the planes and imagine where everyone was coming from or going to."

The sound of planes drowns out most of what she's saying. The dampening roar makes it feel okay to talk. In the lull between planes he asks her why she hasn't been at school much.

"My dad put me in a program. He thinks I'm *at risk*."

"Of what?"

"That's exactly what I said."

"So, are you? At risk?

"Sure, aren't you?"

"I guess, in a way," he says, unsure if he wants to know more, say more.

"It doesn't matter anyways. I got kicked out of group therapy."

"For what?"

"I got into a fight."

"For real?"

"Yeah, this girl was filming me while I was having a moment."

"A moment?"

"Yeah. I was telling the group that self-hate was normal and while I was going off about it, this girl wouldn't stop filming me so I smashed her phone."

"No way."

"Facts. Someone from group posted it," she says and hands Ash her phone.

He watches the video of the girls fighting. "You're fucking crazy," he says, shaking his head and trying hard not to laugh.

"I know, right."

"So do you actually, like, hate yourself?"

"Yeah, sure. I guess."

"Why?"

A landing plane blocks the sun as it crosses over them. The force blows Winona's black hair up and over her face. She sweeps it back and looks at him deadpan. "Because it's my fault."

"What is?"

"Everything."

Day 62

Pavan hasn't worn the Clean and Tidy scrubs for years.

The pants pull at the seams so she loosens the drawstring and slings them down on her hips, love handles bulging over. She grabs the fleshy roll, her fingers pinching like calipers. Disgusted by herself, she opts for leggings and a sweatshirt and pulls her long hair into a ponytail. She stares at her mirrored reflection, moisturizes and puts on her mascara and lip balm. She's always been simple. She's had the same layered haircut for twenty years and only ever wears more makeup on special occasions. She never mastered high heels, a sultry smoky eye, never even had a manicure. When she was younger this all registered as sporty or outdoorsy, but now it simply registers as her having given up. She's like all the other athleisure suburban moms who wear yoga gear without ever seeing the inside of a studio. She turns away from the mirror and heads down the hallway to gather her cleaning supplies, stopping to knock on Ash's door to remind him of the time.

"You're going to be late for school."

"I'm up," he says. She opens the door and pokes her head in. He's still in bed. "Ash, come on. Get going." She crosses the room and raises his blinds.

"Jesus, Mom." He covers his face with his pillow and she yanks it off.

"I'm serious."

"Okay, okay," he says, shooing her away. "Privacy, please. God."

She leaves the door open despite his calls to close it. He gets up and slams the door shut behind her. A few minutes later he emerges dressed.

"Breakfast?" she asks.

"When have I ever. Besides, I don't want to be late," he says, mimicking her.

"Watch the tone."

He throws his backpack on and leaves.

"Love you," she calls after him. He doesn't say it back and she watches him from the window. He has earbuds in, head down, shoulders curled in with the weight of his books as he walks down the street. He doesn't look around, doesn't notice the birds in the trees, doesn't hear their morning song, doesn't see that spring has made way for an early summer. He sees with a fisheye lens, the world curved around him. Pavan reminds herself that the teen perspective is one of ignorance and arrogance. She tries not to take it personally. It will pass. Everything does.

"Was that Ash?" Peter asks, coming in from a run.

"Lucky you, you missed the morning angst."

"What are you up to today?" He's talking loud, headphones still on, and stretches his quads one at a time. He's soccer-player toned, legs chiseled like a doctor's office anatomy chart.

"I'm going to see a client," she says with slow precision so he can hear her over his music.

He takes an earbud out. "Sorry, what?" He's still stretching and this annoys her.

"I'm going to see a new client."

"That's different," he says, bending forward, releasing his hamstrings. "You don't usually go on site anymore. Someone call in sick or something?"

"Yeah," she says. She doesn't want to tell him she's going to Lisa's to pack up the apartment. She hasn't told him about seeing her, the journal — any of it. She certainly doesn't want to tell him that she's been driving Lisa to support group these last few weeks. She knows that if she told him, he'd attempt to life coach her, to try to get at the root of her feelings and pull up the unhealthy attachment, and he'd be right to try. She knows she shouldn't have inserted herself into Lisa's life, but after reading Jay's journal she couldn't stop thinking about him and how it all came to this. She meant to give the journal back to Lisa the first time she drove her to group but then they stopped for coffee, and listening to Lisa talk about Jay, witnessing her pain up close, seeing the serrated edges, made Pavan realize that giving it back in that moment would do more harm than good. What would Lisa get from it other than to see that her son wasn't okay and that she, as his mother, should have noticed and that if she had, he might still be alive. Since then Pavan's kept the journal in her bag, waiting for the right moment to return it.

"What time will you be back?" Peter asks.

She grabs her purse and keys. "Not sure. Go ahead and order in tonight." Though the job won't take all day, she's hoping that maybe she and Lisa will have dinner, order in or go out. She tells herself that she's being a good friend by listening and doesn't name her darker motives — the graceless sympathy, the gratitude of better you than me.

She tells Peter goodbye and walks out. There's always relief in leaving, shutting the door tight behind her. She remembers that same feeling when she was seventeen and walking to school, the brisk fall air, the faint smell of burning leaves, the momentary feeling of freedom. To be alone in her thoughts never seems quite possible — Peter, the boys, the house, the meal planning, the cooking, the cleaning, all of the thankless doing crashes in and crowds her out. Her life is robotic, both empty and full, yet in the rare moment when she's not needed, she doesn't know how to feel. The only time she's ever heard anyone else voice those same thoughts was at Lisa's support group last week. While she loitered by the open door, waiting for the session to end, she stole glances at the circle of grieving parents. "I just don't know how I'm supposed to go on," said the woman who lost her daughter to cancer. "Everything was for her, all of my time, and now I'm just not sure what to do." Pavan knew she couldn't and shouldn't relate, but she did and felt quietly ashamed about it and went up into the chapel to keep from eavesdropping. The church was empty and sad-looking, as plain as she remembered it from Jay's funeral. She walked to the front and stared at the crucifix that loomed above. She knelt down, bowing with her head to the ground as if she was in the Gurdwara. She attempted a prayer but couldn't get beyond the word *help*. A voice from behind startled her and she bolted upright.

It was the minister.

"I'm sorry. I probably shouldn't be here. I was just waiting for my friend Lisa. She's downstairs."

"Of course. Please don't let me interrupt your prayers."

"Oh, no. I'm not . . ."

"Praying?"

"No, I'm not religious or anything."

"Or anything . . . and yet, here you are."

Pavan's mouth tightened into an uncomfortable smile. "Yes, here I am."

"Right, of course. I find a lot of people who aren't religious come in to pray, to talk, to share space."

"Is that so?" Pavan tried to match the minister's calm demeanor but she didn't have his faith, his confidence, and it made her wonder how someone as young as him could have so much assurance unless he was just a born believer. Maybe he was an easy baby who slept through the night and never cried, and maybe some people were just lucky that way, bestowed with a wellspring of certitude.

"I've seen it time and time again: loss makes people question everything, and over time they look to the church for guidance." He took a few steps toward her and she instinctively backed up.

"Yes, I can see that might happen, but I haven't lost anything."

"Haven't you?" He looked at her in a way that made her feel entirely exposed. Her knees felt weak and she grabbed the top of a pew to steady herself. "The whole community has lost something in Jacob's passing."

"Passing? You mean death?"

"You think it's a euphemism, but it's not; he is passing. This life is not the end — temporary, yes, a place we move through as we find our way to God."

"Right." Pavan nodded, remembering her own religious upbringing that left her faithless and alone. "But tell me, where was God when Jay needed him? Let me guess, free will and all of that?"

"God doesn't abandon us. It's us who abandon him."

"But maybe he could just give us a sign once in a while. You know, a signal that everything will be okay."

"Isn't your being here a sign? Bearing witness to Lisa's pain is an act of goodness and healing."

Pavan smiled, knowing that it wasn't God who brought her here. It was fear, shame and guilt — the loveless emotions that edged out hope. "Speaking of Lisa, I should go. She'll be waiting." Without saying goodbye, she headed back downstairs where the group session was ending.

Lisa was putting on her coat. "Thanks for this — for driving me again."

"It's no trouble. I'm happy to help."

"Well, I appreciate it. Most people say they want to help but don't actually want to. It's awkward. It's like they're curious about me, you know? I catch them staring at me in the grocery store, but then as soon as they see me see them, they look away or walk the opposite direction as if I'm contagious or something. But not you. You actually care."

"I do care," Pavan said, shame crawling up her neck. It was true: she did care, but she was curious too. Curious the way people are when they watch 60 *Minutes* or *CSI*, always taking mental notes on how not to be a victim.

She picks up the keys from the building manager and lets herself into Lisa's apartment. The living room is packed, boxes stacked halfway up the window, obscuring the view of transmission towers in the green belt. When the kids were little she'd take them to ride their bikes along the hydro corridor, the buzz and hum of currents running above them, guiding their way. Anik used training wheels when he learned to ride but Ash refused. He'd wobble and fall, push along with his feet, the pedals scraping his tender calves. It took him just as many weeks to learn as it took Anik and he came through it bruised and scraped like a warrior, while Anik had systematic precision. Very little has changed. Ash pushes through the difficulties, forging ahead while Anik always processes the way before he begins. Despite the challenges, she reminds herself to be grateful for everything she has, especially now.

She looks around, life packed up in boxes, the compartmentalized space of moving on. Jay's room hasn't changed since she was last there. She cracks the window, and the smell of the neighbor's torka comes in, the cooking of onions and curried spices reminds her of growing up. To her, it seems unfair that she survived her childhood and Jay wasn't able to survive his. She looks at his small desk and wonders if that's where he sat to write in his journal. She'd kept a diary when she was younger, and when she reread passages, she was always ashamed for having written them and immediately tore out the pages. Something about seeing her thoughts in ink made them all too real and she decided it was better not to admit things, not to confess. Some things are better left unsaid. She once heard Peter encouraging a client to write out his feelings, saying that unexpressed emotions create dis-ease in the body and mind. She wonders if this is why she always feels unsettled even though she has no great secrets, nothing beyond her ordinary story of neglect and want.

She sits on Jay's bed, reaches for the stuffed bear propped up on the pillow and inhales the matted fur. It smells like cigarettes and kitty litter. She hasn't seen a cat and wonders if they have one and if that's why her allergies are acting up. Lisa didn't mention it but now she can't shake the feeling of being watched.

"Here kitty, kitty." She wanders around the apartment until she finds the black cat hiding under Lisa's unmade bed. It's scrawny and nimble, an unlucky-across-your-path type of cat, and hisses at her as she shuts the door. She never got used to being in someone else's home without them, and though it's her job, there's something cold and ghostly about inhabiting their space when they aren't there. When she was a little girl she peered into house windows and glanced at people as they drove by her in the rain, always wondering what their lives were like, where they were going in such a hurry. Now, having been inside hundreds of homes, having looked inside countless medicine cabinets and kitchen cupboards, she realizes that everyone is living some variation of learning to be okay.

In Jay's room, she starts with the closet, folding all of his clothes into boxes labeled accordingly. She tries not to think about it, to not pay attention to his things, to not think about the journal, to not think about him, not in a solid way at least. Thinking about him like a person makes things hard, so she prefers to think of him only as an idea, an example, a simile. She reminds herself that movers and cleaners are efficient because they're detached; they don't assign memories to things so they can simply categorize. She tries to do the same, dumping the contents of his dresser drawers into boxes and quickly folding and sorting them so that when Lisa is ready to donate she can go through them just as quickly. After she finishes with his clothes, she untacks the posters, boxes up his tae kwon do medals and trophies and clears the dusty bookshelves. He has stacks of old *National Geographic* magazines and a collection of secondhand books with cracked spines and yellowed pages. She sits cross-legged on the dingy carpet and thumbs through his leather-bound collected works of Shakespeare, the dog-eared copy of *To Kill a Mockingbird*, and tries to imagine him reading them. The *National Geographics*, all old library copies, have pictures and even whole pages torn out, and she wonders if he was using them for some art project. She remembers that he'd always been artistic. Jay loved to doodle and he and Ash spent one summer making comic strips. She wishes she'd kept some of them, but of course it's hard to know what's important in the moment, what evidence of daily life will be rendered meaningful when the time comes.

She places them all in a box and seals them with tape before taking a moment to survey. With everything packed and the walls stripped of personality, the room feels decidedly abandoned. She's disappointed. She expected to find something, some clue, another journal or a letter, offering some insight into what made Jay different from any other boy. The longer she looked through his things, the more normal he seemed, the more tragic it all is or was. The only thing left on the wall is a photo of Jay and his mother at his grade school graduation. She remembers that day and how excited Ash and Jay were to be heading to high school that fall. She stares at the photo, thinking of all the plans they made, and leaves the picture hanging there.

She sits at the desk and takes his journal out of her purse. She planned on putting it in one of the boxes for Lisa to find in due time. She imagined a year would go by before she was ready to go through them and by then maybe it would be easier to read. But now, as she rereads it, she knows that time won't make it any easier. How can you accept that your child was not who you imagined him to be? That the light you felt for them was matched by some darkness, some shadow life? If only he had left her a note or a letter, something just for her that could be of comfort. She examines his penmanship, the curve and line of each letter, the erratic spacing,

the fragmented thoughts. Pen in hand, she turns his journal to a
new page and begins to write his final entry.

April 2

Dear Mom,
I'm sorry. I never meant to hurt you.

Dear Mom,
If you're reading this, it means I'm gone. Please don't think
that you could have or should have done something. This
is on me.

Dear Mom,
By the time you read this, I'll be gone. There's no way I can
explain it to you that will make sense. I'm sorry.

Pavan drops the pen. She can't find the right words, his words,
and the failure, the forgery, makes her jittery, as if electricity is
running through her looking for an outlet. She opens her purse
and from the inside pouch takes out his remaining joint. Her
hands shake and fumble as she lights it. She inhales until the swell
and current of emotion subside. She puts the journal back in her
bag and reaches for her phone, mindlessly scrolling. She sits on his
bed and types *Jacob McAlister* into Facebook. His profile pic is him
looking straight into the camera, tongue sticking out, hand in the
air in a peace gesture. She scrolls down. His wall is full of condo-
lences. His posts, all boarding and parkour videos, him and his
friends skating and scaling walls. His Instagram account is more
of the same — parkour, thrill-seeking, dangerous locations. As she
scans through, seeing what he liked, who he was, she realizes how
strange it is that even though he's gone, his digital self still exists in
a cloud, all bits and particles and uploads and downloads. It seems
depressing to her that online lives go on. Every year his friends

will get a reminder that it's his birthday, memory notifications of past events and friends of friends will see him listed as "people you may know." She puts the joint out on the mattress frame and lies down on top of the covers. They smell stale, in need of a wash, like gym clothes left in a bag. She wonders if that's how Jay smelled and if Lisa sleeps here just to be close to him.

She stares at the cracked ceiling, mapping the water damage, connecting the stains like landscapes until her eyes feel heavy with sadness and sleep. She dreams that she's moving boxes into a U-Haul, and each box is heavier than the next. She grabs a dolly and stacks them in the truck but each time she returns to the truck with more boxes, the others have fallen open, the contents of clothing and collectables spilling out. She panics and tries to stuff them back in but can't. Suddenly the truck is a boat and the boxes fall off the deck one by one and sink. She jumps in after them, thrashing about, but can't save anything. She wakes to the sound of Lisa's voice calling her name with an upturned concern.

Pavan sits up, confused and embarrassed. Lisa is standing in front of her, holding the cat.

"Oh my God. I'm so sorry. I must have fallen asleep. I finished packing and then I . . ." Pavan glances at her watch. "I'm so sorry. I guess . . ." She pauses, aware of the skunky odor in the air and how it all must look. She closes her eyes for a second and tries to regain her composure. "I should go." She gets up and reaches for her purse but drops it open-mouthed onto the floor. "Shit, I'm sorry." Pavan kneels down to pick up the contents, stuffing the journal back in her bag before Lisa notices it.

Once in her car, she locks the door and exhales in short breaths. It's all she can manage. Her chest is tight, her pulse racing and the more she tries to talk herself down, the dizzier she feels. A numbness sets in and she presses her head against the side window. "It's okay," she tells herself. "Just breathe. You're okay." She closes her eyes and focuses on her breath, counting it in and out. She opens her eyes and locks in on the children playing on the jungle gym in the park across the street. She watches as two boys race to the swings and propel themselves into the air, heads thrown back, legs pumping, higher and higher they go, until finally they can go no more and their legs go limp and they free fall.

Day 65

Anik fills his backpack with ten textbooks and slings it over his shoulder.

He steps on the treadmill and starts to walk, keeping pace with the hiking program that changes elevation and speed every few minutes. After ten minutes his legs feel heavy and his breath labors. He keeps pace and pushes on, knowing that his body will adjust; the first two kilometers are always the hardest. He's walked fifteen kilometers, in three sets of five treks, every other day for two weeks. On alternate days he uses the stair climber and does high-intensity interval training with lunges, squats and sit-ups, a routine he found on YouTube that's meant to build core strength. He's ordered his travel backpack and hiking boots online and has ransacked the shed, locating Peter's camping and outdoor supplies from his tree-planting days. Peter worked in the camps all summer to pay for his university tuition and said that digging in the dirt, planting trees he wouldn't see grow, was metaphoric, life-changing even. Anik didn't understand at the time, but now he can see that the dredging and sowing was all a spiritual excavation, a karmic act of giving and unearthing.

He used to love to dig in the dirt; he planted the magnolia tree out front and for a time tended to a vegetable garden with Peter and Ash. They planted tomatoes, zucchinis, carrots and spinach in raised beds in the corner of the backyard. Anik watered them daily and watched closely for signs of life, measuring growth with his wooden ruler. When critters started nibbling at the leafy greens, they made a scarecrow, repurposing some of their dollar-store Halloween decorations. They named the scarecrow Oz and even pretended the critters that they were trying to keep away were the flying monkeys. Despite their best efforts, Oz did not deter whatever was feasting in their garden and within a few weeks the bounty was decimated, trampled through and eaten. It was likely a deer. Though they weren't native to the area, a few had been spotted roaming around. One had even made it on the front page of the local paper when it attempted to cross a busy intersection during rush hour, motorists and pedestrians alike helping it to safe passage. Peter and Pavan dismantled the raised bed and built Ash a wooden playhouse that still sits in the corner of the yard, with wisteria, groundcover and bleeding hearts lining its perimeter.

When Anik opens the basement blinds, he sees the yard at eye level, and imagines that he too must look like something growing in the garden. His head aboveground and his body rooted below, tucked into the foundation of the house, buried in thick cement. Even now, from the treadmill he can see Peter, spreading a thin layer of seed and fertilizer on the grass. Peter, like most of the neighborhood dads, is obsessed with lawncare and reads countless blogs on how to have a golf-green lawn. The clerks at Home Depot know him by name and he always stops and chats with them, asking for advice, coming home with some new spray or mulch. In the years since the vegetable garden, he's built the playhouse, a trellis for the wisteria, a fire pit and even a pergola. Anik, seventeen at the time, helped him with the pergola. He liked the smell of the pressure-treated lumber and even the chemical scent of the stain, but what he loved most was seeing the project complete. They spent that first summer eating outside under the pergola, barbecue dinners and badminton in the backyard. Ash was only twelve at the time, and even though he hadn't hit his growth spurt, he seemed to have escaped the awkward phase of adolescence. Unlike Anik, who couldn't swing a bat or throw a baseball, Ash was good at all sports, including badminton. He and Peter counted how many times they could rally the birdie, and Anik just sat out and watched from beneath the pergola. The following year Pavan planted honeysuckle and trained it along the beams, creating a fragrant canopy for hummingbirds. While the other two played some sport, she and Anik sat beneath and watched the birds hover and drink from the trumpeted flowers. They could sit in silence together like that for what he remembered as hours, only it wasn't that long at all. His focus on a bird, suspended midair, its wings beating too fast to see, put him into a reverie. He hopes that his pilgrimage will take him to this place of contemplation. It's not about finding himself. It's about finding something more.

Sometimes he wishes he could be like his peers and settle into his Insta twenties, but he isn't satisfied with cheap drinks, expensive lattes, snowflake sentiment and trigger warnings. He doesn't understand when adults say that their twenties were the best time of their lives. There has to be something better than pretending you're something you aren't. He knows that Jay must have felt the same way and at times that's a comfort to him; at others, that shared isolation is frightening.

He presses stop on the treadmill and dismounts, wiping the sweat from his brow as he crashes on the couch. Exhausted, he closes his eyes to the sounds of the suburbs — crows cawing, cars starting, a distant lawnmower and somewhere a chainsaw hacking. Sounds of busyness, efficiency, productivity. The sound of living on a conveyor belt, rolling on, every stage and station bringing something new to spoil what was good at the start. Ash, in his early teenage angst, tried to explain the futility of progress and perfectionism during the family's annual "what we are thankful for" Thanksgiving Day ritual. "Michael Jackson is a perfect example. He was the king of pop before he started to mess with his face. All that plastic surgery made him ugly. He should have appreciated what he had. Instead he messed it up."

Anik, having never been a fan of MJ, could only partly agree with his brother. "So what you're saying is things go from *bad* to worse?" He laughed at his own pun and stood up, attempting to moonwalk around the table.

"But seriously," Ash said, "I'm saying, we should be grateful for what we have and stop trying to change it into something we think it should be."

There was a collective *aww* followed by laughter, followed by "Pass the gravy" and it was another good wholesome Thanksgiving. Anik had a nice childhood, he had everything a boy could want, and yet he went on wanting.

As he watches Peter tending to the grass, Anik thinks that it's the wanting that is his downfall. It's not a pursuit of perfection or success but a pursuit of truth. Perhaps knowing something would fill up the empty space of wanting something.

Day 69

It's seven a.m. and Winona hasn't slept since she saw Jay's posts.

She tried to hack his account to delete them, to stop him from haunting her feeds but she can't figure out his passwords and so there he is commenting from the afterlife, wishing her a happy birthday and posting throwback pics. People from school have been screenshotting the posts, adding them to their stories with ghost stickers and exclamation points. Every year he spammed her, going to great lengths to get the timing just right, writing and scheduling posts in advance, so he could be there to watch her reaction unfold. Mostly she acted annoyed but he knew that secretly she liked that he remembered. She hadn't celebrated her birthday since her mom died. Though her dad tried to keep up the ritual of birthday cake for breakfast and breakfast for dinner, it wasn't the same as when her mom did it. Her mom filled the kitchen with streamers and sat her down at the table like she was royalty. She played music and they'd dance around the kitchen, making up their own lyrics to popular songs. Her dad was usually there, camera in hand, recording it for posterity but never really participating.

Her tenth birthday was only a few weeks after the funeral and her dad tried, but it was obvious that he was trying. Trying to celebrate and trying to forget at the same time. When she turned thirteen she told him that she was too old for dumb birthday parties. She mocked his attempts to plan a slumber party and returned the gifts he bought her for cash. She was mean about it on purpose. She can still see his face, how he had to look away when she said, "You're the worst dad ever. I wish you had died instead of Mom."

"I wish that too. Every day," he said.

After that, he surrendered, giving her cash or over-the-top guilt gifts. She got what she wanted; nothing would replace her birthday memories with her mom. The bright white kitchen, the glare of morning sun, time so slow that she could see particles of dust float in the rays. It couldn't possibly have been how she remembered it. Jay thought she was being dumb for not celebrating. He never bought into what she said she wanted and saw through her lies. Ever since he died she's all tangled up in them. Unsure. A mess, and here he is, still counseling.

"Chill. It's your birthday."

She repeats this to herself when she's at school, when people point and whisper, when randoms say "Happy birthday" with mock cheer. She keeps her head up.

Ash walks toward her. "Hey, birthday girl!" She expects him to keep walking but he stops right in front of her. "You doing okay?"

She nods, aware of the double takes and head-craning around them, people wondering.

Ash doesn't seem to notice or care and keeps talking. "I saw the Snaps."

"Yeah."

"Intense."

"Obviously."

"I didn't think you'd be at school today."

"Can't keep missing. My dad's on high alert since the thing at group."

"Does that mean you can't skip?"

"I probably shouldn't."

"Too bad. I was thinking we could go do something."

"Like what?"

"I don't know."

"Why you being so nice to me?"

"Am I not supposed to be?" He backs up and makes some awkward face, an on-purpose *this is my weird face* look. "Just thought it's your birthday and all."

They head out and walk down the street toward the 7-Eleven, where they load up on sour keys, gummy bears and Slurpees. Sugar-high, they cross the field and sit down on the skate park bleachers and toss gummies into their mouths.

"Have you ever skated before?" she asks.

"Nah, not my thing."

"Brian," she yells and stands up to get his attention. He skates over. She introduces them. He was a friend of Jay's. "Can I borrow your board?" she asks.

"I don't know," he says, looking up at her and then at his scuffed-up Chucks.

"Come on, just for a quick one." She smiles the way other girls do when they want something.

"Alright." He hands her the board. "Just a few minutes."

Ash watches as she pushes off, gathering speed and skimming the bowl. After a few turns around the course, she pops back up and over the rim, handing the board back to Brian who high-fives her before pushing off.

"You should try it sometime. It's such a high — unless." She digs through her backpack, retrieving a plastic bag. "Unless you prefer a different sort of high." She opens the bag and hands Ash a brownie. "I made them."

"I don't know. That shit messes me up."

"Come on, you have to. Think of it as my birthday cake." She holds it out to him, singing a few bars of "Happy Birthday."

"Okay, okay." He takes a bite.

They lay out on the bleachers, until the sky seems fuzzy and the clouds form pictures at will. Winona's arm is extended, moving to and fro as if she's conducting a symphony. She points at the cloud-layered sky.

"It's a cake!" She pretends to blow out candles. "Have you seen that movie?"

"What movie?" Ash is laughing. He can't stop.

"That '80s one. *Sixteen Candles*. It's got that girl with the red hair in it — Molly somebody."

"You watch a lot of old shit."

"My mom's movie collection. It's funny. It has this guy; his name is Long Duck Dong. Jay and I watched it last year when I turned sixteen. Long Duck Dong — see if you can say it ten times fast," she says, trying to string it together, her tongue tripping. She's laughing so hard she rolls off the bleacher and onto the step. She's still laughing but now it's soundless and after a few seconds it turns into ugly crying. She repeats Long Duck Dong between sobs.

Ash tries to help her up, but she won't move. She just lies there crying until the high softens and deflates. She wipes her eyes and sits up next to him, both of them staring out at the park.

"I'm sorry. I don't know what the fuck is wrong with me."

"It's okay. It's just the brownie."

"Yeah, you're probably right."

"At the airport when we were watching planes you said everything was your fault. What did you mean?"

"I don't know. It just feels that way." She pauses, eyes window-glazed. "Like, I can't do anything right. Not at home, not at school — I wasn't even there for Jay."

"You were."

"Not when it mattered."

"You didn't know. No one did."

"I should have. He'd been talking about it. I should've gotten help."

"How could you have known he was serious? People say shit all the time."

"Yeah, but he was different. He'd been different for a few months — you know the whole blue whale thing?"

Ash nodded.

"He actually wanted to do it. He'd been looking for a way in, trying to find the game curator. He got mad at me for not going along with it. I let it go because the game was probably just a hoax. I figured he wanted to find it just for something to do, another adrenaline hit, you know."

"You can't blame yourself for what he did."

"No? Then who can I blame?"

"Everyone else. The world." Ash pauses for a minute and stares out at the boarders weaving and popping. "Yeah, blame the world for spinning like one of those fucking metal playground roundabouts. You know the ones?"

She nods.

"When we were little my brother and I went on one, and some fat fuck pushed it really fast. All of the kids were screaming and some jumped off, scraping their knees and bumping their heads in the process. But Anik and I, we just hung on, white-knuckled, until my mom saw what was happening and stopped it. Both of us staggered and tripped off, all dizzy. Anik threw up in the bushes and I just stood there, the world spinning. My hands were cramped up from holding on so tight," he says, making a fist, "and when I unclenched them, they were pulsing, as if the metal and sweat of holding on had turned into an electric current." Ash is quiet for a moment. "You hear that," he says, gesturing toward the transmission towers beyond the park. "That buzzing . . . close your eyes and listen."

Winona closes her eyes. A cool wind brushes over her. She's calm, almost meditative, as she listens to the current, its linguistic clicks and zips.

"I figure that's the sound the world makes when it's humming along. That's the sound of all of us holding on as we go around and round."

She turns to him, her stoned face cracking with laughter. "That's so fucking deep."

"I know, right?" He shoves her and she shoves him back until their laughter softens.

"So what do you want to do now?" Her high feels thick, the fuzzy feeling turning into a low-grade headache. She rubs her temples and takes another bite of brownie.

"You decide. It's your birthday."

"Jay and I would have gone shoplifting for my gift. You know, like in true Winona Ryder style."

"Why? Your dad's loaded. You can have anything you want."

"For the thrill of it! Come on." She grabs his hand and starts running across the field, flapping her arms as she races toward the gulls pecking by the overturned trash cans.

The dollar store is wall-to-wall jammed with made-in-China crap, each aisle sign categorizing clutter: Baking and Food Storage, Party Planning, Housewares, Beauty, Candy and Food. Ash avoids looking directly at the security cameras but stares at his distorted reflection in the large surveillance mirrors in the corners of the shop. "Maybe we should just go?"

"Rookie," Winona says, pulling him along, leading him down the toy aisle where she pulls a plastic sword from a bin and stabs him with it.

She laughs and says, "En garde, you swine!"

"Huh?"

She looks annoyed. "Sword fight." She hands him a knockoff lightsaber from the same bin. He presses the button on the handle and it glows green.

"Game on," he says, imitating the sound the saber makes as he strikes her. She grabs a nearby plastic shield and holds it against her chest. They pivot back and forth, up and down the aisle, jabbing each other in the ribs, slicing shoulders and arms, part sword fight, part Jedi battle.

"Hey, no playing with the toys unless you buy them," yells the cashier from the front of the store. She's staring at them, her arms crossed over her uni-boob, and if it wasn't for her apron that says *How can I help*, she'd be a deterring force or at least someone to avoid, the same way you avoid the weird aunt who pinches your cheeks and hugs too hard.

"Sorry." Ash puts the lightsaber down. Winona follows suit and they proceed down the cramped aisle, checking the surveillance mirrors as they drop random stuff in their backpacks and jam candy into their pockets. Just as they're about to leave, Winona runs back to the toy aisle and grabs the lightsaber.

"Run," she says to Ash.

They push through the doors as the cashier yells, "You have to pay for that!" Winona glances back as the cashier bolts through the door. "Stop, thief!" People in the parking lot look up, noting the commotion, but no one intervenes.

"Come on!" Ash is still running.

"It's okay," Winona says, her run slowing down to a jog and then a walk by the time they clear the parking lot. "No one even cares."

When Winona gets home, Trish is asleep on the couch and the twins are in the playroom on their tablets. She likes it when they're quiet like this, sedated by the lure and glow of screens and interactive games. She's glad they're over the *Caillou* phase. That cartoon kid was a whiny brat and what was with his bald head — it's not like he had cancer or something.

"What's going on, Thing One and Two?" Neither of them looks up from their device. "Hello!" she says, raising her voice.

"Mom was acting funny when she picked us up from school and then she came home, ate all the snacks and went to sleep."

"She's been sleeping since three?"

They both nod in their weird twin way that always makes her think of the little girls in *The Shining*.

"I'll go check on her," she says, trying to stay calm. She walks normally until she's out of sight and then rushes to the living room, where Trish is sprawled out. "Trish, wake up." When she doesn't stir, Winona shakes her. "Wake up, wake up, wake the fuck up!" She pulls out her phone and dials her dad. No answer. "Shit, shit, shit." She kneels down, her face next to Trish's and listens to her breathing. "Good, still alive." Winona tries to wake her again, shoves her, pokes her, pulls her hair, but nothing. She calls 911 and waits for the paramedics to arrive.

"Is Mommy dead?" Thing One asks. For a minute Winona disappears into the past, remembering when her mother was taken to the hospital for the very last time. How she watched from these very steps, her face looking out between the slats. Thing Two starts to cry.

While Jon is at the hospital with Trish, Winona orders pizza, plays I spy with the twins and watches *Frozen* for the millionth time. At nine o'clock, she tucks them in and reads them stories until they fall asleep. It's the most time she's ever spent with them and as she looks at their identical pale moon faces she thinks they're not so bad.

She's binge-watching when her dad finally comes in. "How is she? What did they say?" She turns off the TV and waits as he hangs his jacket up. "Well?"

"Tests came back positive for drugs."

"What? That's got to be a mistake."

"That's what I thought, but then she told me she ate some of the brownies you made."

"Oh fuck."

"Yeah, fuck is right. What the hell were you thinking, making that shit and leaving it around. What if the twins ate it?"

"I didn't leave it around. I put them in the basement fridge. I didn't think she'd go in there."

"Yeah, well. She did." Jon sits down across from her. "What even possessed you to make them? Isn't your life messed up enough?"

She doesn't say anything.

"Well?"

"I thought it was a rhetorical question. Didn't realize you wanted an answer."

"Well, I do."

"I don't know. I just felt like it, I guess."

"You felt like it?" He pauses, his jaw tightens as if he's holding back. "Where did you even get the marijuana? Never mind, it doesn't even matter. What matters is that you're fucking up your life and you're fucking up everyone else's too. You know, if she hadn't told me that she ate those brownies, the doctors would think she's a user and could even report her to child protection or something."

"You're overreacting. Doctors are so used to seeing rich white women using way worse than that. Besides, edibles are practically legal now."

"Can you even hear yourself? For God's sake, Winona. Your mother would be so disappointed in you if she were alive."

"Nice one, Dad. Real nice." She gets up to leave.

"Sit down. We aren't finished."

"Then let's skip to the end where you tell me that I'm a fuckup and that I'm grounded and then I'll nod, take your bullshit and apologize."

"Aren't you the least bit sorry?"

"Of course I am. But you're acting like I did it on purpose, like I force-fed her. How was I supposed to know she was going to stuff her face with my birthday brownies? Yeah, that's right. It's my birthday today. Happy birthday, Winona!" She runs up the stairs and slams her door. She just stands there, back against the wall for a minute, trying to get a grip, trying to keep herself from spiraling but nothing works, not the breathing techniques and not the mantras. She reaches under the bed and pulls out her cut box. She looks at the knife, runs her fingers along the blade and without thinking makes one quick swipe, striking the blade on her forearm as if she's striking a match. She stares at the shallow cut, the dotted blood line, and palms it, applying pressure until she's filled with the sweet relief of feeling on the outside instead of on the inside.

Her phone pings. It's another message from Jay. A picture of a tiny gift-wrapped box captioned "Hope you liked it!" She wonders what was in the box and accepts that she'll never know. There's so much she'll never know.

She scrolls back to his first message. "Chill, it's your birthday." She hurls the phone across the room.

Day 74

It's Saturday morning sleep-in. Ash's favorite.

His parents are out — getting groceries, running errands, all the weekly boring. They used to bug him and Anik to go with them, but Ash figured if he made a fuss or acted dumb the whole way, they'd leave him out of their ritual chores and for the most part he was right. Sometimes Ash feels bad about it. He thinks that he should be a better kid, especially now with Anik being the way he is. But usually, if he waits long enough the lazy part of him wins and he camouflages into the house like some slow-moving lizard, sliding by, shifting colors.

Ash reaches over and grabs his phone from the bedside charger. He scrolls, stopping to like and comment. He makes himself into an *I woke up like this* meme and snaps a photo of his bedhead, eye jam, surprise face and sends it out there. He waits for the hearts and smiles to roll in and when they do he feels good and accomplished, self-satisfied even. He hates that he feels that way, but it's a natural reaction, a dopamine hit, an *I can feel good even when I feel bad* parachute. He turns on some music and drifts off into nothing thoughts. He's light as air, feeling like sunshine against the crisp piano melody on Tyler, the Creator's "Sometimes . . ." He listens to the first fifteen seconds over and over and thinks about going downstairs to ask Anik to splice it together and make him a personalized mix.

His brother used to do that all the time when he started music school. He could rip apart any song and put it back together, attaching his own piano melodies, backing up a harmony with a new beat, choosing weird intervals and loops that repeated and snaked, like a symphonic infinity symbol. He was god tier at it. He'd post them on YouTube and had millions of views. His best one was him playing a hang drum, layered with piano and violin, and a looped Sinatra vocal from "I've Got You Under My Skin." He posted under the name GOD is DOG and was so internet famous that for a while he even got death threats from a right-wing evangelical group. His parents got all weird about it and asked him to stop posting under that name. He's only posted under his real name once since he's been a shut-in. When Ash texted that he'd listened to the new track, Anik replied that "3.14159" wasn't really a song, it was more like long-form sound, an unending narrative to match our own mortal coil. Ash simply replied "big brain," explosion emoji and then waited for Anik to text back. He saw the three dots but then after a few seconds they disappeared. He feels like those dots all the time — waiting, anticipating and then nothing. Those dots are everything. Every time he sees them, he holds his breath, wondering.

He gets out of bed in his sloth-like way, taking too long to go through the basic motions of brush teeth, have shower, get dressed. Truth is, the bathroom is his favorite place, not just because it has a lock but because of the small luxury inside the utility. The seashell-shaped hand soap meant for guests, the vanilla-scented after-shower lotions, hair products that smell like coconut and the plush Egyptian cotton towels that make him feel like he's living in a hotel. It's all steam and dream in there and for a while it makes him feel good and new until eventually he has to open the door and leave the warmth behind.

He picks the wet towels up off the floor so his mom doesn't freak and heads downstairs to throw them in the laundry room. As he tosses them into the machine, he strains to hear what Anik might be up to, but there's nothing — not the one-sided talk of him gaming, no music playing, not even the sound of nature loops. The silence is weird; Anik's always needed ambient sound. When he was little he slept on the couch in front of the TV until Pavan bought him one of those dream machine clock radios that had endless loops of birds chirping, rainstorms and ocean waves. Most people would just pick one sound and listen to it on repeat, but he cycled through every setting endlessly. He doesn't use it anymore; he can download pretty much anything and now prefers binaural beats. He says the frequency patterns of the delta, theta, alpha and beta reduce his stress and help him sleep.

He's always into some new thing. When he was seventeen he collected crystals and ordered them from eBay, spending all of his burger-flipping money on them. Sometimes he'd work twelve hours on Saturday and Sunday just to pay for a dumb rock. He totally geeked out on them, and like any little brother would, Ash wanted in on it. Every week he'd sit and watch Anik unpack the boxes and reveal his newest geologic find. Ash's favorite was a giant amethyst Anik bought from a guy in Brazil. While Ash turned the rock over in his hands, examining the jagged laven-der, Anik read out the one-page document about the spiritual and chakra-balancing qualities. For Ash's birthday that year, Anik bought him an amethyst amulet to help with his anxiety. He wore it until some dumb kid at school called him Gandalf, and ever since then he kept it in his bedside drawer. It never helped with his anxiety anyway and none of it ever balanced Anik's chakras. So after blowing all of his savings on rocks, Anik moved on to aro-matherapy. His room smelled like witches' brew his whole senior year. "It's probably why you don't have a girlfriend," Ash told him after Anik smudged the house with sage and cedar. "You smell like a fucking hippie."

By the time Anik started university he was more normal. Full into his music again, he left the weird New Age shit behind. Until this past year. Pavan's convinced Anik is special because when she was pregnant, she had her tarot cards read and got some high priest card. Ash thinks Pavan's like Anik that way, sometimes super normal and practical and then completely flaked out in auras and fate. He's more like his dad. Grounded. Peter's into everyday stuff and helps people. He's basic and common sense. He whistles while he does yard work, talks to neighbors, makes small talk matter and likes cooking. He takes actual pleasure in watching cooking shows, practicing his knife skills and trying new recipes. When he's in the kitchen, he even walks around with a tea towel on his shoulder as if he's Gordon Ramsay. He seems genuinely happy with life and that is a mystery to Ash, because although he feels grounded, it's more in a tied-down, wearing-cement-shoes kind of way.

Sometimes Ash thinks they all need an intervention, a reckoning, and at first he thought Jay's dying was that, but life kept marching along in its plotless pace, a never-ending nothing parade.

Ash turns on the washing machine and opens the door to the basement suite. The front room is pretty much as it always is, only cleaner, as if Anik made an effort before going to bed. He moves through the kitchenette toward Anik's room and still he hears nothing, even when he presses his ear against the door. He knocks. No answer. "Anik?" Still nothing. He tries the door but it's locked and now he's banging on it with a fist and then a flat palm. "Open up." He's filling up with fear, with panic, a high-octane feeling from imagining what silence is on the other side of the door. Anik's dead. He thinks it instinctively. "Please open up." He races upstairs to his parents' bathroom and roots through Pavan's drawers, looking for a hairpin or any sharp object to jimmy the lock. Every breath he takes feels like a bomb — blue wire, green wire, boom. "Not again," he says, thinking of Jay. He tries and keeps himself moving, focused on the task until he finds something useful and heads back down.

Holding the hairpin like a switchblade, he works it into the lock, jiggling the knob until the door swings open to nothing. Anik's not there. He exhales and closes his eyes, pretends he's holding that amethyst crystal and tries to calm down. He keeps his eyes closed until he can breathe right again, until all the dead

Anik images have been erased from his mind. It was dumb to even think it. He's not the killing type. That saying "He wouldn't hurt a fly" is actually Anik. He used to catch and release spiders while Ash would stomp on them and then take credit for the rain. Anik wouldn't hurt himself or anyone else; he's not capable of that kind of cruelty.

Ash hasn't been in here for months, and as he looks around, it's clear how shut in his brother's been. His dirty clothes are all over the place. There's a bunch of used coffee mugs stacked on his dresser, a half-eaten pizza at the foot of the bed and at least a dozen empty soda cans. Ash opens the window. The room reeks of old man and bad hygiene. He reaches for the air freshener on the dresser and sprays until the stink is gone and then sits down on the bed, accidentally kicking over a stack of books piled Jenga-high. Ash stays there for a while looking at the mess, wondering where Anik went. He tells himself that maybe the fact that he's not here means he's finished with this reclusive act and, like a hermit crab, he's emerged from the molting period.

Day 74

Errands are as close to date night as Pavan gets.

After Peter's loaded the groceries into the trunk they sit and eat their ritual checkout chocolate bar. Today, their usual Twix Bar — made for easy sharing — wasn't there so they settled on the peanut butter cups, one each. She saves the third for Ash. She imagines he'll be happy, thankful even, just as he was as a child, but of course he won't be. He'll be a surly teen, reminding her that it's not his favorite and that she could have at least picked him up a pack of Skittles, and the short exchange will unsettle her day, his few words a hacked code for *you are a bad mother and I hate my life*. She tries to steel herself against her own anticipatory self-talk and armors up by stuffing the last cup in her mouth. The chocolate and creamy peanut butter coat her tongue and throat, forming some sweet barrier between her thoughts and feelings.

When they get home she calls Ash to help them bring in the bags, but he doesn't answer. From the foot of the stairs, she calls to him again before grabbing a bag in each hand and carrying them to the kitchen herself.

"Where's Ash?" Peter asks, dropping the remaining bags on the island.

"I don't know. Probably in his room. I called him but — the things they get away with, I would never have dreamed of. When my parents asked me to do something, I did it."

"Times were different then."

"I suppose."

"Guess it comes with the territory. Teenage angst," Peter says, unpacking the produce.

"I get the angst. I can even appreciate rebellion. It's the apathy that gets to me."

"Consider it the new rebellion. They have everything so there isn't much to rebel against other than having everything."

"Very wise. Where did you read that?"

"Heard it on a podcast, a parenting expert said that it's in a child's fundamental nature to assert themselves as an individual and reject belonging and possessive parenting. It was really good, actually. I ordered the book, figured I could use some of the content in my next workshop."

"Of course you did."

"What's that supposed to mean?"

"Nothing." She hands him the milk to put away. "It's just that you're always thinking about the work angle. Sometimes it feels like we're just research material."

"That's not true and you know it. You're just projecting."

"Projecting what?"

"Look, let's not get into this now."

"Oh no, we're in."

He shuts the refrigerator door and slowly turns toward her. "It's just that you've been on edge since the whole thing with Jay. Ash is probably picking up on it, acting out even."

"So it's my fault." As she says this, she imagines herself on the bridge, a flashbulb thought gone as soon as it registers. "Tell me then, how am I supposed to be?"

"I'm just saying your concern isn't helping things around here. Maybe you need some time to get your bearings. Maybe go to the spa, take a weekend away."

"I don't see how a massage or a pedicure is going to help."

He doesn't say anything and she focuses on folding all of the grocery bags into a neat bundle.

"Forget I said anything," Peter says, leaning against the counter next to her. "I know you're just worried about the kids."

"You're right. I am. We've got Anik holed up downstairs, a complete failure to grow up, and we've got Ash who pretty much ignores us and yes, Jay — he's on my mind. Everyone says he was fine and then he wasn't."

"Look, they aren't him. They'll figure it out." He puts his hand on her shoulder. "It'll be okay." She's aware of their physical awkwardness, the weight of his hand on her. There's something missing between them, something she can't name. She blames it on the stress, on her inability to balance the needs of others with hers.

"Coffee?"

"Sure." She sits at the kitchen island, scrolling through the news on her phone while he brews a fresh pot. Ash wanders in, headphones saddled around his neck. He opens the fridge and stares. "Do you want me to make you something for breakfast?" Pavan asks.

"I don't know," he says, still staring into the fridge.

"Maybe French toast?"

"Uh, no, I hate eggs." His words are all one long, irritated sigh.

"Oh, it's just you were eating them for a while so I figured."

"You figured wrong."

Peter and Pavan exchange weighted looks but say nothing.

"Didn't you guys just go shopping?" He closes the fridge and opens the cupboard.

"Yeah, we did. That's why I was calling you. To help unpack."

He closes the cupboard. "There's never any good food in the house."

"Well, next time you can come with us and tell us what you want," Peter says, smiling though frustration.

"Yeah, right." He takes his phone from his pocket. "I think I'll just order something."

"What are you going to get?" she asks.

"I don't know. McDonald's or something."

"They deliver, since when?"

"Since it's 2019."

"They must charge a fee?"

"Obviously." His face is still buried in his phone.

"I would have picked it up for you had I known."

"Stop. Please."

"You don't need to be rude, buddy," Peter says. "Your mom's just trying to be nice."

"Yeah, sorry," Ash says on reflex. Pavan says it's okay, even though she knows he's not sorry; it's just his way of ending it before she starts talking about anything that matters.

"Why don't you text Anik and see if he wants something while you're at it?" Peter suggests.

"He's not here," Ash says, face still down, scrolling through combo choices.

"What do you mean, not here?"

"Like, not here. As in not at home."

"Well, where is he?"

Ash looks up. "How should I know? I went downstairs this morning and he wasn't there."

"Are you sure he's not just sleeping and didn't answer?" Pavan asks.

"Uh, no. I actually went in. He's not home."

"Why didn't you tell us?" She rushes to the basement, Peter and Ash following her, and pushes his door open, tripping on a heap of books. "Fuck!"

"What are you doing?" Peter watches Pavan rummaging through the papers on Anik's desk.

"I'm looking for clues on where he may have went." She's scattered the papers around, looking for a Dear Mom and Dad letter, thankful that there isn't one, but then she remembers that Jay didn't leave one either. "Did he leave a note?" she yells to Ash who's standing in the doorway.

He shakes his head. "I didn't find one."

"Why would he just leave and not tell us?" She opens his closet. "Some of his clothes are gone." She combs through the drawers. "Same with his laptop."

"Calm down." Peter grabs her by the shoulders. "He probably just went out to get air or something."

She pulls away. "Someone who hasn't left the house in months just decides to go get air and takes their clothes, laptop and guitar with them." She points to the empty stand. "Don't tell me to calm down. He left and we don't know where he went."

"I'm sure he'll be back."

"We should call the police."

"Pav, he's twenty-two; he's not a kid"

"He's *my* kid," she says emphatically.

"Come on, let's just take a step back. We haven't even tried calling him yet."

"So, call then!"

Peter sighs, his mouth skews to one side the way it does when his patience thins.

"Fine, I'll do it myself." She tries to grab Ash's phone out of his hand and he pulls away.

"Use your own," he says, pushing her away. She loses balance and stumbles backward, the wall breaking her fall. For a fleeting moment all she wants to do is lunge at him, to smack him, to show him how it feels to be pushed around and used up but instead she starts to cry.

"Oh my God. Mom, I'm so sorry. I didn't mean to . . . I'll call him." He tries to help her up but she swats his hand away.

"Don't."

"Mom, please."

"Ash," Peter says, "it's fine. Just go."

He doesn't move for a minute, just stands there, watching Pavan unravel, her face stretched out and melting like in that painting *The Scream*.

"I said go," Peter repeats.

"I heard you. Fuck!" He slams the wall and storms away.

Peter closes the door behind him and helps Pavan up. "It'll be okay," he says, preempting her thoughts.

Pavan sits next to him on the bed, taking in the mess. "How did it get like this?"

"Who knows?"

"We should have known. I should never have let him lock himself away."

"You can't blame yourself. Pushing him never seemed to work."

She stares at the question mark and wonders why he wrote it on the wall. Was he questioning life, having an existential crisis, or was it something more than that? "You're right, the more we tried, the worse things got . . . but to do nothing — it's like we gave up."

"No, we let go — big difference. He's got to find his own path and so will Ash, and so did we. We're just seeing it from the other side now."

"Why does it have to be so hard?"

"You know what they say — tough times never last, but tough people do."

"Is that what they say?" She used to love the wise little interjections, his repertoire of quotables, but she finds they make her twitch now and she has to hold her reaction back the same way she stems a sneeze. "You know, when the kids were small, I would have told you that all I wanted was for them to grow up and be happy. But that's not true, not really."

"What do you mean?"

"I thought being happy was the same as having things easy. I didn't want them to struggle the way I did, not with money or acceptance or love. But there's no living, no real life without struggle, is there? In my own misguided way, I was wishing on them a life less fulfilled."

"Come on, you're being way too hard on yourself."

"No, I'm not. I made their life too easy. I took away all the friction, all the spark of hard work and yearning. I meant to give them freedom but inadvertently I gave them futility."

Peter turns to her. "Freedom can't be given, it's meant to be taken. That's all this is — a battle of self. We all fight it."

"But do we ever win?" She looks up at him, almost hoping he has a quote at the ready, a one-liner that'll make it all okay, but this time he doesn't.

Day 74

Anik sits on the ferry's sunshine deck and takes in the view.

It's a layered horizon, slices of sea and sky, a distant mountain surround. He takes a photo but can't quite capture the feeling and plays around with a filter, adding in light and rays. He used to hate overstylized photos but he's come to realize that while some people use filters to look younger, to look like animals, to enhance what's there, all of them are trying to capture the feeling. We feel different than we look, and we look different than we are. Everything is a distortion.

He snaps some photos of the people around him — the preschoolers sitting with their grandparents eating ice cream, the little girl in a tutu holding the railing as if it's a ballet barre, the couple with dreadlocks sitting on the deck boxes and the pink-haired girl who's asking around for a smoke. He stares at her a few seconds. She looks like cotton candy, pale-faced with sugar-spun hair. He takes a few shots, but now she's walking up to him, filling the frame.

"Did you just take my picture?" Her voice is deeper than he expects. "So what are you, some kind of pervert?" She's talking loud and he's embarrassed.

He shakes his head vigorously. "I was just taking pictures of the scenery."

She grabs the phone. "Let's see then."

"Hey, give it back."

"Scenery, my ass," she says, panning through the photo gallery. "This one is a good one of me, except you didn't get my angle just right. Try it again." She hands the phone back to him and poses by the deck railing, making a surprised laughing face. "What are you staring at, just take the picture."

Stunned, he takes the photo and shows it to her. She takes the phone from him and adds the nostalgic filter that makes it look like a '60s Polaroid. "That's so much better." She passes it back and Anik puts it in his jacket pocket before she can take it again. "I'm Rose. Who are you?" she asks, sitting down next to him.

"Anik." He's careful not to make eye contact.

"And what's your story?"

"No story." He doesn't want to encourage her.

"Oh, come on," she says. "Everyone has one. I'll go first . . . so, I'm Rose, but you already know that and I'm an artist too," she says, looking at his guitar case. "I play the violin, dabble in rap and spoken word, and last week I thought it would be a good idea to move to the island so here I am — moving."

"What, wait, you just decided?" Anik shakes his head. Spontaneity has always confused him.

"Yeah, pretty much."

"So where will you live?"

"In my van."

"In your van?"

"What are you, deaf or something?"

"No, just surprised is all. Never met anyone who lived in a car."

"Not a car, a van. Big difference. It's like one of those *Scooby-Doo* mystery machine type vans. It was my grandma's, from when she was a hippie. She left it to me when she died."

"That's cool. I mean, not that she died but that she left it to you."

"Yeah, she was a neat lady and it's a pretty sweet ride. I figure I'll just live in it until I can scrape up some cash to get a place. I got a job waiting for me on the coast, in Tofino. Toe-feen-o." She starts to laugh and repeats *Tofino* in slow syllables again.

"Are you high?" Anik asks, staring at her pupils.

"Just a little."

"Thought so." He gets up and shakes her hand. "It was nice meeting you, Rose."

"Oh, come on! Don't be like that." She grabs his hand and swings it back and forth. "I thought we were friends. After all, you have my photo in your phone so we're either friends or you have some weird trans fetish."

"Friends, we're friends for sure." Anik laughs in a nervous machine-gun way.

She looks him up and down. "Cool. So where are you going, friend?"

"I'm gonna grab something to eat. You wanna come?"

"God, yes, I am starving."

Over a burger and fries, Rose tells Anik that she decided to leave home because she thought space would make it easier for her parents to accept her. "It's not like they're religious or something, it's just hard for them. I mean they try, but I just can't deal with it, you know. So I figured a fresh start would be good. Got a job lined up cleaning Airbnbs. It's the perfect gig. I don't have to deal with anyone. I used to work in retail but got so tired of the weird looks and remarks, the transphobic bullshit, you know. Got tired of being asked if I was a guy, or if I was a girl, or what I was into. I'm talking too much, aren't I? Everyone says that I do and that I overshare but I can't help it. What about you?" She jams a few fries in her mouth. "What's the tea?"

"Nothing, really."

"Really? Because you've got runaway written all over you. Broken home, shitty parents?"

"No, neither. I mean my parents are alright, but I guess somewhere along the way I got stuck in my own head, so I decided to walk to the ocean to see if I could get unstuck."

"Wait, what? Back the fuck up."

Anik tells her about his attempts at spiritual awakening, his self-imposed exile, Jay's suicide and his pilgrimage to Tofino. She listens with rapt attention, her eyes bugging out, head nodding. She has the most expressive face, and at times, she doesn't look real to him but like some Japanese anime character who rides a scooter and has eyes that turn into love hearts or daggers.

"What?" she says, noticing a change in how he's looking at her. "Is there something on my face? Do I have ketchup on my chin, food in my teeth?"

"Nah. I was just thinking that you are the first real person outside my family that I've talked to in months."

"And?"

"Honestly, it's a bit awkward. I'm used to typing, texting. Being whatever version of me I feel like that day. Online I always know what to say, and if I fuck up, I can just ghost."

"I hear you; I spent a lot of time on Reddit before I made the decision to become Legit Rose."

"Legit Rose?"

"Fuck, there you go repeating me again."

"Sorry."

She throws a fry at him. "Just messin' with you. Legit Rose instead of my online persona of Rosé, you know, like the wine. I tried that out for a while, but it felt too costumey. You know, like what a cis person might name their trans friend if their trans friend were a pet."

"You are so weird."

"Says the guy who's walking to the ocean on a spiritual quest."

"It's not a quest. A quest is like what Frodo does in *Lord of the Rings*. This is low level compared to that."

"Yes, my precious," she says, in a Gollum voice.

"Like I said, weird."

"So back to you and this dude who jumped off the bridge, how's that go together?"

"He was my kid brother's friend and I guess it took us all by surprise. He was a good guy."

"You think that only bad people kill themselves or people who kill themselves are bad?"

"No, that's not what I mean. It's just no one knows why he did it, and it made me think that if a pretty chill guy like him can just off himself, maybe I could too. Maybe we're all one step from the edge."

"Damn, that's intense, Anakin."

"Anik."

"Right, so not like Skywalker," she says, appearing to make a mental note.

"Anyways, I figured I needed to do something about my own shit, figure things out, so I'm walking."

"So, how long will this nonquest of yours take."

"Probably two weeks, give or take."

"That's a lot of steps."

"Yeah, but I don't plan on walking all day every day. I'm gonna stop along the way and compose." He pats his guitar case. "I figure I'll let myself be inspired by my surroundings. Take my time. Be in the moment, you know."

"Eckhart Tolle–type shit."

"Sort of."

"So what will you do when we dock?"

"I figure I'll walk a bit and find somewhere to sleep."

"Like a park bench or something?"

"No, I have a sleeping bag and a pop-up tent and stuff." He kicks his pack with his foot. "It'll be fine."

"You're fucking crazy. What if it rains?"

"I've got a tarp."

Rose is shaking her head. "I'm getting major Reese Witherspoon in *Wild* vibes from you right now. What trail are you taking?"

"There isn't one. The only route is the highway."

"So, you'll walk on the road like some hitchhiker?"

"Well no, but yeah."

"You'll get killed."

"No, I won't."

"Yes, you will. Have you seen the logging trucks that speed down that mountain?"

"I'll just keep to the side."

"You'll be roadkill. Dead man walking!" She says it so loud that people turn their heads to look.

"You sound like my mother."

"Speaking of — what does she think of this?"

"She doesn't know."

"What do you mean, you didn't tell her?"

"No. She'd flip."

"So, let me get this right. You haven't left the house in months, your existential exile prompted a walk to the ocean, you haven't told anyone where you are, and you think this is a good idea."

"I have my phone," Anik says sheepishly. "For emergencies."

"Fuck, you are an emergency. Thank God Rose is here." She tosses her pink hair over her shoulder.

"Jesus, what's next, are you going to *Legally Blonde* bend and snap?"

"You wish. But lucky for you, I have an incoming idea," she says, poised to make her proposal. "Why don't you just come with me? I could use the company and we could split the gas money."

"That's nice of you. But it's not a pilgrimage if I'm driving. I have to walk."

"Oh," she says, opening her eyes wide. "Is this according to the dos and don'ts in *Pilgrimages for Dummies*?

"Ha ha, very funny," he says, his tone flat. "I just think I should stick to my original plan."

"Well, I think your plan sucks. You are seriously going to get run over by a truck and then I'm going to read about it in yesterday's paper in one of the Airbnbs I'm cleaning and then I'll feel guilty about it for, like, ever, or at least a month, and that's not fair to me."

"I see. This is about you."

"Yeah, everything's about me." She pretends to think, tapping her index finger to her temple for a few seconds. "Okay, plan B. You walk, I drive, and we meet up along the route. On the windy roads I drive behind you with my blinkers on. Just like the brother did with Terry Fox, you know?"

"Yeah, but this isn't a marathon of hope."

"Isn't it, though? I mean, sure, you aren't dying of cancer, and you aren't raising money for a cure but still . . . isn't this about hope? We could even get a banner made. Hope for the future?"

"No," Anik says.

"Okay, whatever," she says and sips the last of her soda really loud. "But you have to admit, it's a good idea. A win-win. You're safe and I have company, and if it rains, you can sleep in the van if you want."

Anik chews on the end of his straw, contemplating. "I don't know. Besides, what about the job you have lined up?"

"Well, I don't *actually* have it yet so . . . And this is way more interesting. It'll be an adventure. Come on, pleeease," she says, making prayer hands and puppy dog eyes.

Anik imagines her with Snapchat-filtered ears and can't help but laugh. "Oh what the hell, sure, why not."

"Yes!"

"But there have to be rules."

"Of course!" She says it like it's so obvious. "Like what?"

"I don't know yet. But I know we have to have some."

She pulls out her phone, mapping a route. "So what's the first checkpoint?"

"I was thinking something close. There's a rest area not too far away." He zooms in on the map and shows her. "I could meet you there and we could set out again in the morning."

"Sounds like a plan. Synchronize watches!" She holds up her bare wrist.

"So weird."

The ferry's docking announcement plays over the intercom.

"Well, I guess I should go," she says and takes a quick selfie with him. She looks at the image and deletes it. "Let's try that again." She takes more care this time with her angle and a well-placed peace sign. "There, perfect! Okay if I post?" She doesn't wait for his answer. "I'll see you at seven-ish! So exciting." She high-fives him in a way that's more patty-cake than high five.

Just as she leaves, Anik's phone rings. It's Ash. He answers but no one's there — call failed, no bars. He'll call back when he's in network range, when there's enough space between him and home that they can't just come and rescue him. Pavan's notorious for intercepting his life, removing roadblocks, finding solutions for problems he didn't even know he had. She won't understand why he left, even if he explains it to her; to her it will be running away, a projection of her life onto him. She was the one who was always moving away from what she didn't want. Her family, his father — he wonders if she ever took a step toward something, the way he was about to, or if her life was all go-go-go and no peace. Sometimes he feels sorry for her; he could see the exhaustion hanging on her like rags, a slave of doing and no being. When she was working all hours she'd say that she was doing it for them, and he figures that's the only way she could make peace with the sellout of getting older and giving up. He thinks of his new friend, Rose, and all that she's been through. He can't relate but does understand; Aristotle said that knowing yourself is the beginning of wisdom. Jung said that life's greatest privilege is in choosing and becoming who you are. He wonders if anyone has ever really chosen, or if they just stumble into themselves, the sum of all the things that happen to them.

Day 74

The call goes to voicemail. Every time.

He keeps on for another ten minutes, and when that doesn't work he spam-texts Anik question marks. His parents haven't come upstairs yet. They're still sitting in Anik's room, discussing what to do. It's obvious to Ash that there's nothing to do but wait. Some things have to be left alone.

He checks his phone. Still no response from Anik. He opens Find My and searches for him. Location unknown.

He can hear his parents talking, the hum of their voices, murmurs and tones. It reminds him of the piano's lower register, all vibration and doom, and it makes him wish he stayed in lessons. He dropped them after a few years; Anik was so great at it that his good felt below average. It's not that he was jealous; he was actually in awe. Most of his life has been him orbiting Anik, and for the most part he was happy that way. The four of them were their own perfect universe.

Sometimes when Anik played piano, Ash would sit next to him on the bench and watch the way his fingers laddered over keys, scaling up and down like they weren't even attached to his body. Whenever Anik practiced, he'd let Ash play the opening bars of "Clair de lune," the only bit he knew, and then Ash would shuffle over and give him space to move through the rolling chords that now remind him of waves, up and over, up and over, up and over. Pavan loved it when he played that song. She'd always tear up and never be able to say why but now Ash gets it; that song sounds like life. Anik said Debussy was to the piano what Monet was to Impressionism and since Pavan loved Monet, she could never get enough of it.

Ash lifts the black lacquered fallboard, sits at the bench and dusts his fingers over the keys. It seems strange to sit here without Anik, sad even. He rests his hands, looks for the starting position. That's what Anik always said. "Once you find the starting note, you'll know what to do." He finds his place and hums along as he plays. He messes up and starts over, pacing himself in that slow descent, semitones up-and-down, fingers scaling and then . . . he's lost. He stops and closes the lid.

He doesn't know how to go on without Anik.

Day 74

Winona's not eating.

She does this from time to time. It's not out of protest, or an attention-seeking thing, it's just something she does to reset herself the same way someone might unplug their router to reboot their Wi-Fi. Jon still insists she be at the dinner table, and so she sits there staring at her plate, eating a few spoonfuls just to make him happy. While she listens to Trish talk about the twins' new teacher, she pushes her mashed potatoes into a mound, encouraging the twins to do the same.

"Don't play with your food," Trish says and then continues talking in her pitchy way. Ever since the brownie thing any goodwill from Trish is gone. She feels bad about it. All of it. Everything. It's not Trish's fault that her mother died, and as far as stepmonsters go, Trish is harmless — the trying-to-be-friends type, the mani-pedi type, always advocating for Winona when she wanted to dye her hair or get a piercing. But now that's gone — Winona had heard her father and Trish arguing about it. "I tried, Jon. I really did" was what she told him and to that all he could say was "I know you did." And that was that. What more could he ask of her, of either of them. Winona feels sorry for him. For all of them. As she sits at the table looking at her food, looking at their faces, the wine glasses drained and filled, the twins speaking in their newly learned pig Latin, the only thing she knows for sure is that they are all an apology personified.

Winona holds up her fork like a wand and with a flourish runs it through the middle of her potatoes forming a four-lane highway. The twins follow suit and Winona leans over the table to help them, accidentally knocking over a glass of water in Trish's direction.

"Sorry, sorry," Winona says and sops up the mess with a napkin.

Trish stands up and blots at her lap, slapping Winona's help away.

"It was an accident, Trish," Jon offers in a pleading but calm tone.

"Isn't it always?"

"But it *was* an accident, Mommy," Thing One says.

"If it was, it was because you were playing with your food. I have half a mind to send you to bed without supper and then you'll learn that dinner is not playtime."

Winona watches the twins sink into their seats just like the starving orphans in *Oliver Twist*. Last week she watched the movie with them and then later they reenacted the scenes and songs in the playroom. She hums the "Food, Glorious Food" song under her breath and the twins begin to giggle.

"What is so funny?" Trish asks.

"Oh come now, sweetheart. She's just having a bit of fun with the girls."

"Fun — right. She's always having fun at my expense. The counselor, the brownies . . . all. of. it." She storms off.

Winona gets up. "I'll go."

"No, I think you've done enough lately," Jon says and follows after Trish.

Winona makes an *I'm in trouble* face and the twins giggle. "Come on, help me clear the plates." Ever since Trish ate the brownies and ended up in the hospital, she feels closer to them, almost the way a big sister would. It's just a bonus that the newfound attachment seems to annoy Trish. "Now scrape the food off the plates and throw it in the garbage."

"We're too little." Their twin unison makes them sound cute and creepy at the same time.

"No, you're not. My mom made me start doing chores when I was your age."

"But she's dead," Thing One says.

The other nudges her in the ribcage. "That's not nice."

"It's okay. She is dead."

"Does dead hurt?"

"I don't know. I don't think so," Winona says, stacking plates into the dishwasher. She's thinking of Jay now, imagines him lying in a coffin, hands crossed over his chest, forever dreaming. "Maybe it's just like sleeping."

"Like Sleeping Beauty."

"Sort of, but without the kissy ending."

"Kissing is gross. I saw Mommy kissing Daddy and it was, like, yuk." Thing Two opens her mouth wide and demonstrates on the back of her hand.

"That is gross." Winona shuts the dishwasher.

The twins are eyeing each other like they have a secret. "Give it to her."

Winona crouches down to their level. "Give me what?"

Thing One pulls Winona's phone out of her pocket.

"Where did you get this?" Her dad took it away after the whole brownie thing as a punishment.

"Dad's office," Thing Two says. "If we give it to you, can we go play?"

Winona agrees and the twins skip away. She scans through her notifications. Two missed calls from Ash in a row. She FaceTimes him back. "Hey, you called. What's up?"

"My brother's gone."

"Your brother? I thought he never left the house."

"Exactly."

"Shit. Where did he go?"

"Don't know."

"He didn't leave a note?"

"Nope. My parents are freaking out about it. They're out looking for him."

Winona, having watched too many true-crime shows, imagines them walking through a forest with flashlights and bloodhounds. "Where do you think he went?"

"I have no clue. I thought you might have an idea."

"Me, why would I? I've never even met him."

Ash sighs, in that distressed way that people do when their insides tornado and they shut their eyes tight. "Because you know shit. Like about the hik-o-mor people you were talking about in Japan."

"The hikikomori?"

"Yeah, them."

"Sorry, Ash, I don't know what to tell you."

The line goes quiet.

"I don't know what to do. I've just been sitting here."

"Do you want to go look for him? I can come by and we can drive around."

A long pause. "No, I should probably stay here in case he comes back."

Another silence. Winona doesn't know what to say; she only knows that she can't hang up. "Hey, I was going to watch *One Piece*. You want to watch with me? You said you like anime."

"Sure, why not."

She keeps him on the line as she goes to her room to set up her laptop. She places her phone upright on the pillow next to her and he does the same, both of them pressing play at the same moment.

She watches him watch the episode, the side of his face lit up by screen glow, grainy and sad. There's nothing she can do but stay.

Day 77

The first few kilometers each day are the hardest.

It's not just the walking, the bandaged blisters on his heels, the sunshine haze on asphalt and the near-death SUV sideswipes, it's the quiet. After three days, he's grown accustomed to Rose's non-stop chatter; she can talk about anything. She's read everything and in this way he's found both a match and a missing piece. She's him without the fear and cynicism and sometimes when their talk drifts into sleep, he dreams that she's the stuff of fiction, conjured like *A Christmas Carol* spirit. But when he wakes each morning, she's still there and has already made coffee on the camping stove. "I trained myself how to get up early," she told him that morning. "I made it my new norm and never let myself sleep in. The sleep-ins will kill you, break your circadian rhythm and stuff like that." She was already on her second cup of coffee, full caffeine stream of consciousness, explaining how she once had insomnia for a week and realized how much time there really was in the day. "I'd been sleeping half of my life away, you know." Anik did know, and in a way he felt that he'd been zombie-walking his way through life, never really noticing anything outside his purview. He'd been a slave to his own impulses and this walk was a remedy, a way to take purposeful steps, to gain clarity. But so far nothing was clear and any inspiration he was hoping to find was blocked out by the fatigue. Though he hadn't been walking more than a few hours a day, his legs felt stiff and his mind fogged over in ego and fear.

On day one he ended up reciting every song lyric he knew just to block out his negative self-talk. He thought he'd be able to clear his mind of its numbing monologue, but he found his brain buzzing like a housefly trapped inside, zipping from thought to thought. Even now, he's counting steps and counting breaths to stop the incessant thinking of thinking. It's meditative, he tells himself. The fact that he is even aware of his thoughts is a reminder that he is not the thought, he is the seer. He looks around waiting for a revelation, but there's nothing but a raven perched on a nearby tree. He's seen it every day, and though ravens aren't uncommon for the area, he takes it as a sign and twirls the silver ring on his finger, whispering his mother's inscription. "The world has its own magic."

With his thoughts momentarily quieted, he stares out at the horizon. Postcard-like with its towering trees, all different textures and shades of green, so beautiful that it almost hurts to take it all in. He follows their tapers toward the sheet of gray sky. He knows it'll rain soon and veers off the highway onto an adjacent wooded path.

He's only been walking for an hour and already his heels hurt from the chafing at the back of his shoes. He hopes that Rose remembers to go to the drugstore to get more bandages. The walking is harder on his body than he expected, and that's without most of his belongings. He can't imagine how impossible it would have been without Rose, without a place to leave his gear, without warm food, without company. Without. That's his first lesson. He makes a mental note of it. He's learned what he cannot do without. It's all Maslow's hierarchy type stuff: physiological, safety and belonging. He remembers the textbook pyramid and lists the layers: "food, water, air, clothing, shelter, security, resources, friendship, connection." He smiles, satisfied with himself for having experienced the foundational basics of existence, and repeats the sequence as he walks. "Food, water, air, clothing, shelter, security, resources, friendship, connection."

A few raindrops hit his face and he stops to look up at the opening sky, twirling in a slow circle, arms outstretched as rain seeps through the canopy. He inhales and smells dirt and worms, root and rock. It's distinctly elemental and reminds him of his mother, of planting the magnolia tree. "The deeper we dig, the stronger the roots," she said. He drops his pack and guitar case, takes out his phone, and snaps a selfie, sending it to Pavan without a caption. Somethings don't need explaining. She'll hear the ping, see the photo and know all is well. It's the first thing he's sent her since he called her that first night.

He remembers the sound of frantic relief in her voice, the way she said his name in a long drawn-out exhale. It's the way she used to say, "There you are," if he ever came home late from school. Though it would've been only twenty minutes, he knows now that it was just enough time for her to imagine a hit-and-run accident or a kidnapping. She gravitates to worst-case scenarios, and he can't imagine what she must be thinking now, only that she must be thinking it. She gets this far-off glassy look, and everything about her is downturned as if she's melting into the floor, quicksand thoughts eating her up, and yet from a distance it reads like portrait serenity. It's easier to not talk now, to just send this picture, to reassure her that everything is fine in a one-sided thread that keeps him free of her fear and guilt.

He leans up against a tree to wait out the rain. Sharp light passes through the thick of trees, cutting the forest dark and bright. The sound of rain steadily dropping from boughs and leaf, the white noise of cars slicing by, his own breath, and distant birds signaling that somewhere the rain has stopped. He holds out his phone and presses record, hoping he can layer it into a loop. Already he's recorded a dozen soundscapes and plans to hide them in his tracks so that only the astute listener will be able to detect them. He imagines that one day people will discuss his music, try to uncover what made it feel so alive, and when interviewed he'll say this walk was a turning point in his creative process. He will be famous in certain circles and will be featured in a documentary that premieres at Cannes. The fan sites and bloggers will discover early recordings and digital files of his GOD is DOG recordings and debate their merit as precursors to his seminal work. He'll be asked about those recordings and why he stopped, and he'll say because he read the comments. Though he knew that the comments section was a troll bridge, he couldn't help himself. There were the obvious comments lacking imagination like "God is DogSHIT" but those didn't bother him, not really. It was the ones that came from a guy who went by Jzsthe2N. Every day without fail, he'd spam post, "You should just kill yourself," over and over. To Anik, the repetitive harassment, especially when read aloud, felt like a directive, or worse, a mantra. He'll tell this story in the documentary, and they'll film him close-up, so that the faraway glint in his eye shines like light on water. He'll be in his late forties when they interview him at his off-the-grid cabin, an old shipping container on stilts anchored on a low cliff, the front cut away and replaced by a picture window looking out onto a forested inlet. He'll be sturdy and rugged, a person who has become a landscape. The documentary will win an Oscar. A new generation of music lovers will embrace the unclassified genre that he defined. People will say his new music is evolved and his early music was raw. Posthumously he will be inducted into the hall of fame. He can see it all, this future life, and as silly as it is to be thinking it, rehearsing who he could be feels better than who he is, and so he indulges, believing himself into being.

Rose is waiting at the campsite when he arrives. She hands him a beer, toasting the end of another day's walk.

"You did it! You did it!" she says, singing in a mock cheer way. She has a way of disarming him, and he quickly forgets his deeper thoughts. He strips off his damp coat and sits down in the camping chair and slowly takes off his shoes and socks. "Where do you get the energy?"

"I'm not the one walking," Rose says and takes his picture.

"What? Why?" he asks, as she takes a close-up of his dirty boots.

"For posterity." She snaps a few of him. "So how was the walk today?"

"Tough. My feet are killing." He takes off the bandage and shows her his blisters. "But good too. I feel like I finally got beyond my brain fog, you know, and now it's just going to be step-by-step from here."

"One foot in front of the other." Rose zooms in on the open blisters on his heels.

"Are you filming this?"

"Yeah."

"No way. Come on, cut it out," he says and pushes her phone away. For a minute he imagines her photos becoming part of his imagined documentary. He hasn't told her about his daydreams; some things are too embarrassing to share.

"Trust me, you'll be glad I did." She hands him a pack of Band-Aids. "You'll want there to be a permanent record of this. People will want to know."

"What people?"

"Like all people. You're doing something that matters. Even Carol thought so."

"Who's Carol?"

"The barista at Starbucks. Sidebar: I was there for most of the day, nursing my tall caramel macchiato and using their Wi-Fi. Anyways, after a few hours she told me that I had to get another drink or leave, and while she made me an espresso, I told her all about you. She was amazed. Thinks what you are doing is big time. Oh, speaking of big," she says, putting her phone down, "I picked up a whole chicken dinner from the grocery store, complete with biscuits and mashed potatoes. Tonight, we are going to eat like kings — I mean that in a nongendered way, of course."

"Okay," he says, trying to follow along.

"Courtesy of Carol," she says, opening the bags. "She donated to the cause."

"The cause?"

"Yeah, you. You're the cause. You're the cash cow, cha-ching! Chicken dinner, it's a winner!"

"You monetized me?"

"You make it sound like a bad thing!" She starts to lay out the spread on the portable picnic table.

"It would be, if I wasn't so hungry," he says and grabs a drumstick.

After dinner they sit in front of the fire, listening to each other play their instruments. Rose is someone else when she plays the violin, so upright and aristocratic, her spine and neck hinged in place as she draws the bow. She starts with something classical and melancholy and then screeches the bow across the neck to create some gritty fusion. Anik claps and whistles and she pretends at modesty. She knows she's good. It's in her genes. Her great-grandfather was a virtuoso who died in the war while playing in the trenches. She has a lot of far-fetched stories, and sometimes Anik wonders if she's making them up. He's decided he doesn't care; everyone tells stories about who they are and how they've come to be — sometimes it's the only way to make sense of anything.

"Your turn."

He picks up his guitar and tunes it. "I recorded the rain today, and well," he says sheepishly, "it inspired the start of something." As he finger-picks the song, she nods along and picks up her violin, adding in layers. They play like this until the sky is dark and the embers die.

Though there's plenty of room inside the van, Anik prefers falling asleep under the stars. He knows their names and lists them off the same way Pavan did when they used to go camping. He has an affinity for remembering detail, memorizing and cataloging things. It's given his world order and peace, edges and borders.

Rose hears him calling out the stars and joins him. "Can't sleep." She lies down next to him, her sleeping bag wrapped around her and together they stare at the deep blue and silver ribbons of light.

Anik points out the slow arc of a satellite crossing and watches it until it falls away, wondering what it might be transmitting. He hopes that it has a noble cause, something beyond GPS and television, some important mission like taking pictures of the Earth. He holds his hands above his head as if he's framing a shot. "A mote of dust suspended in a sunbeam."

"*Pale Blue Dot*, Carl Sagan. Well played," says Rose.

"You know it?"

"I was a space geek for a while." She giggles. "My first crackpot therapist said I was infatuated with sci-fi because I felt like an alien in my own body."

"That's messed up."

"I know, right." She pauses. "Whenever I see the Hubble pictures, I think that no matter what we look like, we're all made of the same stuff."

"Stardust?" Anik laughs.

"I know, so lame, but I was a confused thirteen-year-old. Bill Nye and Britney Spears were my idols."

"Fair."

"But to be honest, even now I get all emo about the Mars Rover dying. 'My battery is low and it's getting dark.' Damn little robot gets me every time."

"You know it didn't actually say that."

"I know, I know. Bubble burst on that one, thank you cynics and Snopes."

"So — since you were a space geek and all, did you ever listen to the Golden Record?"

"No, I didn't know you could."

"Yeah, they released a boxset a couple of years ago."

"I take it you have it."

"Yeah, bought it online while I was on my sit-in at home."

"Oh, that's what you're calling your little hermit stint now? Much better; has a protest ring versus a pathetic ring to it."

"Are you done?"

"Yes, please continue."

"So, it's amazing. Fifty-five languages, nature sounds, hours of music and all of that. But what's crazy is to think that the original is just out there, billions of miles away, drifting through space, waiting to be intercepted."

"It's sad in a way."

"Yeah, but hopeful too," he says, his voice catching.

"Too serious," she says and sits up. "Time to lighten things up. What would you put on the record today, if you had to choose the music?" She's animated as if she's a game show host and this is a skill-testing question.

"Tough one . . . Maybe Bon Iver."

"No, oh yuck. That's not Voyager quality. Voyager," she says, pausing. "That's it. Voyager. That should be the name of your quest."

"I told you already, I'm not on a quest."

"Odyssey, pilgrimage, whatever . . . I think you should brand it as Voyager 3; the first two were outer space and now it's all about inner space, self-exploration." Her face is wide open as if she's made some big discovery. "It's the perfect brand, good story." She gets up, grabs her phone and takes a photo. "Too dark, we can try again in the morning, but you do photograph well, your broody artsy vibe, so that's a plus."

"Brand it, story? What are you even on about?"

"Just figured we could start a little blog, maybe something on socials about the journey, you know? It'll give me something to do while you're walking and, besides, a walk without a name is just a walk. All of the great pilgrimages have names — you told me yourself. El Camino, Pilgrims' Way, Abraham Path — if you don't like Voyager, or V3." She stops and cringes. "No, never mind, V3 sounds too much like V8 — you know what, we could just call it Anik's Way. Yeah, that's it. Not sure why I didn't think of it before."

"Sure, sounds great," Anik says mid-yawn. "Now can we go to sleep? I've got an early start tomorrow."

"For real? You're cool with Anik's Way? I can use that?"

"Yes, yes, whatever. Just go to sleep."

"Sweet," Rose says, and with her sleeping bag caterpillared around her waist, she shuffles back to the van, mumbling to herself about Anik's Way.

Day 79

Ash is waiting in the office.

He's been here before, sat in the same worn chair, picking at the flaked pleather armrests, waiting for Principal Carter to call him in. The room reeks like coffee and brown-bagged leftovers — all kinds of smells climbing on top of each other, Chinese food and fried chicken, maybe even pizza. It's gross blended up like that, but since Ash missed lunch, it's making him hungry. He takes a piece of gum out and chews it for a while but reflex-swallows. That was his last piece. He tries to peek through the unfrosted part of the office door but can't see anything. The others have come and gone. Their parents collected them and they all shuffled by, one by one, head-down ashamed or embarrassed, who can say if there's even a difference. Another ten minutes goes by before the principal calls him in and tells him to sit down. Ash looks at the family pictures on his desk. Mr. Carter has two kids, both girls, one's in university and one's in grade eight. He told Pavan about them the last time Ash was called in, maybe his way to say he understands kids, parenting — all of it.

Mr. Carter doesn't say anything for a minute; he just sits on the edge of his desk. Ash leans back and pushes the chair away to avoid the direct inhale. Mr. Carter smells like ass. Apparently, he has some medical condition and this is a symptom or a drug side effect, like those ones they read out at the end of a pharmaceutical ad. *This drug may cause vomiting, dry skin, heart attacks, ulcers, diarrhea, nausea, cancer . . .* Ash has never heard them say *shit stink* as a symptom but he's never really listened all the way through either.

"Ash." Mr. Carter sighs and stands up. He stares at the framed print on the wall as if it were a window. It's one of those crappy inspirational posters with penguins and an iceberg. Ash has looked at it a dozen times. *A leader sets the course for others to follow.* He still doesn't know what penguins have to do with leadership, but now his mind is wandering and he's thinking of *Happy Feet*, remembering watching it on DVD as a kid with Pavan. Good times. He's smiling now, the way he does when he's nervous, and he covers his mouth with his sleeve so Mr. Carter doesn't mistake his expression as insolence.

"We've called your mother and explained the situation."

Ash doesn't say anything.

"Vaping on school grounds is a serious issue. One that we can't take lightly."

"I understand." Ash knows that arguing with teachers only makes them angrier so he lets them talk for as long as they want. Usually they feel better about things after they've said their piece and he can get off with a warning but not this time.

"Suspended?" he repeats.

"Just for the rest of the day."

"I won't do it again."

"I'm sure you won't. Especially after you take the day to think about your actions. While you're away, you'll write an essay on the dangers of substance abuse."

"Substance abuse? It was just . . ." He exhales. "Okay."

"As I said, we've talked to your mother and she's given us approval to send you home."

Ash nods, wondering who the *we* is. Why don't adults take responsibility and just say *I*? I called your mother, I decided your punishment.

Mr. Carter opens the office door, signaling that Ash can leave. "Tomorrow's a new day, Ash, fresh start."

Pavan's waiting in the living room, just like Ash knew she would be. He doesn't give her a chance to tell him she's so disappointed and quickly tells her, "It's not my fault."

"It never is," she says, arms crossed. "What were you thinking?"

He doesn't answer; he knows it's a rhetorical question, her jump-off point for the next ten minutes. He buckles up. He tries to listen but can't. Anyways, the words don't matter. He just watches her face, the way it twists up as if he's done something to cause her physical pain.

"You know that stuff is dangerous, right?"

"Mom, it's, like, one time. It's no big deal."

"You were suspended. That *is* a big deal."

"It's not fair; it wasn't even mine. I just happened to be there and some kids asked me if I wanted to try it and obviously I wasn't thinking so I did, just once, and then Mr. Carter came by and . . . you know the rest."

"I do know the rest. I know exactly how it goes with you."

"What's that supposed to mean?"

"Nothing."

"Nice. You didn't even give me a chance."

"Pot calling the kettle."

"What?"

"It's an expression, never mind." She stands up and looks out the window. It's sunny but the glass has streaks all over it so the light looks hazy and only halfway bright. "I just didn't really need this today. Between you and your brother it's exhausting and with you — it's always something, isn't it? Some issue at school to deal with. I was just hoping we could get through the last few weeks of school without anything else going wrong."

"Sorry I'm such a disappointment."

"Don't be like that."

"Like what?"

"Like you're the victim."

"No, that's all you, Mom." Ash hears himself say this, he can feel his mouth moving, saying things he doesn't mean but he can't stop it. "You're a victim, always playing the martyr card, blaming us for your life, your decisions. Everything's about you and what you want and how you feel and how we should act for you."

"That's enough, Ash!"

"But I've never been enough, have I? That's how you think of me, right?"

"It's not what I think. You don't know what I think."

"And you don't know what I think. You never even ask me how I am."

"That's not true."

"Asking how my day was is not the same as asking me how I am. Maybe if you cared more, paid more attention, I wouldn't be so messed up." He knows this isn't true, but shifting blame feels so much better than carrying the burden.

"Oh, is that what this is — your way to get my attention? Well, you have it."

"I wasn't doing it to get attention."

"Then why were you?"

"No reason. It was dumb, I know. I feel stupid about it." He's yelling and not even aware of it. "It's just been hard lately, especially with Jay and Anik. It's all so confusing and then I can't think straight and . . . and I fuck up and . . ."

"And you act out," she says, her voice low.

"Maybe. Act out? I don't know." He stops and reconsiders. "No, if by act out you mean I'm trying to get your attention, then no."

"It has been hard lately." She pauses for a long time. "Maybe you should see someone."

"What? Like a therapist? No, I don't want to do that again."

"You said it helped."

"I just said that so you wouldn't make me go again. I'm not going to some shitty little office to talk about my feelings."

"We could try someone else."

"Look, I don't want to go. Is that okay?"

"Of course." Her words are clipped, expression tight like a drum.

"I'm sorry," he says, filling her silence. Whenever she gets quiet, whenever she stops talking, that's when he knows things have gone too far.

"I know you are. I just wish this hadn't happened." She turns toward Ash and then looks back out the window. "We'll talk more when Dad gets home."

"Okay. I *am* sorry." He waits, wishing she'd say it's okay, but he knows she won't. She's not an instant forgiver that way. "I'll just go start on that essay then."

From where he's standing he can see the upturn of her mouth, the slight nod of her head, yet she doesn't look away from the window; she just keeps staring out at the hazy blue.

Day 81

No one likes the serious person.

Pavan knows this because she's always been that person and today, for Peter's sake, she wants to lighten up and make a good impression. She leans into the backseat and grabs the gift bag and balloons. The helium stork bashes her in the head, ribbons tangling around her as she gets out of the car. She shortens the string and uncoils herself from the balloon bouquet, which now that she looks at it again makes her wish she didn't buy it. It's so clownish and infantile, but then these baby showers with their pastel hues and silly themes make no sense to her. According to her invitation (which was full of pink and blue confetti) the shower would have a gender reveal announcement. She didn't want to say it to Peter, but she couldn't help but think what a nuisance it was to make guests buy gender-neutral gifts only to have the gender revealed at the party. It didn't seem practical and she was a practical sort of person. She had always been that way; as a child she was textbook smart and always in after-school study groups, and as a young adult she was a wife and then a single mother and then a wife and mother. Her time was never her own; it was always an investment in some future possibility that has yet to pay a dividend.

As she walks up to the house, she reminds herself to smile, to embody a doe-like innocence, to fake her interest in all things baby. She takes a breath and rings the bell. No one answers so she rings it again. From inside, someone yells, "It's open," and she shakes her head wondering what happened to manners and good hosting.

She lets herself in but no one takes notice, and for a moment she just stands in the open doorway, balloons in tow. She scans the room of chattering women. They're all the young moms you'd expect to see at school pickup and drop-off, all the moms who have time to volunteer on boards and class trips, all the moms who worked until they had children, all the moms — so white. She's thinking about leaving, just backing away slowly but then: "Pavan dear, shut the door. Such a draft." Her mother-in-law mispronounces her name even though she's corrected her for years. *Pavan* rhymes with *oven*, how hard can that be to remember? Diane is wearing her signature cashmere twin set and although her style is old-fashioned, she doesn't look her age and she knows it. She tells anyone who asks that her secret to staying young is a few drops of lemon juice and a sprinkle of cayenne pepper in water before breakfast.

"Jane will be so glad you made it," Diane says and air-kisses Pavan's cheek.

"Where should I put these?" Pavan asks, holding up the gift and balloons.

"Just over there is fine." She points to the mountain of presents piled in the corner of the living room. "You haven't been here since they renovated, have you? Wait until you see the nursery. Jane had the sweetest Peter Rabbit mural painted on the wall. You know I used to call Peter 'Peter Rabbit.' I told you that, didn't I?"

Pavan smiles. "Yes, a few times actually."

"Jane, look who's here!" Diane says.

Jane looks up from her friend group and mouths, "Hi." It's just enough to make Pavan smile and reciprocate the faux friendly. Though she's Peter's younger sister, half sister actually, they've never been close and only see each other for obligatory holiday dinners. Pavan stands at the edge of Jane's circle, waiting to say a proper hello. Jane is talking pregnancy details and baby shopping, and her friends all look like cult-member variations of her, the same highlighted beach-wave hair, the same cute petite frames, the same Pinterest perfection. Pavan had met women like this at book club — so entitled that they showed up not having read the book, using the occasion to drink cheap wine and complain ever so lightly about their life but never in a way that couldn't be brushed off as a joke. They were inauthentic bobbleheads just like these women who tilt their heads and seem to "aww" on cue.

"Only two weeks left," Jane says.

"Aww."

"You're so lucky you don't have to go through the summer pregnant," one of the friends says. "I was miserable. My ankles swelled so bad I couldn't even walk!"

Collective "ohs."

"I'm definitely ready for this baby to come. At this point, I just want it out!" Jane says, palming her belly.

"Careful what you wish for. Once it's out, it's out," Pavan says.

Everyone stares.

"I just mean once it's out, life changes."

"Of course it does, silly. Has everyone met my sister-in-law, Pavan?"

"Oh, yes. I remember you from Jane's wedding," one of the identical friends says. "And what a wedding it was, so beautiful, and now this! A baby. Jane, can you believe it, you are having a baby." Her friend reaches over and touches Jane's belly and then all of them do as if they are making a secret pact, swearing on the life of her unborn baby.

"Pavan, do you want to feel?" Jane grabs her hand, placing it on her stomach. "Did you feel that kick?"

"Oh my." Pavan pretends that she did so she can pull her hand away without offending.

"Amazing, right?" Jane's wide-eyed and hopped-up on her own hormones. "But you've been through this already, so you know all about it. You're way ahead of me on this. How are Peter and the boys?"

"They're good." Pavan's glad that the canned response is enough for Jane, who quickly moves the conversation back to baby talk. She can't imagine what Jane and her clone friends would think of her, the ignorant mothering judgments they would cast if they knew that Anik was on a spiritual walk to the ocean and Ash was suspended. All they can imagine at this point is all that she could imagine at that point — raising the perfect child swathed in goodness and light, a child whose existence would make theirs worthwhile.

"So, how are my grandchildren?" This time it's Diane asking.

Pavan stuffs her face with an artichoke-dipped chip. "Good."

"Details, dear." She hands Pavan a glass of punch. "How's Anik?"

"He's doing really well with school. He's got less than a year left in his degree."

"Oh, I'm glad to hear that. Last time I talked to Peter he said that Anik had been depressed. And then I heard about that boy in Ash's school who killed himself," she says, lowering her voice. "Of course, I don't like to talk about such things, but I can tell you I was worried when I heard Anik might be depressed."

"I appreciate your concern, but he's fine. It was just the usual young adult 'finding myself' ups and downs of life." She doesn't want to get into it with Diane. She doesn't want to hear about all the things she should have done differently, all the things she already knows. "You must remember that phase? Peter said he was a handful at that age."

"Oh, don't I know it though." She places a hand on Pavan's arm. "But honestly, maybe it was easier then, none of this social media pressure kids have now. You know my niece — Peter's cousin Jessica — her daughter had a heck of a time. She had a full breakdown at university, ended up in the hospital psychiatric ward. They say she may be a schizophrenic. I feel for Jessica — all of her hopes for her daughter gone . . . but then I wonder if they missed the signs. I mean, surely there must have been clues that something was wrong?"

"You'd think."

"It's hard to parent these days. So much to worry about and you, as a working mom! I'm not sure how you do it all. Something has to give." She's smiling in her casserole-charming, string-of-pearls-superior way that annoys Pavan but today she won't let it get to her. She's trying.

"It definitely has its challenges, but you needn't worry yourself, Anik is really coming through. In fact, he's thinking of doing his master's at Berklee College of Music." Pavan hears the lie come out of her mouth and knows she shouldn't have, but she can't bear the idea of Anik becoming a gossipy tidbit like Jay or Jessica's daughter.

"Boston, how amazing."

"Oh, I know. I'd miss him, but what an opportunity," she says, doubling down on the lie. "And Ash, he made the honor roll this year." Another lie. "A four-point-oh GPA, can you believe it?"

"Oh!" Diane shakes her head with staunch affirmation. "Of course I can, he's so bright. You know Peter was an excellent student, so I'm not surprised. Speaking of surprise, I think we better move this party along. Everyone," she announces, "please take your seats for the reveal." She picks up a tray of cake pops and asks Pavan to pass them around.

Jane stands at the front of the room and makes a speech: she feels so lucky . . . all she wants is a happy healthy baby . . . she's so blessed . . . she's full of gratitude and love. She goes on and on. The sweetness of it, the overflowing entitlement of it, sits in Pavan's throat like indigestion, so much so that when she's instructed to take a bite of the cake pop to reveal the gendered batter, she spits it out into her napkin.

"It's a boy!" Jane yells, holding her cake pop like a chalice.

While everyone toasts to the newborn to be, Pavan slips away and wanders into the nursery. She sits down in the rocking chair and picks up the black-and-white pregnancy photo that's on the dresser. Jane is practically naked, sitting cross-legged with her hands cradling her abdomen. Her husband is sitting behind her. He too appears naked and his arms are wrapped around her. He's nuzzling her neck and somehow the image conjures up Patrick Swayze and Demi Moore in the *Ghost* pottery scene. Pavan wonders why anyone would attempt a sexy prenatal photo and wants to warn them that their child will be mortified when, as a teenager, he finds this image.

Knowing them, they've probably posted it online for the world to see. So proud of themselves for having a baby, for doing what others have already done, so intent on their belief that they're special and that this is the beginning of their happily ever after. They don't know what she knows, they don't know that ever after isn't a place or a point in time. They don't know that everyone was them once, even Lisa. Everyone starts out with the same dream. She puts the frame facedown and takes one long breath before gathering the courage to head back to the party.

All of the guests are now sitting in a circle, watching Jane unwrap her gifts. Diane motions for Pavan to join the group, and she finds a seat next to a woman who is openly nursing. She tries not to stare, but this woman's veiny boob is right by her arm. When Pavan nursed she always did it in another room, or put a blanket over her shoulder, but times have changed. The group oohs and aahs at the gifts and passes them around the circle so everyone can comment and say, "How cute." Pavan didn't buy anything that was on the registry; everything Jane had chosen was ridiculously expensive and completely impractical. Designer diaper bags, monogrammed linens, a Gucci onesie — no, Pavan could not do it and instead bought a medical kit, which included a digital ear thermometer, nail clipper, eye dropper and a book about baby's first year. She knows it doesn't look like much compared to some of the other gifts, but it's useful and when something goes wrong at least Jane will be prepared. She feels good about that, even when her gift doesn't get as many aahs.

The woman next to her has unlatched and is holding the baby over her shoulder in burping position. She locks in on the baby and watches him drift in contentment. The woman sees her staring.

"How old?" Pavan asks.

"Ten months," the woman says. "His name is Jacob."

Pavan's eyes widen. "Jacob, what a beautiful name. I knew a boy named Jacob once, but we called him Jay." She's thinking of him now, viewfinder images of him as a boy with Ash.

"We're trying to stick with Jacob, but my mother-in-law is already calling him Jake, so that's tough."

"I bet."

"Do you have children?"

"Two. Both boys. They're older now, practically men." She sighs. "Time goes by fast."

"So I've been told."

"Oh I know, people told me that too and I didn't believe them, and now — poof, they're grown," she says, exploding her hands in the air. Pavan reaches over and strokes Jacob's cheek. "Adorable."

"Do you want to hold him?"

"Yes, if it's alright." Pavan makes her arms into a cradle. "It's been so long since I've held a baby."

The woman smiles and straightens her blouse. "I'm sure it's like riding a bike."

Pavan rocks and bounces the baby. She's talking to the woman but still looking at Jacob, her voice flitting in and out of baby talk. "You know, I read this article in one of those parenting magazines the other day that said that raising boys was like a terrible breakup. They need you. You give them everything. You're their world and then one day, without warning, they don't need you anymore and they're gone."

"I can't imagine that. Boys always need their mother, don't they?"

"Of course they do. It was a silly article." Pavan's still smiling at the baby, her own memories of motherhood coming through, a life of perfect little moments, gone. She thinks it's how Lisa must feel too and is filled with guilt for how she left things with her. She tried to make it right. She called, left messages and even went to the apartment but by then they had moved. She managed to get Lisa's new address from the building manager but hasn't reached out again. What was there to say but sorry. She tickles baby Jake's feet and belly. "Oh this little one is going to break your heart, aren't you? You're going to break Mom's heart. Yes, yes, you are. You're going to break her heart in two. Yes, yes, you are."

"Pardon me?" The woman's voice is filled with concern. "Come here, Jacob. Come to Mommy," she says and scoops the baby up.

"I'm sorry. That didn't come out right, I meant that *he'll* be a heartbreaker."

The woman doesn't say anything more and moves to another seat where she whispers to another woman, who then stares at Pavan. For the next thirty minutes Pavan tries not to notice them; she tries to look interested in the gift-opening and then the baby name games; she tries to fill her voice with airy enthusiasm but can't keep it up and eventually she slips away.

She's glad that Peter's not home when she gets back. She doesn't feel like talking and fabricating stories about how great the shower was, how good it was to see his mother, his sister, and all of the other little lies that she tells to get through the day. Ever since she held that baby, she can't stop thinking of her own, how soft and tender they were, how loved they were and how they loved her. And now, though they're grown, they'll always be layers of who they were, incarnations of their former perfect selves, their spoken names, an incantation of her deepest desires. She thinks of Lisa and how terrible it is to be denied this, to never know your child this way. Pavan takes the journal from her purse, tears out her failed attempts and finishes writing what she started. She tells Lisa only what she needs to hear, writing only what Jay should have said.

Before mailing it, she reads it one more time to be sure that it's enough.

April 2

Dear Mom,
I'm sorry and I love you.
Always.

Jay

Day 82

It's the sound of clattering metal that prompts Anik to turn around. Rose's van, with tendrils of soup cans trailing like tin jellyfish, skids into the campsite. The sides of the van are draped in colorful flag banners with a vinyl cling beneath them: Anik's Way, A Soul's Voyage! Rose parks and jumps out of the van, arms outstretched.

"Ta-da! Amazing, right?"

Anik circles the vehicle, taking in the banners and the tail. "I don't even know what to say. What is all of this?"

"It's your marathon of hope, your hero's journey to raise awareness."

"Raise awareness for what?"

"That we're losing ourselves, our souls, our humanity, our spirituality, our morality, our sense of decency. It's everything we talked about this week! The rampant post this, like that, follow me culture, the isolation, right-wing politics, apathy, hyperconsumerism as identity, the loss of community — and let's not even start on climate change and our unwillingness to save ourselves. We're all snowflakes, too scared, too easily offended and unable to get past the pedantic and semantic to make real change."

"I said that?"

"Well, yeah. More or less."

"AniksWay.com . . . I have a website?"

"It was Carol's idea."

"Carol from Starbucks."

"You know it," she says with double finger guns.

"For real?"

Rose pulls out her phone and opens a web page. "You know what they say: every movement needs a social media strategy."

"A social media strategy?"

"Yeah, just like we talked about the other night."

"This is insane," he says.

"It gets better." Rose slides the van door open and grabs her laptop. Anik sits next to her as she opens up tabs. "Instagram, Facebook, Twitter, Snapchat." She pushes the laptop toward him, scrolling through the photos, the video clips, the likes.

"Check it, almost five thousand followers on Instagram."

Anik lingers on the word *followers* but says nothing. He hates the idea of it, the individual en masse, some new construct replacing actual community where members contribute to a meaningful society. That's where everything has gone wrong. No longer citizens, people are just followers, cult-like in their pursuit of consumption and now here he is contributing fodder — the irony.

"Hello? Are you even listening?" she says, snapping her fingers.

Anik tunes back in as if his attention were a radio, dialing back to her frequency. "Yeah, sorry. It's a lot to take in." He plays one of the boomerang loops of him cheering his Tim Hortons coffee cup as they set off a few days earlier.

"Even Tim Hortons liked it! If you start trending, maybe they'll sponsor you or give us free coffee."

"When did you do all of this?" He's speed-reading through content, abbreviated versions of their evening conversations, all the bottom-drawer existential matter of life and meaning.

"When you're out walking, I just chill at Starbucks or Timmy's, occasionally A&W — by the way, the Beyond Meat burger is amazing, it made me want to go vegan hardcore."

"Rose."

"Oh sorry, right. Initially I was just sharing stuff on my personal pages but then I figured it would be cool to make a blog and so I kind of started it without telling you and then I thought why not a web page . . . yay free Wi-Fi at Starbucks, and then when we talked the other night it seemed you were cool with it . . . I went ham. Are you mad?"

"No, not mad. Just surprised."

"I know, right? I was surprised too. I didn't expect it to take off the way it did but all it took was one comment, and a few celebrity retweets, and things kind of went viral."

"Celebrity retweet? Who?"

"Tom Hanks."

Rose scans back to the tipping-point tweet that had a split-screen photo of Forrest Gump running and Anik walking. "Here it is." She reads it aloud. "@TomHanks Not Forrest Gump this is the real deal, a soul's voyage #AniksWay #WalkToTheOcean #SaveYour Soul." Rose leans back, smiling big. "Cool right?"

"Yeah, I guess."

"Then he replies and retweets. See here." She points to the screen. "Sometimes you have to go to know where you're going #Anik'sWay." She slaps him on the back, shoving him. "That's Tom fucking Hanks tweeting about you."

Anik shakes his head. "I can't believe it and you . . . you did all of this for me?"

"For us," she says, correcting him. "We're in this together now."

Anik goes quiet and looks down, his face deepening with emotion. He's touched by her efforts and overwhelmed by the attention he's not sure he wants.

"Don't get all mushy on me. It's just a few tweets and pictures. It's nothing. Besides the GoFundMe page will pay for gas."

"Wait — how much have you raised?"

"Just a couple hundred bucks."

"People are giving us money?" He shakes his head, his mouth twisting. "I don't know, this is way more than some pictures online."

"I guess people want to help, be part of something."

"Yeah, I get that, but I just don't get *this*. I'm just walking. That's not much of a cause."

"It's not *just walking*. It's metaphoric, it reminds people that they have a choice to walk out on the shit in their life that doesn't work."

"And you know this how?"

"DMs," she says, squinting.

"Serious?"

"Yep. You have some fans. Like I said, people are inspired."

Anik sighs, thinking of the way crowds react to Peter, hanging on his every word like it's gospel. "I'm not trying to inspire people. I'm just out here trying to figure things out."

"I know it's not what you had in mind, and maybe I went too far but . . ." She pauses for a moment. "It's kind of been fun for me, you know. It's given me something to do and I'm actually good at it."

"No, you're great at it," he says and walks around the van, thinking of what he wants compared to what she needs. "Can we at least get rid of the soup cans? I'm pretty sure that's some kind of road hazard."

"Can I keep the banners?"

"Really? They make us look like local politicians at a ribbon cutting."

"Anik for mayor!" She yells it with her hands cupped around her mouth.

"I don't know, Rose."

"Come on, the banners are fun! Please," she says, making prayer hands.

"Fine, banners can stay but the streamers go and you shut down the GoFundMe page. We aren't a charity."

"Deal," she says and tells him to stand by the van so they can take a selfie. "Three, two, one, Anik's Way!" After she posts the photo she says, "There is one other thing."

"What?"

She scrunches up her face. "Don't be mad."

"Mad about what?"

"The local news wants to do a piece on you."

"Seriously?"

"It's just a human interest, five minutes of fame type thing," she says.

He thinks about his momentary internet GOD is DOG fame and wonders if the onslaught of negative comments was the start of him feeling crowded out of his life; he doesn't want to invite that in again. "What could I possibly have to say that would be of any interest?"

"Just tell them why you're walking."

"I don't exactly know, remember?"

"Just quote some of that Ram Dass shit we were talking about the other night."

Anik looks at her confused, trying to catch up to her train of thought.

"You know — he said something like, We're all just walking each other home."

"Yeah, but that was about the meaning of life."

"Exactly," she says as if it was so obvious, as if there was never a question.

Day 86

Winona's been grounded ever since the brownie incident.

An incident, that's what Jon's calling it, rather than what it actually was — the worst birthday ever. Since she's not allowed to use her car, Jon has been driving her to school, and since she's not speaking to him, she just endures his all-news-and-traffic radio for the duration of the twenty-minute car ride, wondering why adults like listening to the same thing over and over. Traffic every five minutes. Newsflash: not much changes. What neither Jon nor Trish seems to realize is that being grounded isn't much of a punishment for Winona, or really any other teenager. If they really wanted to punish her they would make her do something, like actually do something. She renegotiated the retention of her phone and laptop under the guise of educational necessity, so she was perfectly content and her life went on in the same boring way it had before. She came home, watched YouTube, did her home-work while watching YouTube, doom-scrolled her way down rabbit holes that started with a variety of innocuous self-help, makeup or gaming tutorials. What her father doesn't realize is that she doesn't really have friends. Yes, she knows people, but other than Jay, no one really thinks of her as a friend. She's awkward; she says what she thinks and realizes that people other than Jay, and maybe now Ash, find that unsettling. So in that way being grounded is less of a punishment and more of a relief.

She spends her time working in her mother's art studio out back. It's a glorified shed, rustic but equipped with everything she needs — a small table, an armchair and good lighting. She hadn't created anything since the installation, but last week after spending hours watching stupid videos, she went from zoned out to zenned out and found herself inside the kind of boredom where her thoughts weren't her own and new ideas seemed to pass through her until they took hold in the back of her throat, in the pit of the stomach, an urgent calling to do something.

She found a vintage TV in the free section of Craigslist and when no one was home, she convinced Ash to go with her to pick it up because safety. They drove to East Vancouver and, to Ash's surprise, dismembered the TV in the alley behind where they picked it up. All she needed was the wooden shell and screen, and so with his help she gutted the electrical components, sorting them into use and throwaway piles. "It'll be an expression of how we consume ourselves, you know like the individuals feeding on themselves, echo chambers and ignorance." Ash nodded but she knew he didn't quite get it, so she pulled out her phone and showed him her rough sketch. "Inside will be a head that I'll mold out of these electrical components, and when you look at it, you'll see your own reflection superimposed on the junk head. Get it?"

"Yeah. Garbage in, garbage out."

"Exactly," she said, shoving stripped wire into her bag. "We are what we watch, what we consume. I suppose it's similar to the other installation. I'm thinking of it as a series."

"What are you going to do with it?"

She looked up at him with a pensive expression. "Not sure, really. Isn't making it enough?" As she said it she realized she was asking and stating the thing at the same time. Was it enough for it to exist without a purpose, and if it was, could that be true for people too? It was then that she decided she would model the head after her own, and now that she'd been working on it for a week it was finally starting to look like something.

She'd started with a mannequin's head whose face she melted off. She rebuilt it with metal and plastic and is now sewing in long thin black wires with stripped copper ends into the skull. By the time she looks up, hours have passed the way they always do when she's being creative. When she was working on her installation, life around her seemed to stop and now as she sits, stretching her back, she wonders if it was that creative flow that made her miss all the signs. Jay was with her the whole time, and she was with him, but maybe neither of them were there. She was buried in creation; Jay, in undoing. She didn't see his texts that day until it was too late. By the time she replied he was already gone. Though she's memorized them, she reads them every morning as if her attention now could make up for it. They were just regular *what are you doing, want to chill later, need to talk* texts. There was nothing to suggest that he would do it. They'd talked about killing themselves but maybe he always knew she wasn't serious because sometimes he talked about the future — hers, not his.

Like little girls imagining their weddings, she'd spent hours fantasizing about her perfect funeral and had told him about it. It was something she started to do after her mother died, and though most would think it morbid it gave her a sense of peace, reminding her that eventually her life, like all stories, would be made clear at the end. When Jay died she added new layers to her imagining and now sits down cross-legged, eyes closed, disappearing into a Gothic cathedral with limestone arches and a ribbed interior that makes her feel like she's been swallowed by a gigantic whale. She wears her black A-line mini dress with the Peter Pan collar and combat boots. Her face is powder-shimmered in pink and silver sparkles; she's wearing false eyelashes, bright red lipstick and black extensions brushed straight over her chest. She's Snow White meets Wednesday Addams meets a Tim Burton Claymation character. People cry. Jon's grief is obscene. They play all of her favorite songs, and when they play "Try Not to Breathe" by R.E.M., everyone rises up from their pews and dances in two rows as if they're at a ball in one of Jane Austen's books. They twirl down the aisles, spinning partners and holding hands, and as the last pair approaches her casket, Jay floats down the aisle wearing a navy blue Regency coat with gold buttons and a silk ascot. He takes off his top hat and bows. Her soul slips out of her body, takes his hand, and she too dances through the aisles singing along with them. Her mother, no longer cancer-ridden, sits, yellow-haired and angelic in an Empire-cut gown, in the back pew and together with Jay they drift above the chapel and into the sky.

When she opens her eyes, she stares at her reflection in the screen, her image floating above the circuitry of herself. She hasn't quite achieved what she'd hoped and takes a modeling hammer, tapping the center of the screen until veined cracks spread out over the surface and she is rendered an abstraction, a cubist reflection, a ghost in the machine.

Day 88

Ash didn't plan on going to Hayley's annual school's over party.

He'd made a point of not going to many parties since Jay died. Something about the bullshit way people act bugs him now and makes him wonder why he didn't notice it before. The girls are the worst; their flirty talk and come-ons are constant and he wonders if they even know they're doing it. Sometimes he's mean to them just so they leave him alone but then they see him as a challenge or something. They act like he's a puzzle or a complex equation, something to be solved, and endlessly send texts and pics waiting for validation. Mostly he deletes them but then they talk shit about him because he didn't comment on their nudes. The only girl he thinks isn't crazy like that is Winona — she's all kinds of other crazy but at least she's interesting. He can see why Jay liked her, even if she's a bit fucked up. His friends have been bugging him about her, but he's not into her like that. "Just friends," he repeats and they stare at him not knowing what to do with that.

After listening to his parents argue for the past few nights about Anik, Ash decides that staying home is worse than going to the party. He can't hear them cycle through the same fight again, using each other's first names like bullet points. "Well, *Pavan*, if you had . . ." "*Peter*, you're not listening . . ."

He texts Winona to come to the party and by the time she replies no, he's already there, saddled between two shorties who are nonstop talking in their high-tilt, Kim Kardashian voices. He's not even sure what they're talking about because the quiver in their voices, that gravel-throated baby talk, pisses him off so bad he can't even think. "I'm gonna get a beer," he says and gets up.

"Ooh, can you get me one too?"

"Me too, pl-ease," the other shouts as he walks away.

Ash maneuvers his way through the kitchen, past the beer pong players, the kegger quarterbacks, and heads outside to the backyard. Some of his friends are sitting around a firepit and others are stumbling around drunk, throwing up in the rose bushes. He cringes. That's gotta hurt — thorns and chunks.

Hayley's mom comes outside, crop top, belly ring and really tight jeans. "Everything okay out here?" she asks, yelling over the deep bass. Everyone turns and stares at the same time, as if their bobbleheads are on a string, as if they're a multiheaded organism. Ash can tell that she was probably the popular girl at school, peaked too early, a teen mom who never grew up. She's probably the type of mom who buys Hayley alcohol because she'd rather her daughter drink at home. As if.

"Everything's fine," Hayley says, running from the side of the house where she was making out with some random. She physically turns her mother around and leads her back inside, her urgent whisper reading as *Mom, you're embarrassing me.*

"Move," Ash says to the geek who's stone-cold drunk and sprawled out on a hammock. "This is my spot." He sits down and texts Winona.

rescue me

wasn't invited

I'm inviting u

can't still grounded

sneak out

not my scene

He calls her, taking her on a video tour of the party. "How can this not be your scene?" he says sarcastically, walking around, telling people to say hi to the camera and wave at Winona. "School's out. Time to celebrate." He takes her by the wasted beer pongers, around the firepit and through the crowded rec room where kids are strung out, drunk, chilling on the couch, heads bobbing slightly out of time with Kanye.

"So Alessia Cara, What am I doing here?" she says, her face freeze-lagged on the screen.

A little buzzed, he turns the camera on himself and sings along with her. She laughs and he takes it as a sign to ask again. "Please come save me."

By the time she shows up, everything is quieter, people are passed out on the front lawn and Ash is helping some guy puke. Ash lies him on his side and slaps his face. "You okay?" The guy doesn't answer and Ash slaps him until he opens his eyes. "Good, you're alive." The guy moans and curls up, face pressed into the lawn next to a laughing Buddha garden statue.

"Who's that?"

"Fuck if I know."

She glances around. "Quality people."

"I know, right?"

They go inside and do a couple shots with his friends. Beer pong is over and hookups are happening all around.

"Awkward," Ash says, not knowing exactly where to look.

Hayley gets up from the table, where she's lining up shots and staggers over to Ash. "One for me and one for you. Cheers," she says and downs it. "Woo!" She exhales and slams the empty glass down on the counter. She stares at Winona. "Heeeyyy, I know you . . . you were Jay's friend, right?"

"Yeah."

"Right!" she says with sparks of recognition. "Wendy?"

"Yeah, that's it." Winona folds her arms over her chest. She's grunged up, a baggy sweatshirt, plaid shirt tied around her waist and ripped jeans, covered head to toe, unlike Hayley and her backup dancers, who are all tank tops and bralettes.

"Sooo? What happened to him?" Hayley's drunk swaying as if she's slow dancing.

"What happened?" Winona repeats. "He died."

"OMG, I know." She's veering forward and for a minute it looks like she's going to pass out. "But how?"

"He fell."

"More like, jumped." Her eyes are tabloid-wide.

"Sure, whatever."

"What do you mean, whatever? I thought you were his friend. Shouldn't you, like, care what happened?" She's talking loud-drunk and wagging her finger at Winona like a reality TV star.

"You want to know what happened?" Winona says, her lips drawn in a straight line. "I killed him. Now get the fuck out of my face or I'll kill you too." She fake lunges at her and says, "Boo."

Hayley jumps back. "Oh my God! I knew it. I knew you were a murderer." She glances at her friends. "I told you so."

Winona nods, mouth twitching as if she's chewing on the inside of her cheek. Ash starts to crack up and can't stop. The tequila shots messed him up and he's slapping his knee, trying to smack the giggles out.

"So how did you do it?"

"I pushed him."

"Noooooo." Hayley's lips are frozen in a perfect zero.

"Yes, yes I did."

"But how?"

"Do you really want me to show you?"

She nods feverishly.

"Meet me on the roof in five."

"Huh?"

Winona laughs and shakes her head. "I'm fucking joking. Jesus, do you actually think that I'd confess if I killed someone?"

"Who killed someone," asks the girl with overdrawn eyebrows.

Hayley points at Winona, slurring. "Wendy did. She killed Jay."

The eyebrow girl twirls her ponytail. "Oh my God, what the fuck?"

"It's Winona and I was joking."

"Why would you even joke about that?" eyebrow girl asks.

"Yeah, why would you even — you're crazy." Hayley's talking loud and staggering. She takes a swig of vodka from the open bottle on the counter. "You are fucking crazy."

"Whatever. I think I'll go now . . . Fun," she says to Ash.

"Yeah, go already. You weren't even invited."

"I invited her," Ash says. "She's cool."

Hayley gets close to his face and puts her arms around his neck and stumbles. "Ash, I like you but she's a murderer. You better be careful or you'll end up like Jay."

"You're right." He unlatches Hayley's arms and backs up. "Someone's gotta do something about this."

"Yeah," eyebrow girl says.

"I'm going to take her to the police station; it's a citizen's arrest!"

Winona makes a show of it and cuffs her wrists behind her back. Ash links his arm in the crook of her elbow and leads her out. The drunken partygoers cheer and raise devil horns and rock on symbols for no reason.

"And this is why I don't go to parties." Winona opens her car door and Ash shuts it before she can get in. "What?"

"Come on, let's walk it off."

They head toward the school playground. The midnight air is sobering, takes the edge off his buzz. They sit on the swings and drift back and forth, their feet dragging on the dirt, making swirls and divots in the mulch.

"Jay and I went to school here. It's where we met," Ash says, breaking the silence.

"I know. He told me. Said you were his first good friend."

"Some friend I was." Ash goes quiet, thinking about Jay and all the things he could have done differently. "Back there, why did you say that stuff about killing him?"

"I don't know. Tequila, it fucks me up."

"True story."

"Besides, they think I had something to do with it so I figured I'd give 'em something to talk about, liven up the party a bit." She squints and tilts her head at a figure walking toward them.

"That's Phil." Ash says.

"You know him?"

"Sort of."

"Kid, you got any money?" He stops in front of Ash. He's missing his front teeth and his words come out all funny, like he's been chewing on them, grinding the vowels to a pulp. He's picking at his beard as if he's pulling gnats out of it.

"Nah, haven't got anything, Phil."

"Why the fuck you calling me, Phil. I don't fucking know you. Stupid kid." He moves like a slo-mo zombie, all twitch and seizure. "So you got any money?"

"No," Winona says.

"Fucking bitch." He spits at her feet. "I don't fucking know you. Why don't you mind your own fucking business. I wasn't talking to you." He wanders off muttering to himself and as soon as he's out of earshot they break into laughter.

"Thought you said you knew him."

"I know of him." He pushes back on the swing. "The whole neighborhood does. His family was hella rich."

"No way." Winona watches as Ash goes back and forth.

"Way. He basically pissed all his money away. He's every parent's cautionary tale of how drugs and alcohol can mess you up."

"No shit?"

"Yeah, my mom's pretty paranoid about stuff like that. She's been all over me since the whole vape thing."

"Still can't believe you got suspended."

"I know. And the kicker is now she won't stop talking about it, says vaping is a gateway addiction."

"That's a bit of a stretch."

"Completely. It's nuts. She's obsessed, sending me articles about kids whose lungs get all messed up and end up in the hospital. She even goes through my stuff when I'm not around." He takes his pen out.

"Wait, what the heck. You're still doing it."

"Only sometimes." He takes a hit. "It calms me down."

"Shit, no wonder she doesn't trust you."

"Like, for real, she's next level paranoid . . . I bet she even has spyware on my phone, she probably knows I'm here right now. I swear, it's like big brother mother."

"Well, at least she cares."

"Yeah, she does — but maybe a little too much. I feel like if she'd just leave me alone, I'd be fine."

"So, it's her fault that you fuck up."

"Isn't everything our parents' fault?" He exhales a cloud of mist. "Even my brother's messed up."

"I wouldn't call it messed up."

"No?"

She turns and their swings drift and tangle, the metal squawking gently. "I think he's onto something, the walk and all. Maybe we all need to go on a quest and figure our shit out instead of having our parents plan our lives for us."

"Not sure a walk can sort that out."

"Sure, it can. In some Indigenous cultures, sons were sent into the wilderness on a walkabout, a spiritual journey to adulthood. They could be out there on their own for months at a time. If they returned, they returned as men."

"What do you mean *if*?"

"Well, I'm sure some of them died. Totally Darwinian in that respect."

"I wouldn't call Anik's journey a walkabout. They're sleeping at campgrounds, eating trail mix and Clif bars."

"Still, at least it's something," she says. "Wait — what do you mean *they*? I thought he was going on his own."

"He was, but then he met some girl," he says. "And now they're together. Not *together* together but, you know, as friends."

"Well, I still think it's cool, what they're doing." She gets off her swing and stands in front of Ash's, bringing him to a stop. "Maybe we should join them."

"What do you mean?"

"I mean, let's go. Let's meet up with them — walk about."

"You're crazy. Our parents would freak."

"So let's not tell them. Let's just go. Like right now."

"No way." Ash starts walking to the car.

"Come on. It could be fun," she says, her voice opening to the idea of it. "An adventure."

"No thanks." He waves his hand over his head dismissively and keeps walking.

"Just think about it," she says, trailing a few steps behind. "Isn't it better than staying here and doing nothing? Aren't you tired of waiting for something to happen?"

Ash pauses, knowing she's right. There's nothing waiting for him but the sameness of home, his parents' expectations, the letdowns.

After grabbing his camping gear from the shed, he sneaks past his parents' room, and with the lights off, he packs quickly and then leaves a note in Pavan's office. He doesn't want them to panic the way they did with Anik. He rifles through her desk drawer looking for her emergency money. That's when he sees it — a box with Jay's name on it. His phone lights up: it's Winona texting him to hurry. He packs the box in his bag.

Winona's house is lit up from the inside as if everyone's awake. The brick house has black-shuttered windows, a golf-green lawn and a bunch of exterior lighting that makes the entire house look like it's on a film set. From the car, Ash can see Winona open the security gate and go around the back. Ten minutes later, she's walking out the front door, a bag slung over her shoulder, her father just a few steps behind. He grabs her by the elbow and yells something. She pulls away, keeps walking toward the car, and this time, he doesn't follow, he just stands there in angry-man stance. Ash can tell she's upset but he doesn't ask.

The ferry terminal is closed so they pull over and wait. The excitement of the walkabout fades into the very real consequences of their parents' disappointment. Ash can feel it already — stomach knots and all. "We can turn back, if you want," he says eventually.

"Too late for that." He can tell she must be replaying whatever words were said before she left. She opens the door. "I'm gonna stretch my legs."

A minute later Ash opens his door. "Wait up." But she doesn't and he ends up standing there, watching her go. For the briefest of moments it looks as if she's walking on water, hovering on the predawn ribbon of light, floating somewhere between here and there.

Day 89

Pavan listens to Peter talk to Ash on the phone.

He is calm and reasonable. He doesn't have buttons to push, or if he does Ash has yet to find them. She's annoyed by the plotless pace of the conversation, the never-ending listening and perspective-taking and she paces back and forth, interjecting "Tell him" and "Did he think about . . ." until Peter glares at her with a quieting look. He cups the receiver. "Did you want to talk?"

She shakes her head, knowing it's not a good idea. *What was he thinking* is the only question she has and no answer will suffice. *Where did I go wrong?* is a much easier question to answer — she has a million things she wishes she'd done differently. All of her decisions have led to this. Looking back, she thinks she lost Ash at fifteen, and maybe in her attempts to get him back, she took her eyes off Anik and lost him too. She tries to pinpoint the moment they left her, the moment they became these cynical, tired people that know nothing and believe in nothing. When did they go from bright, wide-eyed boys with sweet smiles who made pancakes on Mother's Day to these little cannibals feasting on themselves and anyone who gets in their way. Last week she dreamt of being in the airport, holding their child hands, and when she turned around, when she took her eyes off them for a second, they were swept up in a sea of angry protesters. She couldn't keep them in sight and soon they were gone, beaten down by the fisted mob, and she was suddenly alone in the arrivals section, holding a missing persons sign with their names on it.

She sits on the living room couch and wrings her hands, her knee bouncing up and down; she can't be contained. "What is he saying?"

Peter doesn't respond and goes into the bedroom and shuts the door. She follows, listening ear against the door.

"Well, imagine how your mom feels."

Silence.

"I understand."

Silence.

"It's been a hard time. I get it."

More silence.

"We're just worried about you, son."

Pavan presses her forehead against the door. He said "son" and he only ever says "son" when he's not getting anywhere, when he needs to make a point about family, belonging and hierarchy.

"Okay. How about this. How about you keep checking in so we know you're okay?"

Pavan pushes the door open and whispers harshly. "No way. How about he gets his ass home before I drag him back."

Peter puts a shushing finger to his mouth, eyes wide.

"Text three times a day and at least one call. And what about money? Do you have what you need?"

Silence.

"Okay, I'll tell Mom. Yeah, I love you too, son."

Peter hangs up and turns around. "What the hell?"

"What the hell is right. 'I love you, son,'" she says, mocking his tone. "What did he say? What did he want you to tell me?"

"Nothing, just that he took the emergency money is all."

She rushes into her office, flings the drawer open to find the box gone. "Fuck." She shakes her head, wondering what Ash must think.

"Pavan."

"What?" She spins around to face him. "You were supposed to convince him to come back."

"Well, I can't force him, can I?"

"Uh, yes you can." She takes the phone from his hand and starts dialing.

He grabs it. "If you call him, you'll just push him away. Is that what you want?"

"No, of course not. But I can't just do nothing."

"Just take a minute. Let's think this through."

"What's to think through? Both of our kids have taken off. One is walking across the fucking island and the other one is following in his footsteps."

"Look, you're acting like they ran away. They didn't. Anik is an adult, he can do what he wants and Ash —"

"Is only seventeen! He shouldn't be out there, traveling on his own."

"He's not . . . on his own."

"What? What are you talking about?"

"He's gone with a friend."

"When were you going to tell me this?"

"Now, I was going to tell you now. Jesus. If you'd just calm down."

"Don't tell me to calm down!" Pavan sits down, her leg still bouncing. "Well? Who is he with?"

"A girl, some friend of Jay's."

"Winona?"

"Yeah, you know her?"

"No, not really."

"Well, they're together. Apparently, they've become friends. She's driving. Don't worry, she has her license and —"

"And what? Everything will be okay?"

"It *will* be okay." He takes a deep breath. "Look, the school year's over. He's going to text us and check in every day. I say we just keep monitoring the situation."

"Monitoring the situation? Is that so? Is that your professional opinion? For fuck's sake, Peter, he's not one of your coaching clients. He's our son and he should be at home."

"And what do you suggest we do? Call the police?"

"Yes, actually. That's exactly what I think. That's what any parent would think if they weren't so worried about their life coaching career being tarnished for not having a picture-perfect family."

"Don't do that."

"Do what?"

"Make this about my work or about us."

"Newsflash, this is about us. Both of our kids have left. If that's not about us, our parenting, our family, what the hell is?"

"That's where you are wrong. It's got nothing to do with us. Kids do dumb things. They test boundaries."

"That's easy for you to say. You didn't give birth to them."

"You're right. I don't know how you feel. But what I can tell you is that although they are *of* you . . . they are not you. They aren't really yours. They have their own lives to live."

"Are you fucking serious right now? Are you life coaching me?" She smiles, her grin twisting in disbelief. "Fuck, you are, aren't you? You're using one of your profound little zingers to open up a dialogue. Well, let me tell you: I don't need a life coach. I need a husband. I don't want profound, I want pragmatic. But you can't be, can you? Because being practical, that's always been my job — boring bad cop, details and checklists. Chores galore mom, gets shit done. You know what, maybe if you had coached less and done more along the way, we wouldn't be here."

"I can't talk to you when you're like this."

"Like what?"

"You know."

"No, tell me."

"You're spiraling."

"Oh, spiraling . . . is that more of your coach speak?"

"Okay, I'm going now." He grabs his keys.

"What a surprise!" She calls after him, "Go already." She hears herself say this; it's what she always says, what she never means.

She's lost control again and she can feel her anger churning, that old rage of having given and never gotten, the fatigue of having tried and failed over and over.

She heads to the kitchen and pours a glass of wine and then another. The warmth and blur is almost instant, her shoulders relax, she exhales, but then comes regret. She has to apologize. She hates saying she's sorry, not because she wants to be right, but because she's sick of herself. Apologizing only proves how inadequate she is. "Just let it go," she tells herself and breathes deeply.

She tries hard. She always has. When she was pregnant, she read all the books, highlighted passages, made notes in the margin. But even then, she was sure she was failing. When Anik was a baby she went to playgroups where the moms listed off their self-worth in baby milestones and even then she knew she was behind. Every first step, every night slept through, every percentile on the chart was either a blue-ribbon honor or something to be concerned about. "Don't worry, he'll catch up" was the sympathy line from playdate moms who were already treating their children like successories.

Not much has changed. She's still waiting for them to catch up, to be like the other kids on social media who get straight As and volunteer at the local animal shelter. The mentions and likes, the hearts and halo emojis on their parents' Facebook wall. The *I'm so proud of insert overachiever's name here* boast post, humblebrag, #blessed. If she sees another #blessed, another suburban family photo — girl, boy, mom, dad, all in matching plaid shirts walking through autumn leaves — she'll barf. They make her sick. The fact that she's not them makes her sick. The fact that they can pretend so well makes her sick.

She pours another drink and takes it to her bedroom, draws the blinds and sits under the covers. She's crying and can't stop and she hates this, further proof of her lack of control, her failures, the edges of her life coming up sharp around her. She takes a deep breath, counts one, two, and on three, slaps herself hard across her cheek. She does it again and again until all she feels is the sting and shame.

Day 89

Anik hasn't walked for a few days now.

When Rose didn't meet him at the checkpoint and didn't answer his calls, he backtracked ten kilometers and found her pulled over at the side of the road, thumb out, swearing at the cars that rushed by without stopping. The guy at the local garage told them it would be at least a week to get the parts, and so they had no choice but to camp out, waiting until the engine was repaired. Rose worried about the delay, told him to go on without her, but he said he could use the break and she seemed relieved. She too had come to depend on him, and this filled him with a purposeful happiness that he hadn't expected. The next days were like that too. Not having a schedule suited Anik and as they went about their day, hiking and swimming, he found his mind making connections that he hadn't before. It was different than what he'd experienced when he was in his room. When sequestered away he was lonely, the lack of productivity hanging over him like a ticking bomb, and here even though an hour passes in stillness there is no foreboding other, no shadow reminder of *should do*, just birdsong and light. Earlier that morning he and Rose attempted to fish and caught nothing but garbage — even that was fine: the simple act of standing on shore in quiet anticipation felt important to him. Just as he was about to give up he felt a tug on the line and with Rose's help reeled in the catch. Neither of them knew what type of fish it was, and when Anik looked at it close up, hook-mouthed and struggling, he let it go, saying he preferred lentils for supper.

Rose didn't seem to mind the break either, and each morning they walked into town to charge up her phone and laptop, posting about Anik's Way and sharing clips of their musical collaborations. The news piece generated some traffic to the website and, as far as Anik's concerned, Rose is taking things too far when that afternoon she talks about getting T-shirts made.

"It'll become the Pacific Northwest's Camino and people will follow in your footsteps. We may as well profit from it."

"No." Anik grabs a beer from the cooler. "This trip — it's not about money."

"Everything's about money," Rose says. "Okay, if not T-shirts, how about buttons or coffee cups, maybe water bottles — cross-promotion with local retailers."

"No." He stretches his torso, before settling into his lotus position.

"Says the guy in a yoga pose holding a beer."

"I hear you, but this trip is about finding yourself, wherever you are."

"Oh, that's totally tweetable." She takes a photo of him. "I'll crop the beer out."

"Clearly, you should be in marketing and publicity."

"No way. I don't want to sell crap and manage brands."

"But you're good at it."

"It's only because this is something I can get behind. It's a good cause."

"It's hardly a cause."

"Sure it is. Think about it, now that people have seen what you're doing, they are reexamining their own lives. Where they are, where they're going, what they're even doing. I mean, shit, most people are walking dead, workaholics or narcissistic addicts completely absorbed by themselves, like a flesh-eating organism."

Anik enjoys watching her talk, the mounting passion of her monologues and diatribes as if she's delivering Hollywood lines. She's poignant and funny and so assured in every word that when he watches her, he feels better about the world, if only momentarily. "But I'm just like all of those people you're talking about. I'm walking because I was in my head, absorbed by myself, unsure and scared of what I was going to do with my life and now here we are contributing to the *look at me and buy this* culture that has us all trapped. Wordsworth was right: 'The world is too much with us; late and soon.'"

"Whatever, Shakespeare," she says, interrupting. "I don't know why you can't accept that people think what you're doing is cool. It's not an easy thing to do something that doesn't have a point. That sense of being is a radical act in a society that wants you to have a plan, get a job and pay your bills." She makes a eureka face and types something on her phone. "I'm going to save that for tomorrow's tweet."

"Tweet this." Anik flips her the bird.

She takes a photo. "Perfect."

"Maybe you should switch things up, write something about yourself. Your journey. You could call it 'A Rose by Any Other Name,'" he says, panning the air with a *picture it* directorial gesture.

"Ugh, sounds like a bad way-off-Broadway show. No thank you."

"Don't sell yourself short. I think our *followers* would be curious about you." He gets up and holds out his hand like a microphone. "Have you found yourself?"

"You might want to lay off the day-drinking."

He reasserts his pretend microphone. "Please don't avoid the question. Have you made peace with yourself? Our audience would like to know."

"Self, as in singular?" She pushes his hand away and he sits back down as she opens a bottle of water. "Life isn't so this or that for me. It's never has been — I mean look at me."

"Meaning?"

"Sometimes I don't even know what I'm about."

"Everyone's figuring it out."

"It's not the same. Even when I think I've figured out, I've got to deal with other people trying to figure me out. Case in point: did you see how the mechanic guy eyed me up and down when I gave him my ID? He had this little smirk on his face, like 'I can't wait to tell the wife about the girl named Thomas who came into the shop today.' That look on his face reminded me that no matter what I do, people don't see me the way I see myself."

"Isn't that true for everyone though? My dad says that we see the world as we are, not as it is."

"Maybe, but it feels worse because it's so obvious, you know? Another time, this guy came into the grocery store where I worked and when I was ringing him through he asked me if my pronoun was *it*. For a second I imagined taking the bottle of hot sauce in my hand and smashing it on his head, ramming the jagged end into his eye and twisting it until he was all fucked up. I'd been called that before, I'd been called worse before, but that day, I felt like shit. Some days I just wake up hating everything and everybody."

"Yeah, I get that."

"But you don't. Not really. Everyone's lives look so easy; they just get to go about being themselves. Nothing about my life is easy, or normal."

"Fuck normal. Who wants to be normal anyways?" Anik asks and takes a long swig of beer. "Oh, that sounds like the opening number of your Broadway show." He grabs his guitar and gives it a quick tune. He clears his throat and sings, strumming between each phrase, "Normal is herd mentality, get in line, toe the line." Rose nods her approval and he continues. "Normal is Sunday dinner and six o'clock news. It's a two-by-two squared scheduled list of to-dooooos."

Rose jumps up and with a Streisand flourish belts, "Normal is gold-star special, good job, hand job, you can be anything . . . so long as it's safe and productive."

They walk in circles around each other alternating lines on the mundane and absurd.

"Normal is mall shopping, bar hopping, Netflix and chill."

"Normal is politics and policies, numb your pain and take a pill."

"It's mainstream media, mouth breathers, mass shooters!"

Anik palms the guitar and for a moment there is nothing but the sound of birds and the sparkle of sunlight between the trees.

Rose begins again, this time whispering to crescendo: "Normal is doing what you're told, going once, twice, three times, sold." She holds the last note out, arms in the air.

As she bows, Anik claps and yells, "Encore!"

"Normal is brand names and brand *you*."

"Mass migration and starvation."

"Headlines and deadlines."

"Hide and seek, don't ask, don't tell."

"Normal is not me and it's not you."

"Normal is not me and it's not you . . ."

They stop singing when they hear a car coming down the service road.

A black Mercedes with tinted windows comes to a stop and Ash gets out of the passenger's side. "What the hell were you singing about? You sounded like shit."

Anik puts down his guitar. "What are you doing here?" He hugs his brother, cuffing his back twice in that hard-hitting *I got you* way.

"Saw you on the news. We figure we'd see what shit you were getting up to." He gestures to Winona. She introduces herself. Her handshake is strong, like she's making a point.

"This is Rose," Anik says.

"Judd or Ryder?" Rose asks Winona.

"Ryder," she answers.

"*Beetlejuice* or *Scissorhands*?" Rose asks as if her movie preference is a clue to her psyche.

"*Beetlejuice*, of course."

Rose smiles. "Cool." They all stand there staring for a minute before Anik breaks the silence, asking if they're hungry.

"I could eat," Ash says.

Anik grabs the hot dogs. "We can roast them over a fire."

"Rugged. Never pictured you as an outdoors type."

"Well, I guess I'm full of surprises," Anik says, gathering some wood.

"Yeah, like giving Mom and Dad a heart attack by leaving. Big fucking surprise," he says, giving Anik a shove. "You could've at least told me."

There's an awkward silence. "Why don't we get the fixings ready, leave you to talk." Rose motions to Winona to follow her to the picnic table.

Ash looks around the site, noticing the few empties on the ground. "I thought this was a spiritual quest?"

"It is," shouts Rose. "Jesus turned water to wine. We do cheap beer, honey."

"Fair." Ash grabs one from the cooler.

Anik takes it from him. "Mom would kill me. Does she even know you're here?"

"Yeah, unlike *you*, I left a note. I talked to Dad. He's cool with it."

Anik kneels down and starts the fire, coaxing it with kindling. "How's Mom?" he finally asks.

"She's okay. Just regular, I guess."

"She mad?" he asks without looking up.

"No, just worried. She recorded the news. Watched it over and over. You know how she is."

"Yeah, I know." Anik gets up and skewers the hot dogs. "Dad's okay with it though?"

"Hard to say."

"Thought he may be upset or get some blowback on his coaching stuff on account of me being fucked up."

"You aren't fucked up and he's fine. You know Peter, he'll find a way to sell it, maybe use the material for his next book," he says, laughing. "But you should've told me. I could've done damage control."

"Sorry, I didn't want you to get caught up in it."

"How could I not? You know how Mom is; when one of us does something, we both get the lockdown."

"True. I'm sorry."

"I told Dad that I'd text and send pics and stuff. Maybe you should call Mom again?"

"Yeah, I just . . . I don't know what to say."

"Start with sorry. That always works for me."

"Facts."

"She just wants to know you're okay."

"Yeah, I am. I'm figuring things out. It's been good. So what's the deal with Winona? Wasn't she Jay's girlfriend?"

"Yeah, we've been hanging out, like as friends."

"Cool." Anik knows he should have more to say on it, like any big brother should, but he doesn't and so they just stand there in front of the fire.

"So what's the deal with the walking? Is it like a metaphor for life? No matter what, you just gotta keep going?" Ash asks.

"Yeah, sort of. Speaking of which, how did you find us?"

"Rose," Ash says loud enough for her to hear. "She posted the last stop online so we figured you'd be camped around here. Plus I still have you on Find My."

"Good to know."

"That's quite an Instagram following you have, by the way," Winona adds as she and Rose return to the fire.

"It's all Rose," Anik says.

"How did you guys meet anyways?" Ash asks as they sit down to eat.

"I caught him taking pictures of me on the ferry. Total stalker move," Rose says, laughing.

"Originally, we were just going to meet up along the way. You know, keep each other company. But then *Anik's Way* happened," Anik says, sarcastically.

Rose pretends to take offense. "You say it like it's a bad thing. Your brother," she says, looking at Ash, "pretends like he doesn't love all the attention."

"Not surprised. He is the introvert of the family."

"Ambivert," Anik corrects. "I can be social when I need to be. It's just the small talk that gets me."

"I'm with Anik on that one. Who wants to talk about the weather anyways?" Winona says. "And you know what's worse than the small-talkers? The so-called nice people who ask how you are, and since you know they're only asking to be polite, all you can say is 'fine.' It's, like, people are just talking to talk. No one actually listens and —" She stops and looks down at her lap. "I'm talking too much. Sorry," she says, her face *oops* scrunched.

"No, it's fine. We're totally with you," Rose says. "My gran used to say if you suffer fools gladly, you are a fool."

Ash gets up and looks around the campsite. "So where's the van?"

"At the shop," Rose says. "Some mechanical mumbo jumbo. It won't be fixed for a couple days so we're just killing time."

"That sucks."

"Yeah, it put us behind but whatever, right. Shit happens," Anik says. "We'll get there when we get there."

"We can use my car if you want," Winona offers, her voice small but reaching. "I mean, if you don't mind us tagging along."

Anik glances up at Rose, who nods. "Yeah, sure. Why not." He puts another log on the fire and they all settle in. As they talk about the next day's walking route, he observes them as if he's out of body, trying to understand how they've come together, all of them bonded by circumstance and chance, hanging on to each other, desperate for some thread of connection. He wonders if that's all life is: a spinning of thin webs, a silvered way to get from here to there, from me to us.

Day 90

Ash forgets where he is for a second.

When he opens his eyes the first thing he feels is an ache run-ning through him like a rod. He's stiff, tense-limbed from sleeping on the ground, and when he moves, he's suddenly aware of every stone and root beneath the down sleeping bag. He curls up on his side and watches Anik on a tilt. He's making coffee in a French press, which seems like a real grown-up thing to do. Anik hasn't shaved, and the scruff makes him look older, wiser even. Like a Patagonia poster boy, he's wearing a headband, a buffalo check shirt and the kind of khaki pants that can zip off at the knees. As Ash watches him make breakfast, he notices how much he looks like Peter in his old tree-planting save-the-world days and yet the resemblance is genetically impossible. Anik looks like Pavan and a little like his uncle on his father's side, yet somehow all of his man-nerisms are from Peter. Ash wonders what it must be like for him to never have known his father beyond the knowing that Pavan left him. Anik's never talked about it. He's never reached out to his bio-dad, he's never wanted to meet him and he's never made a deal of daddy issues except when he was fifteen and had a fight with their parents and called Dad "Peter," as if it was a curse word. If Peter was bothered by it, he didn't let on and continued to play the part of father whether Anik wanted it or not.

"You hungry?" Anik asks.

Ash groans and rolls over.

"You can't walk on an empty stomach."

"Gotta piss," he says and gets up.

"Here." Anik hands him a bear bell. "Ring it, just in case."

He takes it into the bush with him and walks further into the forest than he needs to; it's cool and full of shadows, the sun filtering through the canopy in a fairy-tale way, all sparkle and shimmer. He feels good to be away from home, away from clockwork boring. As he breathes in the morning air, he realizes there's something about being in nature that just slows you down and makes you see that everything's okay. Winona says there's a name for it — biophilia. She told him about it as they drove through the old-growth forests of Cathedral Grove on their way to meet up with Anik and Rose. She was so into it that they pulled over and hiked the trails for hours. She told him that people are hardwired to connect with the natural world. If she'd told Ash that last week, he wouldn't have believed her but now he gets it; being out here makes everything else small and ugly.

A twig snaps behind him and he freezes when he hears something rustling in the bush. The forest goes quiet. All he can hear is his breath. He rings the bell and turns slowly to see a deer about ten feet away. It's staring at him with wide, lashed doe eyes, just staring, not startled by the bell, not moving. He hasn't seen a deer close up since one was wandering around their neighborhood a few years ago. Ash and Jay had been riding bikes when they saw it cross a busy intersection and leap into the ravine. They followed it for an hour, stopping when it stopped, getting off their bikes and crouching behind trees and fallen logs, pretending they were spies in pursuit. It seemed to know they were following and even looked at them as if to say "this way" before it disappeared into the brush. He thinks this deer has that exact same look and he takes a step closer. It blinks and they lock in, both of them seeming to observe the animal of the other. He is filled with a deep wonder. But then he thinks of the deer head that's stuffed and mounted in the local pub. He thinks of the hunters — those camo men, with their clean shots and prize kills, with their tobacco breath and drink fists.

He rings the bell but it doesn't move.

"Go, get out of here."

He rings the bell again and shouts, but it won't take a step. It simply stares at him. In the distance, Ash hears Anik, Winona and Rose running through the forest calling his name.

"Go, please," he urges, stamping his feet, pretending to run at it.

The deer turns toward their voices and back at him before jumping into the thicket. The forest reanimates and everything is as it was.

"What's the matter? Are you okay?" Anik's looking directly at Ash, his hands on his brother's shoulders. "Was it a bear?"

"I don't think so . . . maybe. I didn't get a good look," Ash says. "It was just some rustling in the bushes. I probably overreacted. I'm sorry."

"We should put the food away and pack up, just in case," Rose says.

They all start heading back to camp.

"You look like you've seen a ghost. Are you sure you're okay?" Winona asks.

"Yeah, sure." Ash looks around for some sign of the deer. He replays the moment in slow motion, zooms in on its eyes, its stance and that overall expression of knowingness, which, as he reflects on it, seems ridiculous because what could a deer know? "It was just staring at me."

"What was?"

"A deer. It was a deer."

She doesn't say anything.

"I felt like it was like important or something." He looks down, shaking his head, trying to decipher what it is he just said. "That's dumb, right?"

"No, not dumb," she says. "Maybe it was a sign."

"Of what?"

"I don't know." She glances at him over her shoulder before continuing on. "But a deer symbolizes peace, so there is that."

After breakfast, Winona and Rose stay at the campsite, cramming everything into the car, while Ash heads out with Anik for the day's walk. Because the car can't fit all the gear, they carry heavier packs than Anik normally does and after an hour Ash feels the weight of it, his body bending forward beneath the load. They walk at a meandering pace, often stopping by the side of the road, or jumping the median to take in the view. Standing on the edge of a cliff, taking in the full expanse of sky makes Ash think of Jay and he tries hard to push it away, to bury it in some other thought as they press on.

"So, what do you think of when you walk?" Ash asks some distance later.

"When I'm lucky, nothing."

Ash links his thumbs around the shoulder straps of his pack and pulls them away from his body. "But I thought the point of the walk was to figure things out."

"I am figuring things out."

"And?"

"And it's not what I expected. I thought I'd realize what I want to do with my life and I haven't, at least not in the way that we've been trained to think about life."

"Not following."

Anik pauses as if calibrating. "It's like we've been taught to think that we need to prepare for life, that there's some big outcome we're working toward, and for some people maybe that's true — but this trip has taught me that if you're too busy chasing some eventuality, you might miss the good stuff."

"But what about your music?"

"What about it?"

"Are you still going to keep doing it?"

"Yeah, sure. It's just that life has to inform my music, not the other way around. Music isn't my purpose; living is my purpose. Look around," he says, his arms outstretched. "Really, take it in. Life is happening all around us."

Ash watches his brother's awe-filled face. He wants to talk to him about Jay, he wants to tell him about the deer, but he knows there's something in the saying that would, like a magic trick explained, take all the mystery away.

Day 91

Winona and Rose have the stereo cranked.

Mitski's "Nobody" has been on repeat for the entire drive. They're right into it, alternating between theatrical lip-syncing and shout-it-out vocals.

Rose turns the volume down. "I swear, she wrote that song for me."

"I feel the same way." Winona says, turning it back up for a few more beats. "I never met anyone besides Jay who's even heard of her before." She goes quiet, realizing that she's said his name as if he was still alive, that for the briefest of moments she forgot he was dead and for that she's flooded with guilt for not having guarded her memory better. Sometimes she imagines him like a bird in her chest, alive so long as she keeps him there, safe and warm, nestled in recollection.

Rose turns the music off. "Anik told me about your boyfriend. I'm sorry."

"It's okay — he wasn't my boyfriend exactly," Winona says, now wishing that they had claimed each other in that way. She stares at the moving dot on the car's navigation screen as if orienting herself was as simple as following an arrow. "This next stretch is really curvy."

Rose adjusts her mirrors and focuses on the snaking kilometers ahead. "So Jay — how long has it been?"

"Three months. People say it gets easier, but it doesn't."

"Tell me about it. People said all kinds of things like that when my brother died."

"Sorry, I didn't know," Winona says, glancing at her.

"I don't talk about it much. He was ten years older than me and it was a long time ago. A car accident."

"Still. That's got to be tough."

"I was seven so I don't remember much. But I do remember the funeral and the way people talked in this lower register and how they kept saying things that were supposed to make me feel better but did the opposite."

Winona nods and stares at her reflection in the side mirror. "I didn't go to Jay's funeral."

"Why not?"

"I don't know," she says, shaking her head. The month after he died, she went to the cemetery. She'd expected more than a modest slab of granite with his name and dates, more than a small patch of earth. For a time she lay down next to him, staring at the muted sky so perfectly painted that it reminded her of her mother, of da Vinci's advice: "That which is five times more distant make five times more blue."

"Did your parents ever talk about your brother after he died?" Winona asks, her gaze fixed on the water and the steep cliff drops. Though she's been to the island before, they'd always taken a seaplane; the aerial view, a relief map, was nothing like the jagged rock face and towering trees that surround her.

"Sometimes. But over the years less and less. I think they were worried about the effect it had on me. You know, being in his shadow type of thing."

"Makes sense, I guess," she says, wondering if that was why her dad remarried, some attempt at giving her a family. "It's sad though — being forgotten like that."

"Yeah, but just because my mom doesn't talk about him, it doesn't mean she forgot him. She found a way to go on. Same way we all do."

Winona sighs, wishing she lived in a culture that revered the dead, that had days devoted to them, that built shrines and made offerings for the afterlife. She traces the scars on her arms. What she wouldn't give.

Outside, the views both distant and near dip and curve around her, and as the road bends again, Winona closes her eyes and exhales long and hard.

"What's the matter?"

"I used to get carsick as a kid."

"Used to? You look a little green." Rose cracks the window. "Fresh air will help."

She presses her head against the cool glass.

"We're almost there. Just keep your eyes on the horizon."

Winona bites down, chewing her gum with harsh precision.

"Bet you're glad you let me drive today. This route is not for the faint of heart." Rose laughs and glances over at Winona. "You don't look so good."

"Yeah, I probably should've walked with the guys." She slides the window right down for a minute and then back up.

"Better?"

"A little." She stares out at the lake, so clear that it's pulled the sky down upon its surface.

"There's an empty bag just behind the seat, if you need it."

Winona grabs it just in case. It smells like the French fries they ate for dinner when they stopped at a creek yesterday. She was tired and hot from having walked all afternoon and waded into the cool waters with Ash. Anik and Rose stayed on higher ground and Anik kept yelling at them to be careful. As she thinks back, she realizes she had barely said a word to anyone. Being outside and exposed to the sun, the heat, the cars whizzing by — it all made her quiet as if that physical ache of walking, that assault of the elements, had matched how she felt on the inside. Yet she was able to continue on in a way she hadn't thought possible, experiencing "the journey in each step" exactly as AniksWay.com said she would.

Rose takes the curve too fast and the blood drains from Winona's face, her stomach lifts into her throat. "Pull over, pull over."

"I can't, there's no shoulder. Use the bag."

"No, it stinks." She muzzles herself.

Rose checks the rearview and pulls to the side. "Quick."

Winona jumps out and heaves over the guardrail, once and then again. She wipes her mouth with her sleeve and gets back in the car.

"Better?" Rose asks.

Winona nods. "Sorry."

"There's some mints in one of Ash's bags, I think."

Winona undoes her seatbelt and reaches into the back as Rose pulls away from the curb.

"Find it?"

"Yeah." Winona takes the mints from the front pouch.

"Check if he has any snacks. I thought he had some chips in there."

Winona digs into the bag and it's then that she sees the keepsake box. She's just about to take it out when Rose slams on her brakes.

"There they are!" Rose points to Ash and Anik who are about fifty meters ahead. "Any luck with the chips?"

"No," Winona says and watches the brothers walk as the car slows. From behind it's hard to know which is which; they both lean forward, as if they're pressing into a wind, all the weight on the balls of their feet. Rose honks and they both turn around. Ash smiles and waves. Winona doesn't wave back.

Winona wanders off toward the lake. She doesn't feel like listening to them replay the day; she doesn't want to hear the jumble of their voices. The nausea has her agitated, but so does Jay's keepsake box. She helped him decoupage it. She'd been working on her installation, cutting pictures out of magazines and he was helping her. "Nothing better to do," he said. He said that a lot — nothing better to do — and it never bothered her but now she wonders if it meant something more, if she should have realized that he was bored by it all, that he was finding it pointless. She sits down and rests her eyes against the light breeze. She's zenning out when Ash plops himself down next to her.

"What's up? You still sick?"

She doesn't move, doesn't open her eyes. "If I said I was, would you leave me alone?"

"What's wrong with you?"

"Nothing."

He's quiet for a minute. "You mad at me? Did I do something?"

"I don't know, did you?" she says, still serene.

He doesn't answer and opens his backpack and takes out a granola bar. "Want half?"

She opens her eyes. "No thanks. Got anything else?"

"Nope, that's it."

"Nothing?" She yanks the bag away from him and dumps the contents out. "Nothing at all in this bag that you want to tell me about?" She hands him the box.

"I was going to show you. I was just waiting for the right moment."

"Where did you even get it?"

"I found it in my mom's desk when I was looking for cash."

Winona shakes her head, confused. "Why did she have it?"

"Who knows? I couldn't exactly ask her." Ash opens it. "It's mostly pictures and stuff but there is this." He hands her the gift-wrapped box. "Probably your birthday present. I thought you should have it, all of it."

She sets it down and picks up the photo booth pictures. She's got her tongue sticking out and Jay's laughing big, eyes squinty shut. "This was last year; we were in the mall just goofing around.

Jay stole a roll of security tags and we put them on people as they walked by, laughing when they set off store alarms." She flips through the rest of the photos and tears up.

Ash leans over and picks up the photo of five-year-old Jay in his Superman pajamas. "It's weird, these pictures, seeing him as a kid again. It makes you wonder what went wrong. How did he go from this to . . ."

"Dead?"

"Yeah."

"Who knows? All I know is that everyone keeps telling me to move on. But's what's his life worth if I can just move on, acting as if he never existed."

"I guess for most people moving on is way easier than dealing with it." Ash gathers the pictures and puts them back into the box.

"He was depressed," Winona says. "I can see that now. He had these crazy mood swings that usually sorted themselves out. I figured he was sad in the regular way. I mean, everyone's kind of depressed, right?"

"Proof. Look around. We're here on a soul's journey! Trying to walk it off as if being sad is a hangover."

She laughs a little and goes quiet, thinking of all the ways things could have been different if only she'd been different.

Ash picks up the gift box and hands it to her. "You should open it."

"I don't know if I'm ready," she says, refusing.

"Come on, he wanted you to have it." He nudges it toward her again.

She takes it from him and unwraps it slowly, holding her breath as she lifts the lid. "It's a Free Winona pin," she says, turning the black-and-white button over in her hands.

"Inside joke?"

"Sort of," she explains. "After Winona Ryder was arrested for shoplifting, there was this whole pop culture moment, her fans trying to save her from prosecution . . . I always wanted a piece of it — the memorabilia. Jay knew that; he knew everything about me." She pins it on to her denim jacket, her hands fumbling. She can't quite get it straight and is overcome with emotion.

"Here, let me," Ash says and leans in to help.

She glances down at the pin and then at him. "What do you think?"

"Free Winona," he says, with a knowing smile. "It's a good look on you."

"It is, isn't it." With her head on his shoulder, they stare out at the water, saying nothing.

Day 92

It's midnight and Pavan's sleeping with her phone on the pillow.

Ash's last text was yesterday and it was a group selfie by the lake, followed by assurance that he was fine. She was relieved to get a message and zoomed in on the photo, inspecting them the way she always did. It started when the boys were little, a primate instinct, grooming and matting down their unruly hair, wiping their dirty cheeks, checking their palms for washed hands. But as they got older, she was looking for something more, some sign of okay-ness, some verification that she had done it all right, but of course there was none and in fact lately all signs suggested to the contrary. Like every other mother, she felt at some point the cause for all their misery but still she tried to be of use. She helped them with schoolwork, science fair projects, and drove them to school so they wouldn't have to walk the four blocks in the rain. When they were sad or angry she couldn't bear it; she felt their hurt so keenly she could think of nothing else. For years, the only questions that mattered related to their well-being. Are they happy? Do they have friends? Are they smart? Will they be okay? And in the upset all was lost. She can't remember the last time she and Peter went on a date, had unscheduled sex or a conversation that wasn't about the boys. She calls them boys but really they are something else entirely. Not men, not boys, but something in between, something raw and unstable.

She checks her phone again for a new notification, hoping that she might have missed a text or post, but still nothing since yesterday. She scans through the threads, rereading their messages, looking at their pictures on Instagram, trying to see the adventure in it all but all she sees is danger — bears and cougars, hiking accidents, hypothermia — she closes her eyes and tries not to let fear eat her insides. She worries about most things and always has without ever really knowing why. When she was seven she saw a made-for-TV movie about killer bees and was so worried, she wore a netting shroud over her clothes all summer. The only way she could cope with all her anxiety was to plan for every eventuality, but her coping strategies were no match for motherhood.

She puts the phone on the bedside table and watches as the screen shuts off, returning the room to darkness. She sits up and punches at her pillow, readjusting it before tucking it tight under her neck. She stares into the dark until her eyes adjust and she can see the shape and outline of the door, the window, the reading chair in the corner. How small it all looks in the night and how small it makes her feel. Helpless. Yes, that's the feeling. Unlike the worry that courses through her, this helplessness is like a tiny blade at her neck — don't move, or I'll cut you.

"Will everything be okay?" she asks aloud, hoping that Peter will stir in his sleep and reassure her the way he often does. He doesn't and she's left on her own to answer.

After another ten minutes, she gets out of bed, takes her phone and wanders down the hallway to the basement, turning on lights, double-checking the locks before heading back upstairs to Ash's room. The room is cold with the suspended animation of his hurried departure. She opens his dresser drawers and closet, looking through his things, but finds nothing. She's not sure what she's even looking for until she pulls down the toy bin from the top shelf — a half-assembled Lego set, a tin of *Pokémon* cards and a broken Transformer. "There it is," she thinks, proof that he, her little boy still exists. For a moment she's satisfied, but then she remembers all of Jay's toys and trophies, all of his clothes that he'd grown out of, all of the things she packed up — all of him. Disappointed, Pavan puts the bin down.

She pulls back the bed covers and gets into bed, lying right in the middle just as Ash would. She imagines him now, sleeping under the stars next to Anik in the cold night. "They have each other," she thinks, remembering how inseparable they were as children. She scrolls through her photo gallery, through their childhood, in single swipes. She clicks on an imported video clip of them playing in the sandbox when they were just five and ten years old. She watches their past selves come to life, their little voices — the sweet timbre breaks her heart. She hears her own voice in the background — they're trying to show her something but her "good job" response is distracted and empty. Her mind was elsewhere. How could she be so careless? Why wasn't she paying attention?

She shakes her head and checks her messages again, but there's nothing and this leaves her wanting. She wants what all mothers want. She wants what Lisa wanted. She wants them to be okay. She wants them to come home. She wants them to find a way to live in the beauty of the world, to leave the harshness to lesser men, but for now all she can do is wait. Pavan hears Peter in the darkened hallway.

He opens the door and peeks in. "Pav, are you okay?"

"I couldn't sleep."

"Was I snoring again?"

"No," she says and switches on the lamp. "You're fine. It's just me, worrying."

He sits on the edge of the bed, his face in shadow. "I worry too, you know." The room feels small with the two of them there, a closeness in the half-light.

"I know." Her nod bounces the way it does when she's thinking, only she's not thinking, not really; her mind is just a back-and-forth of wait and see. He switches the lamp off and lies down next to her, both of them staring at the ceiling.

She takes his hand in hers and it's enough.

Day 93

Anik is the first to spot the ocean through the trees.

The silver beach, the hazy layers of blue sky and ocean like something in a storybook, magical and pristine. He stops and watches from the edge of the highway before making the decision to hike through. He knows it's farther than it seems and the out and back will add more time to this last leg of the journey, but it's a primal calling. Rose parks the car and the four of them hike the forest trail, the sound of their breathing drowned out by the ocean.

They drop their bags on the beach. The sun is so bright that it can't be seen and Anik squints, shielding his eyes in salute. The shoreline stretches for kilometers and the sand is cut in soft gray ripples with ribbons of seaweed and debris scattered by the ocean's last push.

"This is it. You did it!" Ash turns to his brother. "How does it feel?"

Anik closes his eyes, face to the sky, arms outstretched. "Fucking awesome." He unlaces and kicks off his hiking boots, stretches his shirt over his head and throws it down as he runs toward the water. It's farther than he realizes and he pumps his arms and legs harder, pushing himself further still. The others catch up and together they run into the water, screaming and laughing, their voices barely audible above the ocean roar. The tide rolls in and uproots them. They hold hands and count down, catching the jump end of each oncoming wave.

After they dry off, Anik sends the others on their way, watching until they fall out of sight. It's his idea to walk the last leg alone, to have time to reflect on what, if anything, he's learned. He combs through his thoughts and chuckles. So much of his wisdom has been reduced to tweetable sentiment. Life is not a straight line, solitude is a state of mind, noticing is an act of courage, love is many things and being is enough. He shakes his head, amused that after walking hundreds of kilometers, all he has is one-liners that Rose would love and he wonders how much of the journey is about who you're with.

As he treks along the highway he notes the Tsunami Evacuation Route signs and wonders how long it would take to get to higher ground. If an earthquake triggered a wave, there would be no real escape. He saw the 2004 tsunami on the news, saw the waves break over a tropical holiday resort, saw the aftermath and ruin of what was left. How quickly something became the worst sort of nothing, the emptiness of a place ripped away from itself, mutilated and mangled, laid to waste. There he was sitting in the living room, building the Lego set Santa gave him, when somewhere half a world away, everything had been washed away. He had nightmares after that. Asleep in his bed, he was awakened by a steady drip of water from the ceiling onto his face. When he opened his eyes, the ceiling fell open, and he was immersed in water and night. He swam out a window, kicking his legs like a frog, but there was no end to the water, nowhere to take a breath. Panic stricken, he clutched at his chest and his heart burst open, filling the water with tiny red Lego pieces. He woke up gasping and flailing at least once a week.

In an attempt to change his association, Pavan bought him sea creature books and took him to the aquarium, and over the course of a few weeks his anxiety about the ocean was driven out by facts and knowledge. "It's the unknown that's frightening," she told him on a trip to the beach. "The ocean is a beautiful thing teeming with life. Close your eyes and listen," she said. "Do you hear that?"

She breathed in and out, matching the tide. "That is the sound of life." He closed his eyes and followed her rhythm until the two of them fell in sync.

The sun is just a half slice on the horizon when Anik arrives. He drops his pack on the gravel driveway and stretches his arms wide as he looks at the house. When Rose suggested they pool their money to rent it, he balked at the expense but now, after weeks of walking and cold-ground sleeps, the prospect of a warm bed and a hot shower is a relief. He stares up at the cedar A-frame, all lit up and cozy, and watches Ash, Rose and Winona from outside. From where he's standing, it looks like they're dancing or playing a game and for a time he watches their grand gestures and sound-less clapping, the familial way in which they move around each other. He shakes his head, in his soft wizened way, acknowledging his own arrival: "I'm here."

Day 96

Winona hasn't slept much these last few nights.

The sound of the ocean's ebb and flow matches her mind's back-and-forth and she can't stop thinking. Insomnia. It's a side effect of her antidepressants along with nausea, anxiety, dry mouth, consti-pation, dizziness and a whole lot of other fine-print disclaimers. Whenever she can't sleep she tries to focus on her breath, to med-itate and let go the way all the stupid self-help posts say to, but she can never quite get there. She had a moment of letting go the other day in the water, when her feet lifted off the sand and the ocean swirled around her. She can picture that moment as if it was happening to someone else. The sun cast itself into millions of pieces, the water rose and fell, crashed and toppled over them, water dripped from the ends of their hair, teeth-chattering laugh-ter, all of them so awake and alive. She was overcome by it and when she walked out of the water, she was crying, later explaining her red eyes as saltwater sting. The only one who suspected was Rose who, on the following day when they were driving back to pick up the repaired van, asked if she was okay.

Winona turns in the king-sized bed and puts her arm around Rose. It feels nice to be near someone and she snuggles in. Rose's pink hair smells like vanilla and it reminds Winona of the carnival, of holding her mother's candy-apple hands on the Ferris wheel. The wheel had gotten stuck, and they sat in the top bucket for half an hour and though heights made Winona nervous she hardly noticed. Her mother never let her look down.

"Can't sleep?" Rose asks.

"Sorry. Did I wake you?"

She turns on her back. "No, I was up thinking," she says in a half whisper.

"About what?"

"Everything. This trip. Anik's Way. My own journey."

"Oh." Winona doesn't know what to say. "That's a lot." She's quiet and stares at the ceiling before asking. "When did you know you wanted to be a girl?"

"You mean, when did I realize I *was* a girl?"

"Yeah, sorry. When did you?"

Rose turns toward Winona and pulls the blanket under her chin. "Grade two. All of the boys started hating girls and I didn't get it. I liked everything about them, the way they looked, the way they smelled, the toys they played with; they were everything I was. I'd even take stuff from their backpacks when they weren't looking."

"Like what?"

Rose smiles and laughs.

"Tell me, what did you take?" Winona asks, nudging her.

"It was pretty innocent at first, just hairbands and sparkly pencils, but in grade four I was suspended for stealing a Bratz doll."

"Hard-core."

"I know, right. My mom freaked, said that I embarrassed her. Not much has changed. I'm still an embarrassment. Something for her to be ashamed of, her only living son, a girl."

"Do you think she realized?"

"That I was a girl?"

"Yeah."

"No, I don't think so. I don't think it was in her realm of understanding back then. I mean she does try, don't get me wrong. It's just that she'd still rather have me be her son than her daughter. She still calls me by my deadname sometimes. I know she doesn't mean to but still . . ."

"I'm sorry. That must be hard."

"It is but what can you do? Life sucks and then you die."

"That's intense."

"Yeah, but so is life. No one gets out alive, so we may as well stop pretending to be what we aren't. With Anik — the walk, and everything — I realized I needed to stop punishing myself, stop proving myself." Rose reaches for Winona's arm and traces her birthday cut line. "Pretending isn't worth the pain."

Winona pulls her hand away. "I'm trying to stop. I don't know why I do it."

"Sure you do."

"I do?"

"Yeah, you do it to feel something. That's why any of us do anything really." She eyes the faded scars on Winona's arm. "But there are better ways than that."

Winona leans in and kisses Rose hard on the mouth and then pulls away. "I'm sorry. I don't know why I did that. I thought you meant, or wanted . . . Oh shit, I totally misread."

"It's okay." Rose smiles. "It was nice."

"Are you sure? I don't want things to be weird."

"They aren't."

Winona closes her eyes and flops her head back onto the pillow. "I'm such an idiot."

"No, you're not. It's fine. Now come on, I want to show you something." She gets out of bed and tells Winona to suit up. They tiptoe out of the bedroom, past the pullout couch where Ash is sleeping and out to the beach.

"Grab a surfboard," Rose says.

"It's too dark. I'm crap at it in the day. Imagine how shitty I'll be in the dark."

"It'll be fine. We're just going to drift."

"I don't know." Winona follows her into the water. "We're going to die."

"You'll be fine. Trust."

Stomach down they paddle out, and then, on Rose's cue, they drop their legs in the water and sit up. They drift on the ocean, so dark now that it seems to have disappeared.

"Don't you love it?" Rose asks.

"Love what? I can't see shit." Frightened, Winona grips the sides of her board tighter.

"Look up."

Winona stares up from the darkness. Stars swirl from their infinite nothing; clusters of long-ago light map the sky.

Day 100

It's raining and the beach is end-of-the-world empty.

The sky is pulled down low on the water and everything looks tarnished and dirt gray. Even the sand, which just yesterday was piled in sun-kissed castles, is trampled, flattened in the monochrome of quick-set cement. Water pools in Ash's footprints, sinkholes each step, as he walks along the shore toward the group of black rocks that lie on the beach like sleeping giants. When he was little he imagined them getting up and wandering into the ocean, anger shaking their rocky limbs. His mom was always worried that he'd fall when he raced to the top to see the starfishes up close. He buttons his yellow coat against the wind and tucks his face away from the pounding rain and pushes on. The rock isn't as tall as he remembers; at barely ten feet, it's a pretty easy climb even with the rain-slick surface. He stops to check out the fat purple starfish and wonders what it must be like to live such a long life without a brain. No sense of purpose, just the slow-moving act of being, eating and reproducing. He resists the urge to pick it up and moves on, scaling the rock to its ocean face. He perches on top and stares out at the ocean, taking his phone out to record the waves crashing up against the rocks. His hands are shaky so he redoes it and then sends it to Pavan with a couple of emojis for good measure. He feels good about sending it, and waits for a few minutes to see if she gets it but it just stays on sending, so he pockets the phone and turns to leave.

That's when he sees it. From a distance it looks like a giant lava rock, ancient and smooth, but then comes the gust of wind and the stink. Ash knows the smell. He remembers it from his family's whale-watching trip when he was six. While everyone else in the boat was amazed by the whale's breach and spray, he was seasick and puking over the edge.

Ash scales down the rock, slipping down the last few feet onto the beach below. He rights himself and walks quickly toward it, slowing his approach into the tide where it's lying partially submerged.

"Holy fuck." He stares at the creature. He's never seen a whale laid out like this before and is humbled by its sheer size, its prehistoric appearance. As he circles it, he notes the rocky nodules on its head, the grooved throat and elongated fins. He recognizes it from Anik's books — a humpback whale — yet seeing it up close and outside of the illustrated pictures is something else entirely. All of its majesty is gone and all that remains is rot and curiosity.

He steps back, pulls out his phone and takes a selfie, captioning it: "Moby Fucking Dick!" Before hitting send, Ash looks at the photo and studies his stupid face, his fat grin. He's filled with shame, the instant kind, all regret and take-back wishes.

No one knows exactly what to do and for a time they just stand in the water looking at it.

"Is it alive?" Rose is filming.

Anik kneels down, laying a hand on its back. "For now," he says. "But we have to get help."

"Can't make this shit up."

Ash moves inside her frame. "You better not be livestreaming this."

"Well no, not right at this very moment."

"Are you for real right now? Come on, you heard Anik. We have to do something. We need to call the authorities."

Winona still stunned by the sight of the whale, looks up. "What, like 911?"

"I don't think this classifies as a real emergency." Rose covers her mouth. "But fuck if it doesn't smell like one. Shit."

"Be serious, will you? Besides do you have a better idea? No — didn't think so. Anik, what do you think?"

Anik's walking away from the whale, holding his phone in the air. "Who has bars?"

Ash pulls his out and checks. "Nothing. No signal."

"Nothing here either," Rose says, looking at her screen.

Anik continues to walk up and down the beach, arm extended like an antenna, looking for connection. "Got it — nope — it's gone again. Shit."

"Got it, one bar, 3G," Winona says, waving her phone in the air. "Now what?"

"Try googling it." Anik rushes over to her.

"Google what? Like, what do you do when you find a beached whale?"

"It's a start." Ash looks over at the whale, watches the tide roll over it and wonders if it will push it further in or out.

She types as they crowd over her shoulders and after a few long seconds of buffering the results load. She scrolls through, shaking her head, scanning through pages of useless information. "These are all about dead whales," she says. "What are we going to do?"

"Try searching Fisheries and Oceans," Anik suggests.

Winona types it in but the page doesn't load. "Fuck!" she says and throws down the phone.

Ash picks it up and brushes the sand off. "I'm calling 911." He covers his free ear to drown out the ocean sound. After a few minutes of answering questions he hangs up. "I think they'll send someone."

"You think?" Rose asks.

"What the hell, Rose, I don't see you doing anything besides planning your next social media post." Ash shakes his head and storms off.

"Wait up," Winona yells. "Are you okay?"

"Are you?" Ash reaches for her hand and flips it over, exposing her whale tattoo. "You're the one always talking about signs."

"I know, I know." She goes quiet.

They both stare out at the ocean and for a moment there's nothing but the sound of waves crashing and the tide collapsing on itself.

Ash watches one of the marine officials walk around the whale, talking to the others with big conductor-like arms. "What do you think they're saying?"

"Probably assessing its health, strategizing how to move it," Anik says.

"They've been here for over an hour already and all they've done is douse it with water and set up a perimeter and tent."

"I'm sure they know what they're doing."

"Right." Ash looks back at the beach, now crowded with onlookers taking pictures. It reminds him of being at Jay's funeral and how people had treated it like an event, a photo op.

A woman's voice from behind: "Excuse me! You there!" The brothers turn. "Were you the kids who found the whale?"

"Yeah." Anik takes a step forward as if to protect his brother.

"I'm from the local news." She points to a media crew that's setting up just down the beach. "I'd love to ask you a few questions on camera, if you don't mind."

"I don't think so." Ash turns away.

"What's going on?" Rose asks, now inching her way into the conversation.

"Were you part of the group that found the whale?"

"Yes, I can confirm that," she says like a spokesperson. "I'm Rose, this is Winona, Ash and Anik."

"Anik?" the reporter asks. "You're not the same Anik who was walking to the ocean?"

"You bet he is!" Rose dials up her perkiness. "That's us. Anik's Way. Here we are, we made it!"

"And now this. That's quite a story." The reporter beckons to the camera crew. As they set up for the interview, Ash imagines how stupid they all look — a bunch of kids, in rain gear, talking about — what exactly? This isn't hard-hitting journalism. It's a whale and it's almost dead. They shouldn't be talking about it. They should be saving it. End of story.

"I'm out," Ash says and walks away.

"Wait up," Anik calls.

"Don't let me keep you from your five seconds of fame."

"No, you know that's not me." He grabs Ash's arm and spins him around. "That's Rose's thing."

"Right, I forgot. Your thing is walking for world peace or some shit like that?"

"What the hell, Ash? I'm trying to help you."

"Is that what you're doing? Your whole walk was about helping? Looked a lot like running away to me."

"Fine. That's fair," Anik says, hands up in surrender. "Maybe it was but I'm here now. We're here now."

"Isn't everyone?" He motions to the tourists and locals taking pictures and videos. "It's fucking disgusting. No one actually cares."

"That's not true." He takes him by the shoulders and tries for eye contact. "We care and so do they." Anik points to the emergency officials gathered under the pop-up tent. "They're doing what they can. Sometimes things just take time."

"What if we don't have time?" Ash takes a moment and looks back at the chaos — the satellite news van, the reporter interviewing Rose and Winona, the small crowd of people wandering around taking selfies. "Fuck it!" He walks toward the rescue organizers. "Hey, what's the plan?"

An official with an in-charge look about him glances at Ash. "And you are?"

"I'm Ash, I found the whale."

"Right," he says and then continues on with his work.

"I want to help." The man stops and looks at Ash the way people always look at him, like he's a dumb kid who doesn't know anything. "Just tell me what to do. I'll do it."

"Okay." He rubs his beard like he's thinking of how to make something complex simple. "We're going to dig a trench around the whale, then we're going to harness it up with rope — we'll need a lot of volunteers to help pull the whale out of the shallows. Once it's clear, we'll attach the rope to a boat and pull it back out."

"Cool."

"For it to work we're going to need dozens of people ready and organized. If you and your friends think you can get a jump on getting the volunteers prepped that would be a big help."

"On it!" He waves Anik over.

"Oh, and Ash, water's cold. It could be a while out there, so we're going to need wetsuits."

"Okay. No problem. Where do I get them?"

"You wanted to help, right?"

"Yeah," he says, head bobbing.

"Then figure it out."

It's Winona who suggests they call the surf shops for wetsuits and Rose who convinces them to lend them for free in exchange for a mention on the news, along with a tag in the #SaveTheWhale #AniksWay posts. Within a few hours, they're mobilized and local restaurants have set up heated tents with food and drink where volunteers gather and wait.

Ash is focused on the official giving the instructions. It's hard to hear over the sound of the ocean yet he knows the actions aren't complex and he reiterates this to the volunteers. "We just need to pull together." As they wade into the rising water, seaweed brushing against their legs, Ash thinks of Jay and wonders if he died when he hit the surface, if he drowned, if his eyes were open, if the last thing he saw was the sky. It was so blue that day.

Anik calls to Ash and the brothers take their position at the front of the line with Winona and Rose just behind. Ash twists his hands around the rope and holds tight and together with all of the volunteers, they pull in synchronized bursts over and over. After an hour, their efforts barely register, but there's no talk of giving up, there's no talk at all, there's nothing but the sound of the ocean. They're almost waist deep as the tide rushes in, cresting and crashing hard against their bodies. Ash's back and shoulder blades are rolled in knots and his arms ache with the tension of holding on and staying put. A numbness sets in and his fingers tingle as if an electric current is running through them. "It's okay," he tells himself. He digs in, shifting his weight to his heels, trying to hold steady. He glances back at the others, their faces twisted in exhaustion. They keep pulling, even as the water rises. "Hold on," they say to each other, to themselves.

Ash zones in on the whale and imagines it free, calling out in song — that hollow moan, the needle pitch cry, the haunting vibration. He can almost feel it reverberate through his body and then something shifts. The tension on the rope lightens and they're called on to let go. Ash stares out at the ocean looking for a sign. He wants there to be a moment: a slap of a tail, a breach, something to show that it was all worth it, but there's nothing.

On shore, Ash takes his gloves off and looks at his hands. He can't stop them from shaking, he can't tell if he's cold or hot, if he's faint or tired, if he's awake or dreaming. He's filled with the strange sensation of being separate from himself. He closes his eyes, breathing slowly until all of his feelings find a place inside his bones, until everything settles inside him like wisdom.

When he opens his eyes Anik is looking at him. "You okay?"

"Yeah, tired . . . cold," Ash says, pulling his body in tight, trying to get warm. "I think I'm gonna head back."

"You sure?"

Ash lowers his head and nods. His chest swells; he's crying and trying to hide it.

"You know what, I'll come with."

"Let's all go," Winona says and calls to Rose.

As they approach the house, they look back one last time. The sky cracked silver, the ocean near and far, the sunlight filtering rays on a distant horizon.

They take it all in. Everything at once.

Acknowledgments

Thank you, Sat, Amit, Arun and Xena for the love and inspiration. Thank you to my agent, John Pearce, for his limitless faith in this book. Thank you to my brilliant editor, Jen Knoch, who understood this novel from the start and helped me fully realize my vision. Thank you to Crissy Calhoun for an outstanding copy edit. Thank you to Nin and Subby for the day-to-day encouragement, and to Kay for being my trusted first, second, third and always reader. Thank you to Elee Kraljii Gardiner — the walk in the woods gave me courage to stay true to myself and to the stories I wanted to write. Thanks to my friends and family who keep me honest and grounded. Thanks always to Wayde Compton and Betsy Warland for the early encouragement that helped me find a way into a writing life. Thank you to all of those at ECW who do the invisible and important work of bringing diverse books into the world.

If you or someone you know is struggling with suicide, self-harm, or disordered eating, there are places that offer free, confidential support.

In Canada:

- Kids Help Phone: kidshelpphone.ca
- Canada Suicide Prevention Service: crisisservicescanada.ca

In the United States:

- National Suicide Prevention Lifeline: suicidepreventionlifeline.org

1% of the sales of this book will be donated to support Kids Help Phone.